Grim finale /
MYS O'Neill

22030

O'Neill, Dorothy P.

GRIM FINALE

GRIM FINALE

•

Dorothy P. O'Neill

AVALON BOOKS
NEW YORK

Published by Thomas Bouregy & Co., Inc.
160 Madison Avenue, New York, NY 10016

Library of Congress Cataloging-in-Publication Data

O'Neill, Dorothy P.
    Grim finale / Dorothy P. O'Neill.
        p. cm.
    ISBN 0-8034-9798-9 (hardcover : alk. paper) 1. Rooney, Liz
(Fictitious character) 2. Women forensic scientists—Fiction.
3.
Police—New York (State)—New York—Fiction. 4. New York
(N.Y.)—Fiction. I. Title.

PS3565.N488G75 2006
813'.54—dc22

                                        2006013674

PRINTED IN THE UNITED STATES OF AMERICA
ON ACID-FREE PAPER
BY HADDON CRAFTSMEN, BLOOMSBURG, PENNSYLVANIA

To my sisters, Grace Pentz Sloan, Audrey H. Pentz, and Carol Pentz Logan, and to my brother, Arthur H. Pentz, who recall my first poems and stories scrawled in a school notebook; who remember when I declared my intention of becoming a published novel writer when I grew up; who rejoiced with me when, at last, it happened.

Prologue

On an afternoon in late October, in the auditorium/gymnasium of Manhattan's prestigious Chadwick Academy, Marva Malin slumped in her seat just in front of the stage, almost ready to scream from frustration.

Only two more weeks before this pathetic school play was supposed to go on, and today's rehearsal was the worst yet. No dramatics coach could have worked harder than she to tailor the script for the capabilities of the students and coordinate the school orchestra's pitiful attempts at background music, but they still weren't getting it right. The music was much too loud, and take the boy now center stage—over and over she'd told him to get a little action in with his words, but there he stood like a wooden Indian, again.

She jumped to her feet and yelled at him. "Hold it! Are you deaf or just plain stupid? How many times do I have to tell you? Move a little when you're speaking! Turn your head, shift your weight. You're not supposed to be a statue!"

Cringing, the boy stammered out another line. "Uh . . . one sees more, d-devils than, uh, uh, vast hell can hold," before coming to an abrupt halt.

Instantly, all the instruments went silent, too. Snickers

1

from student musicians and from cast members onstage further enraged Marva. For a fleeting moment she felt like quitting this stepping-stone job, going back to the Indianapolis suburbs, and marrying Warren before he got wise that she was stringing him along. Life as the wife of a Midwest banker couldn't be any worse than being an English teacher doubling as dramatics coach in a private school full of rich brats.

Six years devoted to learning and perfecting her craft and another two pursuing her dream of becoming a Broadway theatrical director, and what did she have to show for it? Almost twenty-eight, she was still living in a three-room walkup in a downscale area of the city. Her two degrees in theater arts and drama had gotten her nowhere. She grimaced, recalling how one theatrical agent advised her to take some dance lessons and go after a spot in a chorus line. "With your face and shape you'd be a shoo-in," he'd told her.

Though she'd always been pleased with her striking, brunette looks and figure, recollection of the agent's insinuation angered her all over again. Why shouldn't a successful theatrical director be glamorous? Her urge to quit vanished. Her resolve strengthened. She was going to make it as a Broadway director, no matter what it took. She'd show her parents she was just as talented as her musical genius sister, who played piano and violin and sang like a diva.

She turned her attention to the student musicians, selected by auditions to form the orchestra for the play: an assortment of brass and strings, with drums and piano. They'd been rehearsing under the direction of a faculty member, music teacher Vincent LoPresti, but they sounded no better today than they had after the auditions. She glanced around, looking for LoPresti. Evidently, he was taking a break.

LoPresti should make them practice more. The violins, especially, were a disgrace.

Earlier today, she'd asked LoPresti when he was going to

whip his poor excuse for an orchestra into shape. He'd frowned and made a surly reply in that throaty voice of his with its unidentifiable, almost British accent, unusual for a New Yorker. "Quit complaining. They're coming along."

His attitude had surprised her. Although she'd turned him down flat when he asked her to have coffee with him after a rehearsal a couple of weeks ago, and let him know she wasn't interested, he'd taken the brush-off with an indifferent shrug. But today she sensed strong resentment. Why the change? A delayed reaction, perhaps, but that was his problem. She'd never gone for the swarthy type. She liked Nordics.

After checking the area to make sure LoPresti wasn't nearby, she focused on the blond, teenage girl who'd been playing violin. She didn't know the names of most of the student musicians yet, including this girl, but for the past few rehearsals she'd singled her out for scathing criticism. The best way to get her to practice and improve was to humiliate her, she'd decided, and if LoPresti wouldn't do it, she would. She stepped closer to the orchestra, shook her head at the girl, and scowled. "Was that screeching noise I heard from your instrument supposed to be music?" she asked.

The girl's reaction disappointed Marva. Instead of unshed tears, a look of defiance sprang into the young violinist's eyes. Just as she was trying to think of something she could say to break this feisty girl down and make her weep, a voice sounded from behind Marva. "You're being too hard on the kids."

Even before Marva turned around, she knew the speaker was Headmaster's Assistant Bernice Fripp, who attended every play rehearsal. Tall, skinny, middle-aged Bernice had been aide to a succession of Chadwick headmasters for more than twenty years. If she hadn't been a woman and black, she'd probably have been appointed headmistress by now, Marva thought.

Bernice was a childless widow whose entire life revolved

around the school. Until this year, she'd coached the students in the school play. She'd given it up because her other duties had become too pressing, she'd told Marva, and her arthritis had gotten so bad that some days she had to walk with a cane.

Bernice loved the kids. More than likely, she wished she hadn't given up being the drama coach, Marva thought. Suddenly, the thought became a suspicion. The way Bernice showed up at all the rehearsals, maybe she had ideas about trying to worm her way back. Frustrated as Marva was with the job, the possibility of being replaced angered her.

"Mind your own business, Bernice. You're not the dramatics coach anymore," she retorted. "I'm directing this play, not you."

For an instant, she regretted having lashed out like that. Bernice was about the only person at Chadwick she got along with. She'd made an effort to be friendly toward Bernice, because, as headmaster's assistant, Bernice was privy to Social Security data on all personnel. Marva didn't want it getting around that her real name was Marva *Malinbaum*. She'd shortened it unofficially because Malin sounded classier and would look better on playbills.

She'd have changed the name legally if it weren't for Grandmother Golda Malinbaum Schlotzheimer, now ninety-one and still sharp as a tack. The Schlotzheimer pickle works had made her grandfather rich and left Grandmother loaded. Marva stood to inherit a bundle, but the old girl would disinherit her if she ever found out about the shortened family name. Renouncing her Jewish heritage, Grandmother would call it.

Bernice's voice penetrated Marva's thoughts. "I consider every kid in this school my business. You've been nasty to that little violinist since rehearsals began."

"They all have to learn how to take criticism," Marva said.

"Well, you're making a big mistake, picking on that girl

all the time," Bernice replied. She lowered her voice, adding, "I hope she hasn't told her father."

"Why?" Marva asked. "Who's her father? Some billionaire who's going to give big bucks to the school? What's the girl's name?"

"She's Anna Tynkov. Her father is Boris Tynkov."

Marva stared over at the young blond violinist and replied, almost in a whisper, "Boris Tynkov, the Russian Mafia racketeer?"

Bernice nodded. "That's the one."

Marva kept her voice down. "I'm surprised a school like Chadwick would accept the daughter of an organized crime figure."

Bernice shrugged. "Maybe he made them an offer they couldn't refuse." Glancing toward the orchestra, she added, "Take my advice and say a few kind words to Anna before rehearsal ends today."

Marva considered the possibility of a confrontation with notorious Boris Tynkov of the Russian Mafia. "All right, I will," she replied.

Bernice turned away and looked toward the rear of the room. "I'm going to grab a chair and watch the rest of the rehearsal from back there," she said. "And I think you're overreacting. From what I've seen so far this afternoon, it isn't as bad as you think."

"I don't know how you can say that with a straight face," Marva replied.

"I've been through this," Bernice said. "The kids never do their best in this gym atmosphere. When the athletic equipment and bleachers are removed, and the chairs are set in place, and they start rehearsing in a theater atmosphere, they'll do better. Don't forget, I've been through this."

"I'm not likely to forget, with you reminding me every two seconds that you used to be the dramatics coach," Marva snapped.

Bernice made no reply. Instead, she turned and hobbled over to the folding chairs stacked against a wall. Marva noticed she was using her cane. This must be one of her bad arthritis days.

She watched Bernice unfold a chair and push it to a spot under the balcony. Too late she realized she should have helped her. She dismissed the thought and replaced it with the wish that Bernice was right in believing the kids would improve. Otherwise, her first Chadwick Academy production was headed for Flop City.

None of this would be happening if the headmaster, aided and abetted by the board of trustees and some influential parents, hadn't insisted on a Shakespearean play. But half of the schools in the country were putting on *Romeo and Juliet.* She wanted her first production as school drama coach to be something beyond the usual, perhaps something by Tennessee Williams or Eugene O'Neill—a play with a strong plot, a few vigorous characters, and straight, pithy dialogue. Instead, she was stuck with a fantasy, a cumbersome cast of unrealistic characters and lines of poetic dialogue that most of the students couldn't understand, much less deliver.

The kind of play she wanted to put on would have demonstrated the expertise she'd gained earning her two theatrical degrees. She'd hoped to impress the prominent Broadway producer whose son was in Chadwick's twelfth grade. She would have made sure the producer's boy landed a prominent role.

But Chadwick's powers-that-be squashed that idea. She was told that plays such as *Cat on a Hot Tin Roof* and *Desire under the Elms* were not suitable. Forced to choose from several of Shakespeare's plays, she reluctantly agreed to *A Midsummer Night's Dream.*

The way things were going, she wished her name as dramatics coach and director of this fiasco could be left off the program. Having her name associated with this disaster could undermine her hopes for the future. Fortunately, the Broadway producer's son wasn't interested in dramatics and didn't even try out for a part. Chances were, his father wouldn't attend what was shaping up to be the worst play ever put on in any school, anywhere, anytime.

She'd taken this English and Dramatics teaching job because she'd thought it would be an entrée into the world of professional theater. She'd never have considered it if she'd known she wouldn't be given free rein.

Now she was forced to deal with a large cast, from twelfth-grade students down to kindergartners. And right from the start, there'd been interference from the headmaster, the board of trustees, and influential parents. The teen age girl whose parents endowed the school library had a face like a frog and a voice to match, but she had to be Queen Titania, and the tone-deaf kindergartner with two left feet was the great-great-granddaughter of Chadwick's founder, so she had to be one of the little singing and dancing fairies.

It was inevitable, Marva thought. Only a miracle could save *A Midsummer Night's Dream* from becoming *A Midautumn Night's Bomb.*

Her rambling thoughts were interrupted by the sudden appearance of Greg Jensen, the student stage manager. Greg, a handsome boy in the graduating class, was one of the few students doing a fairly decent job. She suspected Greg had a crush on her. This was understandable. Schoolboys were often attracted to pretty, young teachers, and she knew she was by far the best-looking female on the faculty.

Deciding to brighten his day, she addressed him with a flirtatious smile. "What is it, Greg?"

"Miss Malin, the art department finished the scenery. You want to come backstage and have a look at it?"

Marva nodded. Getting to her feet, she cast a menacing look at the cast members onstage. "Study your scripts while I'm gone," she directed. "By the time I get back, maybe at least one of you clods will be able to speak your lines without sounding like a complete idiot."

Backstage, she stared with disdain at the art department's attempt at a forest scene. She should have known art teacher Cyril Gibbs didn't have the guts to make sure his students came up with anything but an amateurish mess. What a mollycoddle—close to thirty and still living with his mother and two aunts. She glanced around. Too bad he wasn't present or she'd tell him again he was a first-class wimp.

"This looks like something done in the kindergarten," she snapped.

"Shall I tell Mr. Gibbs you want it done over?"

"No, get your crew together and rig it up. Awful as it is, we'll have to use it."

Just as Marva spoke, she heard a voice from the wings. "I'm sorry you're not pleased, Ms. Malin." Art teacher Cyril Gibbs, wearing paint-spattered jeans and a T-shirt printed with a likeness of Rembrandt, stepped into view. She knew he was attempting to sound assertive as he brushed his long, straggly, light brown hair away from his thin face, adding, "The purpose of Chadwick Academy's annual play is not to achieve perfection but to present the creativity of students in all departments."

The wimpy art teacher had a thin skin when it came to criticism of his students and remarks about his passive nature. It gave her a sense of power to push his buttons. Stirring him into anger was great sport. Once she'd goaded him to the brink of rage, and he'd let loose with a couple of out-of-character words.

She was about to say something to get him going when girls' phys-ed teacher, Julia Tulley, appeared, wearing her usual athletic sweats and headband, with her straight hair tied back in a stubby ponytail. Julia was another teacher Marva enjoyed goading into anger. She was coach of the little kids' fairy ballet, which was every bit as sorry as the scenery, and Marva took every opportunity to tell her so.

But this time Julia spoke first. "Cy's right," she said. "If you'd been here as long as we have, you'd realize this isn't about putting on anything close to a Broadway production."

Broadway production. The words reminded Marva of her longtime dream and stirred her own anger. "Julia," she replied, "when the audience sees your students going through the clumsy results of your coaching, there'll be no doubt this play isn't a Broadway production. What gave you the idea you could direct a ballet?"

She turned and headed back to the auditorium before Julia could reply, but she hoped she'd succeeded in making her hopping mad. The gym teacher had been with the school for several years and had a tendency to act superior toward faculty newcomers. This should take her down a peg or two.

On her way back to the auditorium, she noticed the trash bin in the corridor hadn't been emptied again today. Candy wrappers and snack bags from the machine backstage were spilling out onto the floor. Yesterday she'd ordered Duddy, the janitor, to take care of it. Obviously, he'd ignored her orders. She hadn't seen the aging, punch-faced, ex-pugilist since she noticed him mopping up a puddle of spilled milk in the lunchroom. Most likely he was already down in his basement quarters with a six-pack, even though it was still too early for him to go off duty. Several times she'd complained to the headmaster about Duddy's slip-shod ways but was told it was difficult to get janitorial help these days, and at least Duddy was honest and trustworthy.

Back in the auditorium, she called to the cast onstage. "All right, take it from where you left off, and for God's sake try to get it right this time."

She managed to endure the rest of the scene without losing her cool. When the scene ended, Greg approached her. "You want us to put the backdrop in place, now, Miss Malin?"

"Yes, do it before we start the next scene, and take a break when it's done," she replied. *Thank God the next scene was the last. These after-classes rehearsals made her late getting home to walk her dogs.* She smiled, picturing Tina and Trixie welcoming her with joyous yelps when she opened the door to her apartment—two adorable, blond Pomeranians, bought on an impulse straight out of the window of a Manhattan pet shop. Her folks back in Indianapolis pretended to be shocked when she told them. "Two dogs in a three-room apartment? I'll give you a week before you ship them out to us," her father had said.

She knew he was kidding. She'd always loved animals— always had multiple dogs and cats. Her father often joked that she preferred animals to people. Neither he nor her mother realized how true this was. With animals, she didn't have to compete. Their love was always unconditional, and she was always in control.

Her thoughts returned to the students on the stage and the musicians in their places, below. She raised her voice. "The rest of you, take a break, now."

They all began to scatter. A crew of boy students brought the scenery onstage. Watching them put it into place, she again thought it looked like it had been painted by a bunch of five-year-olds. Maybe it looked better from further back where Bernice had taken her chair. "Bernice, how does it look from back there?" she called.

"Come and see for yourself," Bernice replied, somewhat curtly, Marva thought.

Bernice was annoyed about the sarcastic remark a few minutes ago. But Bernice was too good-natured to hold onto it, Marva decided, as she walked to the rear of the auditorium. From there, the forest scene looked somewhat better.

She turned around and started back to her chair near the stage, when another thought struck her. "I'm going up to the balcony and see how the scenery looks from there," she called to Bernice.

"It'll be dark up there. Do you know where the light switches are?" Bernice called back. "Maybe you should get hold of Duddy."

Marva had no idea where the light switches were, but she wasn't about to track down the negligent janitor and ask for his help. He knew she'd reported him to the headmaster, and he'd been grouchy and hostile toward her ever since. "There'll be enough light coming from down here," she replied. "Anyway, I won't be up there long."

She decided to take her bag with her. In addition to the entire script of the play, her wallet and apartment keys and other personal stuff were in it. If she left it on the chair, some rotten kid or one of those teachers might come out from backstage and notice it while she was up in the balcony. She didn't trust anyone around here.

She went and picked up the bag, slung the straps over her shoulder, and walked across the auditorium to the corridor. She climbed the stairs to the balcony and made her way through the semi darkness to the railing. Looking down at the stage, she saw that Greg and his crew had finished putting the scenic backdrop in place. From up here it didn't look bad. She noticed there was nobody on the stage, and the orchestra chairs were empty. Remembering she'd told everyone to take a break, she pictured student actors, orchestra members, and stagehands backstage, hitting the snack and soda machines, sitting around complaining about her. All of them except Greg Jensen would be badmouthing her. At least she had one friend among the students, she thought—if having a crush on a teacher could be called friendship. Too bad Greg wasn't ten years older.

Switching her thoughts back to the scenery, she decided

she'd call to Bernice and tell her it looked better from up here. From where she stood, she couldn't quite see the area where Bernice had been sitting. Was she still down there?

As she stepped closer to the railing and leaned over to look for Bernice, she heard a creaking sound from somewhere in the surrounding shadows. Though it was barely audible, her instincts told her she was not alone on the balcony.

Chapter One

It was almost quitting time. Liz Rooney had just started clearing her workstation when she saw her boss, Medical Examiner Dan Switzer, heading her way. The look on his face suggested he'd been advised of a murder—not the commonplace drug-or-gang-related type, but the kind she liked to follow, generally involving a high-society, political, or showbiz celebrity. If so, he was going to ask her if she wanted to go with him to the scene.

As if he needed to ask. He and her father, a retired NYPD detective, were longtime friends. Dan knew she'd been hooked on homicides ever since Pop took her, a freckle-faced kid with strawberry-blond pigtails, to the station house one day. What had started as an interest in following baffling cases and trying to solve them had developed into an important element of her life. And since Pop had retired and he and Mom moved to Florida, Dan had become a substitute father.

She looked at him with expectation. "What's up, Dan?"

"I just got word that a female teacher at the Chadwick Academy died in a fall from a balcony in the school gym," Dan replied. "EMS was called, but paramedics reported her DOA."

"*. . . died in a fall from a balcony . . .*" Liz looked at Dan in puzzlement. This sounded like an accidental death or suicide, yet she got the distinct impression he believed he'd find out otherwise when he examined the body.

"It was phoned in as a jump or fall," he said. "But I have a gut feeling foul play could be involved. Since the cause of death is questionable, I have to go over there anyway. What do you say, Lizzie—you want to go with me and find out?"

She started closing down her computer, saying, "If you think it might be homicide, that's good enough for me." Moments later, she was ready to go.

"I'll have to make a couple of phone calls from your car," she said on the elevator. "I had something on for tonight with Ike and Sophie and Ralph. We were supposed to meet at my place right after work, then go somewhere to eat. I'll have to call it off."

She knew neither Sophie nor Ralph would mind. Best-friend-since-first-grade Sophie Pulaski, a NYPD patrol officer, shared her passion for following murder cases. Sophie's fiancé, Ralph Perillo, was a cop, too. They'd met in police academy. They were being married at noon this coming Saturday in Our Lady Queen of Peace Church on Staten Island.

Of course, Sophie had asked her to be her maid of honor. Though tonight's get-together was to have included a discussion of final wedding details, this could be put off until tomorrow. She was sure Ike wouldn't mind, either. It wasn't as if she were breaking a date with him. Maybe he could drop by her place later this evening.

Dan's chuckle came into her thoughts. "Call it off? I thought your priorities might change when Ike put that engagement ring on your finger, but I see your interest in homicides is as strong as ever."

"Ike will understand," Liz said.

Dan smiled, as if he were remembering when the possibility of NYPD Homicide Detective Ike Eichle understanding her passion for following murder cases seemed as remote as a friendship ever developing between them—much less a romance. Only a few months ago, she and Ike were adversaries. He didn't think she had any business going to homicide scenes with Dan. Whenever she encountered Ike at a homicide scene, he'd greet her with the same hostile question. "What are you doing here, Rooney?" She and Sophie used to call him Detective Sourpuss.

He'd sweetened up last March, after her amateur sleuthing into a particularly tough case turned up something that helped solve it. Since then, he'd welcomed her help and even cleared it with the squad lieutenant and the DA. Their resulting friendship took off into a romantic relationship. Now they were planning a February wedding. With Sophie's wedding only four days away and her own only a few months off, it was no wonder Dan thought she might be diverted from murders to marriages.

While driving cross-town, she used her cell phone to call Ike in the precinct squad room. One of the other detectives told her he'd left a little while ago on a case.

"He's out," she told Dan. "I don't want to bother him on his cell phone when he's working. I'll try him later."

"The school's in Ike's precinct," Dan said. "Maybe that's where he went. Maybe the paramedics picked up on something they thought was suspicious and phoned the precinct, and when Ike investigated the scene he found out they were right—it was a homicide."

Liz hoped that's how it was. She liked being at homicide scenes with Ike, watching him, imagining what conclusions might be developing in his mind. His keen ability to zero in on the minutest aspect of a murder was a big part of her attraction to him. Pop used to say that Ike was the most perceptive young detective he'd ever worked with.

She called Sophie's cell phone. As expected, Sophie's reaction to the cancellation was total understanding. Not only did Sophie share her interest in trying to solve murder cases, but she was also planning to apply for detective training when she became eligible. The two of them often talked about forming their own private investigation firm, someday.

"A possible murder at a ritzy private school!" Sophie exclaimed. "I'll listen for a bulletin on the news. Call me tomorrow morning and let me know the details."

From the start, Dan had it pegged as a homicide, Liz thought, clicking off her phone. "How come you believe this is a murder?" she asked him.

"In the first place, the building code requires balcony railings to be a specified height to prevent someone accidentally falling over them," he replied. "In the second place, a balcony in a school gym wouldn't be high enough off the floor for the impact to kill someone instantaneously. Sure, this teacher might have sustained serious injuries, but the paramedics wouldn't have found her DOA."

"Are you saying someone could have attacked her and killed her—bashed her on the head or something, then pushed her over the railing?"

Dan nodded. "Exactly."

Liz pondered this for a moment before another thought struck her. "Then you're definitely ruling out suicide?"

"Right," Dan replied. "I don't think a teacher would choose a school gym for a suicide leap."

This was going to be an interesting case, Liz thought. Though the victim wasn't any kind of celebrity, the prestigious private school background made it the sort of homicide she liked to delve into.

"The school's on this block," Dan said, steering his car around a corner.

Just as he spoke, Liz saw a large, gray stone building looming ahead on the right-hand side of the street. Seconds later, she noticed an EMS truck double-parked near the entrance and two NYPD squad cars behind it. A police barricade was stretched across the school doors.

"Looks like my hunch was right, and so were the paramedic's," Dan said, pulling the car up behind one of the police vehicles.

As always, when she was about to enter a crime scene, a familiar excitement gripped Liz. Again, she hoped Ike and his partner had been sent to cover this case. She scanned the vehicles parked along the street. "I don't see Ike's car," she said with a pang of disappointment.

"It could be further down the block," Dan replied.

As they approached the short flight of steps leading to the entrance, the officer on guard recognized Dan. "Hello, Doc," he said, lowering the cordon. He nodded at Liz. She'd become a familiar figure at crime scenes with Dan.

In the reception hall, a small crowd of adults, mostly women, milled around the security desk where a harried guard fielded questions. From what she overheard, Liz gathered that there'd been a school play in rehearsal after classes that afternoon. Most of the students had gone home on the school vans after regular dismissal time, and these people were here to pick up kids who were in the play.

The women were probably nannies or mothers, Liz thought. A man in full livery was undoubtedly a wealthy family's chauffeur. Another man, rather rough-looking and wearing dark pants, brown leather jacket, and a chauffeur's cap was probably a taxi driver sent to pick up one or more kids. She got the feeling she'd seen him before. Had she ridden in his cab frequently? With all the taxis in Manhattan— no way. If she gave it some thought, she might remember. He and all the others waiting looked grim. They must have been informed of the teacher's death. Even if they hadn't been told it was a homicide, the arrival of the police and the barricade would have tipped them off.

She noticed a register sheet on the guard's desk. Anyone entering or leaving the building had to sign in and out and put down arrival and departure times. After pushing the victim over the balcony rail, would the killer have had time to sign out before the guard knew what happened? Or could the killer have slipped out one of the exits? When Dan finished talking to the guard, she asked him about these possibilities.

"Negative on both," he replied. "The guard told me nobody signed out since three-thirty, and he said nobody could have left through one of the exits because they're all hooked up to an electronic alarm system that goes off if anyone attempts to leave the building that way."

Liz felt a pang of excitement. *The murderer was still on the premises!*

A cop, standing at the entrance to a corridor, directed them to the crime scene. "The gym's off this corridor," he said. "Go through any of the doors on the left."

Just as he spoke, a group of young children came out of the corridor, escorted by a tall black woman, perhaps a teacher, walking with the aid of a cane. The kids all looked upset. One of them, a little girl about six years old, was crying.

When they passed by, Liz saw the woman stroke the weeping child on the shoulder, smile reassuringly at the group, and say, "It's all right now, children. You're going home very soon."

This woman was obviously fond of children, Liz thought. Too bad those little kids had to be interviewed, but one of them might have noticed someone in the corridor leading to the balcony stairs, or seen someone following the teacher up there.

Through a cluster of crime scene regulars, Liz glimpsed a slim body sprawled on the gym floor below the balcony and caught sight of long, dark hair. Though she was hooked on homicides, seeing a victim always gave her a sense of regret. As she shook her head and looked away, she spotted

Ike with Lou Sanchez, his partner, seated on a bleacher, talking to a man dressed in coveralls. It appeared as if they'd started interviewing possible homicide suspects, she thought. That must mean they'd completed their investigation and ruled out any kind of accident in the balcony as the cause of death.

Her heart stirred. She'd always found Ike's rangy form, his shock of sandy hair and rugged good looks very attractive—even while he was still Detective Sourpuss. Now that she'd grown to know his surprisingly gentle nature, his unfailing integrity, and his terrific sense of humor, the attraction was intensified.

Seeing Ike mustn't divert her. She looked around for a place to sit while Dan examined the body. When she accompanied Dan to crime scenes, she stayed in the background, kept her eyes and ears open, and jotted her observations in a notebook.

Chairs were stacked against the wall, but she saw one, placed underneath the balcony, a few yards from where the body lay. She sat down, took her notebook out of her purse, and started to put down a full description of the individual being interviewed. Even from across the gym, she could plainly see that the man wearing coveralls was in his late fifties or early sixties, balding, with a bull neck and a squashed-in nose that suggested it had been broken. A tool belt was slung around his middle. Clearly, he wasn't a teacher in this prestigious private school. Most likely he was the janitor, or perhaps an outside workman who'd been doing a job on the premises. Like the little kids and everyone else who was in the building at the time of the crime, he had to be questioned.

She put her notebook back in her purse and glanced around, At the far end of this combination gym and auditorium, she saw a stage and in front of it a piano. Musical instrument cases stood nearby, along with other band items. A group that looked like teachers and students was seated there. Liz noticed a police barrier across the area. This group was probably waiting to be interviewed, she thought. She knew detectives often isolated potential witnesses prior to interviews, but in this situation separating so many of them might have been difficult. She guessed they were being detained together where detectives could keep track of them till all had been interviewed.

The students, mostly boys sitting apart from the teachers, weren't doing much talking, but the teachers appeared to be in conversation. Too bad she couldn't overhear them. If she walked closer to the barricade, maybe she'd pick up on something. From past experience she knew that a chance remark could lead to a clue.

She got up from her chair and sauntered toward the stage, looking all around, pretending to observe the surroundings by glancing toward the rear of the gym and up at the balcony. She nodded at a cop standing near the barricade. He returned the nod—assuming she was part of the investigation, she decided.

For a moment she thought she might get away with walking right up to the barricade and asking the teachers a few questions, but the moment quickly passed. She knew better. She mustn't let her snooping exceed certain limits. Also, she couldn't risk sending Ike right back into his Detective Sourpuss mode.

Still pretending to observe her surroundings, she stepped closer to the barricade—within earshot, she hoped. A few seconds later, her hopes soared. A woman's voice sounded.

"I'm all shook up about this. I keep asking myself who could have done such a terrible thing? But then I remember how she picked on the kids all the time. Any one of the bigger ones could have done it."

The voice came from a muscular woman in athletic

sweats—a P.E. teacher, most likely. Liz was shocked by the lack of emotion in her voice. She didn't sound or appear "shook up" at all. Why, when a fellow teacher had met a violent death only a short while ago?

"Right," a male voice responded. Liz traced the voice to a young man with long, straggly hair, wearing jeans and a T-shirt. He didn't sound upset, either, but she detected a dazed look on his face, as if he were more shocked than saddened by the teacher's death.

Another male voice, with a slight accent she couldn't quite identify—possibly British—spoke with total lack of feeling. "She had an abnormal dislike of children, but in my opinion she didn't care about people in general." The speaker was a swarthy, young man wearing a coat and tie and sitting on the piano bench.

"But she sure loved those little dogs of hers," the athletic-looking woman said. "The only time she ever warmed up was when she talked about them. If you ask me, there's something screwy about a person who likes animals better than humans."

"Especially dogs," the man on the piano bench replied. Liz caught sight of bushy, soot-colored eyebrows coming together in a deep scowl. This guy had something against dogs, Liz thought. Maybe he'd been bitten when he was a child.

Now another voice drew her attention, and Liz noticed the black woman she'd seen with the children. Evidently, she'd just returned from the reception hall. "Julia, all your little ballerinas have been delivered to their mothers and nannies," she said.

"Oh, thanks for doing that for me, Bernice," the gym-teacher type said. "They were so upset, some of them crying—I couldn't handle it, but you're so good with kids."

"This has been upsetting for all of us," the black woman said. Liz waited for her to say something kind about the victim. She said nothing more.

None of the students had said anything, either. She looked them over. They ranged in age from preteens to seventeen or eighteen. A girl, blond and pretty, about sixteen, was whispering with an older boy who looked like an athlete. She pictured him as star of the school basketball team. From the way the two were looking at one another, she imagined they were teenage sweethearts.

At that moment, Liz noticed a pair of dark, deep-set eyes staring straight at her. The swarthy man on the piano bench had become aware of her presence nearby. Something in his steady gaze made her feel uncomfortable. She decided not to linger. The little she'd heard had given her something to work on, for starters. In this group of teachers and students, no one was in deep mourning for the dead woman.

When she walked to the rear of the gym, Liz saw that Dan had completed his examination, a police cameraman had finished photographing the victim, and the body was being prepared for removal. The bull-necked, squashed-nose man was gone, and Ike and his partner were talking to Dan.

As she approached them, Ike turned his head. Their glances met. He smiled.

An unacquainted witness to this encounter would never suspect this NYPD homicide detective was smiling at the woman he was going to marry. Ike wasn't one to let the whole world in on his feelings, nor had he broken any speed records for letting *her* know how he felt. It had taken him way too long to say those three little words. She almost had to speak them before he did.

"I thought I'd run into you around here somewhere, Liz," he said.

Not exactly heart-stirring words, but a giant step forward from "What are you doing here, Rooney?"

"You know where there's a murder there's usually me," she said with a laugh. "This is definitely a homicide, isn't it?"

"Definitely," he replied.

"Then I guess you'll be tied up here a while longer," she said glancing toward the group of teachers and students in the stage area.

Ike must have noticed the glance. "Right, but first we want to talk to the people in the reception hall who came to pick up the younger children," he replied. "We want to get those interviews over with. This has been rough on those little kids. We want to get them out of here as quickly as possible. Next, we'll do the teachers and students in the gym, and then the remaining people in the reception hall. And after we've interviewed everyone in the building, we're going to search the victim's residence."

He paused. "Sorry, but I can't make our dinner with Sophie and Ralph."

"That's okay, I've already canceled with Sophie. But how about you coming to my place when you're finished? I'll rustle up hamburgers or something."

"I might be late. I'll bring takeout, instead. Chinese?"

"Great. So I'll see you later."

"Right." His hand brushed her shoulder in a lingering caress before he left.

She'd have plenty of information to sort out this evening, she thought, as she and Dan left the school building. Soon, Dan would let her know the details of the teacher's death. He'd already told her he believed she'd been killed before being pushed over the balcony railing. Now, after examining the body he'd know the cause of death. Pieced together with what she'd seen and overheard and with what Ike might choose to tell her regarding the interviews, her own investigation would be off to a good start.

"What happened to the teacher up there on the balcony?" she asked as she and Dan left the scene. "Was she bashed on the head before being pushed over the rail, or what?"

"We won't know the full details till we're into the autopsy," he replied, "but there's a discoloration on her throat consistent with asphyxiation from impressment. There's no doubt in my mind this was some form of strangulation."

Chapter Two

By the time Dan dropped her off at her apartment building, Liz's mind was bursting with speculation. The person who'd strangled the victim and pushed her off the balcony might be someone she'd seen in the gym—one of the teachers or students waiting to be interviewed, or the workman with the squashed nose. Since a play rehearsal was in progress, the teachers and students must have been on the stage or somewhere nearby, and the workman might have been fixing something in the area.

Maybe the killer was someone she'd seen in the reception hall, who'd come to pick up a child. Had this person signed in, then entered the gym area and waited for a chance to get the teacher alone? At the time he or she signed in, there was no reason for the guard to restrict anyone to the reception area. She'd noticed restrooms in the gym corridor. The guard wouldn't have thought it unusual if he saw someone going in that direction.

Though the victim seemed generally disliked, the person who murdered her surely must have been motivated by a stronger emotion. Strangulation suggested anger. The slain woman had said or done something to enrage her killer.

With these thoughts whirling around in her head, Liz entered her building, an early twentieth-century Gramercy Park brownstone, converted into three apartments. Owners Rosa and Joe Moscaretti occupied the entire first floor. One flight up were two more apartments. Mr. Klein, an elderly retired gentleman, rented the larger one. The other was the one-room, kitchenette, and bath she'd called home since Pop and Mom sold the family home on Staten Island and moved to Florida.

She'd barely set foot on the second step when the door to the first-floor apartment opened and landlady Rosa Moscaretti appeared, round face all smiles. She held out a plate covered with aluminum foil.

"Hello, Dearie, here's a couple pieces of chocolate cream pie I just baked."

If it wasn't home-baked pie or some other delicious confection, it was pasta and made-from-scratch Italian sauce. Since the day Liz moved into their building, Rosa and her husband Joe had assumed the roles of proxy parents.

The building was not equipped with a buzzer entry system, and the main entrance and vestibule were left unlocked, but the apartment doors were secured with double deadbolts. Who needed anything more with both Moscarettis always on the alert, especially Joe, a Vietnam Marines veteran who kept his service revolver handy?

Rosa and Joe had followed her relationship with Ike from its beginning, voicing constant approval of "that nice young cop." They were as pleased as Pop and Mom about the upcoming February wedding.

Liz took the plate. "Chocolate cream pie! Wonderful! Thanks so much. Ike's coming over later on. We'll have it for dessert."

"What are you cooking for him?" Rosa asked.

Liz knew what *that* meant. If the dinner didn't measure up to what Rosa considered suitable fare for "that nice young cop," she'd insist on providing at least one supplemental side dish from the meal she'd prepared for Joe and herself.

"I'm not cooking anything tonight. Ike's bringing Chinese takeout."

"Oh." Rosa looked disappointed. Liz knew why. The last thing a Chinese meal needed was a supplemental side dish. Besides, cannelonis or eggplant parmesan weren't exactly compatible with chow mein or moo goo gai pan.

Rosa turned to step back inside her apartment. "Well, give my best regards to Ike, and have a nice evening, Dearie."

Liz, continuing up the stairs, smiled, and blew her a kiss. Rosa and Joe had become her good friends, and she was going to miss living here after she and Ike were married. Her place was too small for the two of them. Ike's apartment, further downtown, wasn't much bigger. They'd been looking for larger quarters.

She let herself in and turned on the TV to see if Marva Malin's murder had made the news. It had, and it seemed to be the lead story. In a city where homicides were commonplace, the killing of a beautiful young teacher in a classy private school got media attention not always given to back-alley or drug-related homicides.

"And now, a late-breaking bulletin," the newscaster said. "A teacher at Manhattan's prestigious Chadwick Academy died this afternoon after a fall from a balcony in the school's gymnasium. According to a police statement, her death was not an accident. Further details after these messages. Stay tuned."

Although Liz knew more than the teasing bulletin stated, she'd listen for the rest of it while she got ready for the Chinese takeout. With Ike going to search Malin's apartment after he left the crime scene, she had ample time to set up the gateleg table she always used when he came for dinner. Like her sleeper sofa, chairs, TV, and all her other furnishings, the table had come from the Staten Island house. She liked having things around from the home where she grew up. Also, Gram McGowan, who still lived in New Dorp on Staten Island, had given her what she termed housewarming gifts from her own home. Many of these items Gram had crafted herself, like the patchwork quilt and the needlepoint sofa pillows. Thanks to Gram and Mom, this had to be the best-furnished dinky apartment in Manhattan.

Ike would enjoy wine with their dinner after this extended workday, she thought as she set the table with a lace cloth Gram had given her and dishes and silverware Mom hadn't taken to Florida. But, as she placed two goblets on the table, she realized she didn't have any wine on hand. She should have picked up a bottle the last time she went shopping. All she had were several bottles of fine vintage champagne, given to her a few months ago by Russian Mafia racketeer Boris Tynkov, better known as Big Tiny.

Reviewing the incident, she smiled. Last summer her sleuthing had plunged her into a dangerous predicament. While probing into a baffling murder case, she'd been involved in a botched kidnapping by two thugs. She'd been injured and her captors killed in a high-speed police car chase. When the dead kidnappers were identified as members of Tynkov's organization, Big Tiny was arrested for masterminding the kidnapping. But she'd overheard enough talk between the two thugs to know they'd carried out the kidnapping on their own and Big Tiny had nothing to do with it. Her testimony in his behalf saved him from a prison sentence.

Afterward, she and Ike had been eating dinner in her apartment when a knock on her door brought her face-to-face with four men who looked like characters out of an old gangster movie. One of them could have doubled for Edward G. Robinson. Moments later, she recognized the man in the foreground as Boris Tynkov.

A grateful Big Tiny, accompanied by his bodyguards, had

brought the wine to her apartment in person. She'd always remember his parting words: *"You ever got trouble, you ever need something—I want you should let me know. Big Tiny never forgets."*

She and Ike had decided to save the champagne for special occasions. Ike had popped the cork on one bottle the night he presented her with an engagement ring. Champagne of that rare quality deserved to be accompanied by something more epicurean than tonight's Chinese takeout.

She vetoed her thought of phoning Ike to pick up a bottle of wine. Whether he was still at the crime scene or checking out the murdered woman's apartment, the last thing he needed was a distracting phone call. But the Moscarettis generally kept a variety of wines on hand . . . She reached for the phone.

"Sure, Dearie," Rosa said. "Scarlatta's white should go good with Chinese food. I'll send Joe up with a bottle, right away."

Just as Liz hung up the phone, another TV news bulletin came on the channel she'd been watching, with more details of the Chadwick Academy murder. The newscaster announced that the victim, Marva Malin, age 27, had been strangled before being thrown off the balcony. A photo of her was shown from the school files, a pretty face framed by a cascade of dark, glossy hair. Viewers were advised to stand by for live coverage after a commercial, but Joe was at the door already.

"I had the TV on and heard about the murder at that school," he said, handing her the wine bottle. "I guess you'll be into this one, same as always."

Like everyone else who knew her well, Joe was aware of her passion for following and trying to solve homicides.

She nodded. "I've already been at the scene with my boss."

"Is Ike on the case?"

"Yes."

Joe turned to leave. "Well, I guess the two of you will get it all figured out," he said with a puzzled grin.

He and Rosa would never understand why she'd chosen something so gruesome as a hobby, she thought as she opened the wine bottle and placed it on the table. She didn't fully understand it herself. She only knew she'd always found it stimulating and challenging to try and solve murder cases. Now, matching wits with top-flight detective Ike made it even more so.

The news bulletin came back on with the live coverage. In the darkness, spotlighted shots of the exterior of the school building were shown. She could see cameramen and reporters and curious bystanders gathered near the entrance. While the newscaster delivered a repetitive report, a woman and two boys came out and made their way through a crowd of jostling, shouting reporters and photographers. Ike and his partner must have finished interviewing in the gym and were now working on those remaining in the reception hall.

Liz recalled the people she'd seen in the reception hall and compared them to the group sitting near the stage. After what she'd overheard in the gym, she thought it more likely that someone there was the murderer. None of them had a kind word for the victim. If the news media had arrived at the scene earlier and cameras put into action sooner, she could have gotten another look at the gym group as they left—especially the teachers. Now that she knew the death was the result of some form of strangulation, she could better have speculated who among them might have done it.

Although Dan didn't know exactly how Marva Malin had been strangled, it seemed unlikely that the perpetrator could be one of the younger boys or a girl. But one of the older boys would have been strong enough to overpower a woman the size of Marva Malin, choke her to death with his hands, press something hard against her throat, or tighten a cord around her neck.

If she hadn't been concentrating on the adults, she'd have a clearer picture of the kids, but the only older boy she could recall was the one to whom the pretty blond girl was whispering. She'd imagined them as sweethearts. Then she remembered one of the teachers remarking that the dead woman was always picking on the kids. Had she been especially mean to this pretty blond girl, and was the boy aware of it? Would a lovestruck teenage boy have murder on his mind?

With a shake of her head, she decided to continue concentrating on the four adults. Since she hadn't described them in her notebook, she drew on her memory, picturing each of them.

The woman she thought might be a gym teacher: It wasn't hard to imagine this Olympic contender type sneaking up behind the victim with a length of cord or getting a throttling handgrip on her neck. And she was athletic enough to sprint down the stairs, back to the stage area within seconds after the victim's body hit the floor.

The young man with the long, straggly hair: He was no Mr. Muscles, but from what she'd glimpsed of the victim, he could have overpowered her. He looked agile enough to run down the stairs and return to the stage area while everyone else was distracted by the fallen body.

The swarthy guy with the semi-British accent: Definitely big and powerful enough to do the deed and high-tail it back to the stage before anyone had time to look beyond the victim. She recalled his dark, deep-set eyes, like two brown marbles, scrutinizing her, making her feel uncomfortable.

But the tall, middle-age black woman who walked with a cane and whose manner toward children suggested she liked kids seemed an unlikely suspect. She was slightly disabled. How could she have climbed the stairs to the balcony, strangled the teacher and pushed her over the rail, then gone down again, all within the short time span? Also, would such a kind-natured person be capable of such violence?

She was considering motive, recalling the lack of emotion shown by the four probable teachers in the aftermath of the murder, when another thought flashed into her mind. Had anyone seen the victim hit the gym floor? Any witnesses might be eliminated as suspects. Ike would have gotten that information during his interviews.

Action on the TV screen drew her attention. Another woman was coming out of the school with a boy. A few moments later, two more women and several students came out. At this rate, the interviews would be over soon, Liz thought. A sense of impatience came over her. She wanted to discuss the interviews involving the adults in the gym with Ike and compare her own reactions with his.

The phone rang. Ike wouldn't be calling in the middle of interviews, Liz thought, picking up. It might be Gram. If she'd heard the news about the murder she'd want to talk about it. Liz often thought the genes passed along to her by Gram contained more than red hair.

"I caught a bulletin on TV about a teacher being murdered—thrown off a balcony at a Manhattan school, but I didn't get any details," Gram said, her voice crackling with excitement. "Did Dan take you to the scene of the crime?"

"Yes, I got home a little while ago." She knew Gram would never forgive her if she didn't come up with some details. She filled Gram in on what Dan had told her and promised to keep her up to date. Gram was good at putting things together. If there should ever be a Pulaski and Rooney Private Investigation Service, they'd be smart to bring Gram in on it.

After she said good-bye to Gram, she turned her attention back to the TV. Live coverage was continuing. More people emerged from the school. Spotlights played over their faces. Cameras hummed. News reporters shouted questions.

The phone rang again. It was Ike, sounding hurried. "Liz, if you're not already watching the news, turn it on, quick."

"I have it on. All I see is people coming out of the building."

"Keep watching. We just interviewed a man who'll be coming out any minute now. He'll have a blond girl with him."

Liz focused her eyes on the TV screen. "Yes, I see them coming out. . . ."

An instant later a spotlight swept over the faces of the blond girl and the man. The girl was the pretty teenager from the gym. The man was the one she'd noticed in the reception hall and pegged as a taxi driver. She'd thought he looked familiar. Now, in a flash, she knew she *had* seen him before. He was no taxi driver. *How could she not have immediately recognized that Edward G. Robinson face?*

"Ike—that man's one of Big Tiny's bodyguards!" she exclaimed.

"Right. I was sure you'd recognize him."

"I *didn't* recognize him when I saw him earlier in the reception hall. But a little while ago I was thinking about the night they came with the champagne. I guess that stirred my memory."

She paused, struck by another thought. What if the blond girl had told her parents that the dramatics coach had been especially mean to her? And what if her father . . . ? This thought led to a startling possibility. Far-fetched as it seemed, she couldn't keep from expressing it. "Could Big Tiny possibly have a daughter in Chadwick Academy, and the blond girl—could she be his daughter? Could she have complained to him that the dramatics coach had been picking on her? Could he have sent one of his bodyguards over to the school that day to . . ."

Ike broke in. "Yes, she's Tynkov's daughter. But the bodyguard doubles as a driver. He picks her up at the school every day. The security guard verified this. Also, I don't think Tynkov would have ordered any kind of violence in the school gym. He must have known his daughter would be at the play rehearsal with the orchestra."

Liz nodded. When she'd observed Big Tiny with his family in court, she'd noticed signs of his deep affection for them. "I guess he wouldn't have," she said, though she wasn't convinced. Then Ike's next words told her any further ideas he might be willing to share with her about this would have to wait.

"We're ready to leave for Malin's residence," he said, "See you later, Liz."

Chapter Three

Liz found it difficult not to fire questions at Ike the second he set foot in her door. Knowing that a member of Boris Tynkov's organization had been in the building at the time of the murder had added another ingredient to the mix.

Ike managed as good a hug and kiss as possible while holding the bagful of Chinese takeout cartons. "I'm so hungry, I almost started eating this on the way over," he said.

She took the bag and headed for the kitchenette. "I'll get this on the table right away. Meanwhile, pour yourself a glass of wine." He'd had a long day. She'd let him relax a while before jumping in with queries and comments about the Tynkov henchman. "And maybe there's something about the case on the TV news," she suggested.

"There won't be anything but rehash for a while," he replied. Goblet in hand, he joined her behind the screen that separated the cooking area from the rest of the apartment. "I've been a bachelor too long," he said, watching her scoop moo goo gai pan, shrimp lo mein, and rice into serving dishes. "I was getting too accustomed to takeout boxes on the table. You got me just in time."

"I'm very glad I got you at all," she replied. "But serving

GOODLAND PUBLIC LIBRARY
GOODLAND, KANSAS 67735

out of cartons is okay if you're in a hurry. You don't have to eat and run tonight, do you?"

He shook his head. "Nope. We can have a nice, leisurely dinner and talk about the case."

Her face must have lighted up when he mentioned the case, because he laughed. "Ah—the magic words," he said. "I guess you want to start with the man who came to drive Tynkov's daughter home."

"Yes," she said, carrying the serving dishes to the table. "I don't think he can be ruled out. Maybe Big Tiny didn't know his daughter was rehearsing in the gym."

"Do you believe Tynkov would order a hit just because his daughter had a beef with a teacher?"

"It's possible," she replied, as they sat down at the table. "I observed him with his family the day of his hearing. I could tell he's devoted to his wife and daughters. That means he's protective, too. I remember I was surprised that someone with a reputation for being ruthless and hard-hearted could have a tender side."

"You don't miss anything, do you?"

"Not when something is so obvious."

"Well, ruthless as he is, Tynkov generally draws a line when it comes to outright killing," Ike said, digging into his food. "Remember, he's a loan shark. He just has his thugs break a few bones on the poor slobs who can't ante up."

Liz recalled that kidnapping was another crime Big Tiny would not commit. After her kidnappers had been identified as two of his thugs, he'd made a strong statement to the news media. "I do not do kidnapping," he'd said. "The men who did this, they should be thankful they are dead."

Boris Tynkov was capable of ordering his thugs to administer unspeakably cruel retributive justice, but somewhere in his dark nature lay a spark of decency, she thought.

Ike's next words indicated he was on the fence regarding Tynkov's thug as a suspect. "In our interviews with the teachers and students, we got bits and pieces of information about the victim," he said. "She was coaching the school play—*A Midsummer Night's Dream,* and evidently she took it very seriously. Nobody could do anything right. Nothing but harsh criticism all the time. She'd been especially mean to the Tynkov girl, who plays violin in the school orchestra. We got the distinct impression that Ms. Malin picked on the poor kid constantly from the first day of rehearsals."

"So you agree the girl could have told her father about it?"

Ike nodded while helping himself to another portion of rice. "She could have. But even if he didn't know his daughter would be in the gym, I don't believe he'd have the teacher eliminated. More likely a couple of black eyes and a broken nose."

"Maybe that's what was supposed to happen, but it got out of hand."

Ike shook his head. "The condition of her face and body didn't indicate a roughing-up. She sustained at least one fracture from the fall, and injuries at the points of impact, but the only distinct mark on her was the discoloration across her throat that Dan said was the result of the strangling."

Although Liz wasn't fully convinced that Tynkov had nothing to do with the murder, she decided to table this for now and proceed with the gym group.

"I happened to overhear the teachers talking in the gym," she said. "What I heard ties in with what you picked up in your interviews."

He cast her a sharp look. She knew he was thinking she had to be pretty close to them to overhear what they were saying. He might even think she'd questioned them—a distinct no-no. She hastened to assure him there'd been no verbal exchange.

"I was just wandering around the stage area, and I don't think any of them even noticed me," she said.

A moment later she recalled one of them *had* noticed

her—the swarthy man with the bushy eyebrows. She recalled his scrutiny made her feel uneasy.

"Actually, one of the teachers saw me," she admitted. "He gave me sort of a dirty look, and I decided not to hang around."

Ike looked interested. "Yeah? Which one?"

"The dark man, wearing the coat and tie. He was sitting on the piano bench."

Ike took a notebook out of his coat pocket and consulted it. "Vincent LoPresti," Ike said. "He's the music teacher."

"I wonder why he looked at me like that."

"If he hadn't been very cooperative with Lou and me, I'd say he believed you were part of the investigation and he didn't want to be questioned."

"So he cooperated with you?"

"Fully. Answered all the questions without hesitation. Said he'd let us know if he thought of anything we might be interested in. He was quite friendly."

"There was nothing friendly about the look he gave me," Liz said.

Ike grinned. "Maybe you reminded him of an old girlfriend who dumped him. Did you pick up anything interesting from the other teachers before that dirty look sent you packing?"

"Only what you got. None of the teachers liked the victim."

Again, Ike consulted his notebook. "Only three of them are teachers," he said. "The tall black woman is assistant to the headmaster. Name's Bernice Fripp."

Something in his voice gave Liz the impression that his interview with Bernice Fripp had been especially interesting.

Ike's next words bore this out. "She told us she coached the school play up until this year and still attends all the rehearsals. We got the feeling she likes kids and misses being the dramatics coach."

Liz contemplated this. "I guess it would be too far-fetched to think she had a double motive for murder."

"What, that she'd kill to stop the kids from being harassed and to get back her job coaching the plays?" Ike asked with a grin.

"Forget I said that," Liz replied. "It was a silly notion. She has a very kind disposition and, besides, she has to walk with a cane. How could she have gotten up and down the balcony stairs?"

His answer surprised her. "She doesn't have to use her cane all the time—only when her arthritis is especially bad."

"Who told you that?"

"We picked it up from the kids. Seems she's very well liked by all of them. They feel sorry for her when her arthritis flares up, and she has to use her cane and they're glad when she has a good day and can get around without it."

Liz set her fork down on her plate and looked at him in disbelief. "Are you saying she might have been *faking* a bad arthritis day today?"

He nodded. "Think about it, Liz. The woman's relatively young—in her fifties, I'd say. She's tall and she looks wiry. Her hands are probably strong enough to have choked Malin. If this was one of the days when she didn't need her cane, she could have made it up the stairs to the balcony and down again on her own."

"Wouldn't someone have noticed her following the teacher?"

"No. She told us she was alone in the gym when the victim went up to the balcony to see how the scenery looked from up there. Everyone else was taking a break. She said she called after Malin, telling her it was dark in the balcony and she'd better get the janitor to turn on some lights, but Malin said she'd only be up there for a few minutes."

Malin was one hundred percent correct about that, Liz

thought, in a stroke of dark humor. "So, assuming Bernice was telling the truth, she'd be the only one who saw the victim hit the floor."

"Right. She said she was sitting in a chair under the balcony when it happened."

"But she could have been on her way down from the balcony."

"It's a possibility."

"If what she told you is true, and she *was* sitting under the balcony when the victim landed, that must have been an awful shock. Wouldn't she have screamed? Wouldn't someone have heard it?"

"She said she remembers screaming, but evidently nobody heard it. However, the male teacher with the long hair said he was coming out of the men's room and saw Bernice heading for the reception hall. This corroborates what Bernice told us. She screamed when the body hit the floor, then went to notify the guard."

Liz looked at Ike with a frown. Was he playing games with her, first making her think Bernice was a strong suspect, then insinuating she wasn't?

He must have noticed the frown and guessed the reason for it. "Sorry," he said. "I get a kick out of your reactions."

She felt herself bristling. "Well, I'm delighted you find them amusing, Detective."

"Whoa! Hold on to your redhead temper! Sure, I get a little fun out of your reactions, but that doesn't mean I don't value them. I haven't forgotten how often they've helped me crack a case."

Not fully placated, she asked, "Can we discuss the other possible suspects without you setting me up for an amusing reaction?"

"Yes, ma'am. You choose who's next."

"The male teacher with the long hair."

"He's the last one we interviewed. I remember his name's Cyril Gibbs. He's the art teacher. He and his students painted the scenery for the play."

"He told you he was coming out of the restroom when he saw Bernice going to notify the guard, but he could have been coming down from the balcony."

Ike contemplated this for a moment. "Right, but there's something I haven't figured out yet. The victim would have hit the deck before the killer could make it down the stairs and into the corridor. Whoever he or she is would have bumped into Bernice on her way to notify the guard. But she didn't mention seeing anyone."

Liz pictured Bernice, shocked and horrified when Malin's body landed on the gym floor. Like anyone else, she would have gone immediately to notify the security guard. But on a bad arthritis day, it would have taken her extra minutes to get up from her chair and hobble out of the gym, into the corridor. "Bernice wouldn't be very fast on her feet if her arthritis was kicking up. Maybe she didn't get to the corridor till after the killer was down the stairs and home free."

Ike shot her an approving look. "Some detective *I* am! I was still into the concept of her faking a bad day. You're absolutely right. The time she'd have taken to get moving would have given the killer time to clear the stairway area."

She knew it wouldn't have been long before he thought of this, but she loved his approval.

"So the art teacher can't be ruled out?" she asked.

"Not at this point."

"How about the other male teacher, Mr. Dirty Look?"

"LoPresti told us he was backstage during the break, talking to his music students most of the time, except for a trip to the men's room."

At the risk of providing him with another amusing reaction, she asked, "Did he tell you what time that was?"

42   *Dorothy P. O'Neill*

"We asked him, but, understandably, he wasn't sure," Ike replied. "But taking Bernice's arthritis into consideration, *anybody* could have made it down from the balcony and away from the stairway area before Bernice hobbled into the corridor."

He paused with a grin. "Getting back to LoPresti—how about that accent of his? I never heard an Italian-American New Yorker who talked like that. Did you notice it?"

"Yes. I thought it might be a British accent, but I wasn't sure."

"It's closer to British than anything else. I think he must have taken speech therapy to get rid of an especially strong *Noo Yawk* accent."

Liz nodded. "Maybe he really wanted to land a job in a classy private school and thought he'd have a better shot if he sounded like Prince Charles."

Ike laughed. "Evidently, it worked. Well, let's get to the female teacher." He consulted his notes. "Physical education teacher Julia Tulley. She's the choreographer for the little kids' dancing scene. According to what we picked up in the interviews, she and Malin weren't on the best of terms, and they'd had words not long before Malin's body came down off the balcony. Several of the kids told us Malin made an insulting remark, and the gym teacher was still very angry during the break backstage."

"The restrooms are near the foot of the balcony stairway," Liz said. "She could have been on her way there or coming out and seen Malin going up to the balcony."

"Though she told us she stayed backstage during the break, two students remembered seeing her leave," Ike replied. "They didn't notice how long she was gone."

Had Julia Tulley forgotten she'd left the backstage area, or had she lied?

"Well, that covers the adult interviews," she said. "How about the kids?"

"Nothing suspicious. Most of them are too young or lack the strength to perform a strangulation."

While I was in the stage area I noticed the blond girl you say is Big Tiny's daughter," Liz said. "She was whispering to a good looking, well-built older boy. I got the impression there's a teen romance going on."

Ike didn't have to consult his notebook. "I recall the boy's name—Greg Jensen. And you're right, according to what we picked up from the kids, he and Anna Tynkov have something going."

An idea sprang into her mind. Their glances met. He shook his head.

"If you're thinking the boy might have gone after Malin because she was mean to his girlfriend, I don't think so. He impressed both Lou and me as an easygoing kid—too easygoing to commit murder. Of course, we could be wrong. He's not much of a suspect, but we're keeping him in mind."

Liz recalled the squashed-nosed man wearing coveralls and a tool belt. "How about the guy in the work clothes you were talking to on the bleachers?" she asked.

"The school janitor," Ike replied. "He claims he went to his basement quarters around four o'clock and stayed there till one of our cops brought him up to the gym to be interviewed." He glanced at his notes. "Dudley Baca. He told us everybody calls him Duddy. Nice old guy. Used to be in the ring."

"Any reason to suspect him?"

"No more than anyone else, but he admitted he had a run-in with Malin. Seems she reported him to the headmaster for not removing trash. After Lou and I go over our notes and put a few things together, we'll be doing some second interviews."

Liz looked at Ike's empty plate. "If you're ready for dessert, Rosa gave me two pieces of her homemade chocolate cream pie."

He smiled his approval. "What are we going to do for desserts after we're married and you're out of here?"

Liz gave a sigh. "I don't know." The sigh wasn't as much from the thought of moving away from Rosa's desserts as from knowing they'd never find landlords like the Moscarettis.

Ike must have had the same thought. "Too bad this apartment doesn't have a little more space," he said. "Even one more room would be enough."

They finished their pie and took mugs of coffee to the sofa.

"You haven't asked if we found anything interesting at the victim's apartment," Ike said, settling himself among Gram's needlepoint pillows.

"Did you?"

"Would you call two little dogs interesting?"

"Two dogs? Are you serious?"

"Absolutely. A pair of Pomeranians. We fed them and Lou took them out for a walk while I was checking the place. We were going to put them in a shelter, but the super said he and his wife would look after them till Malin's folks get here."

"I guess you were surprised when you found the dogs in the apartment."

"No surprise. When I talked to Malin's parents they told me about them."

"You talked to the parents? Under such circumstances, isn't it customary for the local police to break the news to the family?"

"Right—I didn't break the news," Ike replied. "I phoned the Indianapolis police and they took over, but I left word how I could be reached and the parents phoned me while I was on my way to the apartment. They were shocked and dazed, of course, but they had questions. After I answered them as best I could, we talked a while. They mentioned the dogs and said they were going to take them back home with them."

"They sound like nice people. I wonder what made their daughter so hateful."

"In cases like this, it's not unusual for family members to

talk freely about the deceased. It's as if they have a need to do this. Listening to Malin's parents, I got the distinct feeling that she was always extremely jealous of her younger sister. Abnormal jealousy can poison a person's nature."

Liz nodded. "That could explain everything."

"And here's one more sidelight on Malin," Ike continued. "The first cops at the scene went through her purse and took out her ID and address book before bagging the purse. They turned the items over to me when I got there. When I looked up the phone number and address of the parents, I found out their names are Marvin and Ethel *Malinbaum*."

"She changed her name! Do they know that?"

"Yes, but, understandably, they didn't go into it."

Another thought struck Liz. Ike said the cops gave him the victim's ID and address book, but he hadn't told her where they'd found the purse.

"It was on the floor of the balcony," he replied, when she asked him about it.

"How was the purse styled?" she asked. Dan didn't know yet if the killer choked Malin manually or used cord or something, she thought. If the purse had long strap handles, maybe this was used in the strangling.

"I haven't examined it yet," Ike replied. He gave a teasing grin. "Sorry I'm not into purse styling, but when I go to the evidence lab I'll keep this in mind. I promise I'll report back to you with all the styling details."

He glanced toward the TV. "Want to see what old movie's on?"

She knew he'd gone as far as he wanted with the case tonight, and she loved watching old movies with Ike. "If you're sure there's nothing new about the case on the news channels," she said.

"Trust me. Unless some media cameraman spotted Lou walking the Pomeranians, there's nothing that hasn't been reported," Ike replied. He turned the TV to a news channel anyway, adding, "We'll make sure."

The familiar facade of Chadwick Academy flashed onto the screen. A commentator was repeating the spiel Liz had heard earlier.

"You're right—no updates," she said.

Seconds later, the commentator made an announcement. Chadwick Academy's headmaster had put out the word that the school would be closed tomorrow due to the death of teacher Marva Malin.

Ike gave a wry smile. "Make that *due to a police order.* We're giving the premises another going-over tomorrow, concentrating on the backstage and balcony. Until that's done with, the school's a crime scene."

"I guess the headmaster didn't want to remind people of that," Liz said. "Especially the parents. They must be in a furor, knowing the killer might be someone their kids come in contact with every day."

"That's classified information," Ike replied.

"I guess you mean the general public, including the head-master, doesn't know your suspects are all connected to the school in some way. If you let that out, you'd be tipping the killer's hand. You'll have to keep the news media in the dark, too."

"Right. We have to insinuate the idea that we think the murderer could be a rank outsider."

"That's going to shake up the school's security system."

"It already has. Parents are calling for an overhaul of the exit alarm system and an intensive investigation into the se-curity guard's background."

He turned the TV to the movie channel. *Mrs. Miniver* had just started. "Are you up for some World War Two?" he asked.

"Oh, yes, I haven't seen that one in ages," Liz replied. "It's one of my favorites, and so is Greer Garson."

"I have to leave as soon as the movie's over," Ike said,

drawing her close to him. "Busy day at the school tomorrow, and the victim's parents will be in town. We'll need to talk to them."

There'd be more such days before he finally zeroed in on Marva Malin's murderer, she thought, snuggling closer. Homicide was a hobby for her—she could choose which ones she wanted to follow—but for Ike it was a constant grind. It would do him good to get his mind off killings for a little while. At least the bloodshed of World War II was blurred by time.

Chapter Four

Liz awakened the next morning with the sense of anticipation she always felt when she became involved in a new
murder case—while she showered and dressed, while she
made coffee and thawed a bagel in the microwave, while she
folded up the sofa bed, she reviewed what she and Ike had
discussed last night.

She got the feeling Ike hadn't held back, but this was
only the beginning. If his investigation produced evidence
he considered too sensitive to divulge, he'd clam up.

Sensitive or not, he'd have ample time to dig up evidence
before she could try and get it out of him. They weren't seeing one another tonight. Ralph's male cop friends were
throwing a bachelor party at a favorite NYPD hangout, and
Sophie's women friends were hosting a dinner party for her
at a Rockefeller Center restaurant. Meanwhile, with a strong
lineup of possible suspects and a common motive, Liz
thought she couldn't ask for a better beginning.

Dan usually got to work earlier than she, but when she
glanced into his office on the way to her workstation, he
wasn't at his desk. Good, she thought. Marva Malin's au-

topsy was probably underway. Dan would soon know if the killer had choked Malin with his hands or used some sort of implement to strangle her. Once she knew, she could start matching possible murder weapons with possible suspects. How lucky she was to have a job where her boss was both medical examiner and Pop's longtime friend.

Sophie phoned during the morning. She and her partner were on their way to a domestic fracas. "I know you said you'd call me, but I won't be answering my phone for a while," she said. "I saw the coverage of the school murder on the news last night, but there wasn't much to it. You have about two minutes to fill me in."

"Dan said the victim was strangled before she was thrown off the balcony," Liz replied. "He won't know exactly how till they're into the autopsy."

"Any suspects, or to use the current term, persons of interest?"

"Several potentials. Ike and I discussed them last night. None of them came out on top." She knew if she told Sophie too much, she'd be betraying Ike's confidence. Anyway, Sophie was sharp enough to figure things out for herself.

Sophie's next words proved her right. "The way schools are beefing up their security with guards and electronically controlled exit alarms, nobody could come into the building and slip out without being caught. I think this has to be an inside job."

An instant later she added, "Oh, we're at the scene. Gotta split. Call you later when we can talk."

With Sophie's wedding coming up this Saturday, they had much more to talk about than a homicide, Liz thought. Ralph's family would be arriving on Staten Island from Yonkers on Friday evening, and Sophie had been trying to find overnight accommodations for his parents, grandparents, and other relatives. The only local hotel had been booked solid for months because of the annual Curtis High School Alumni reunion scheduled the same day.

Sophie's parents had a spare bedroom plus a sofa bed in their basement recreation room. Neighbors and friends offered bunk beds and sofa beds, which took care of everyone except Ralph's grandparents.

"They're both elderly," Sophie said. "I want them to be comfortable, and that means double deckers and foldaways are out. I guess I'll have to give up my room and sleep on the living room couch."

Sophie had told her this a few days ago. With her mind occupied by Marva Malin's murder, Liz had forgotten to tell Sophie that Gram had offered her guestroom. It was the room Liz always slept in whenever she stayed with Gram. It was to have been her headquarters the night before the wedding.

"If you don't mind sleeping on the daybed in my sewing room, Ralph's grandparents can have the guest room," Gram had told her.

"Of course I don't mind," Liz had replied. "Thanks, Gram. This will take a load off Sophie's mind." She'd tell Sophie the good news when they talked later.

"I should have a bigger house," Gram said. "When you and Ike get married, your mother and father will be staying here, and it would be so nice if I could put Ike's folks up, too."

The comment stirred a thought that had disturbed Liz almost from the moment she and Ike got engaged. Months ago, before their relationship became serious, he'd mentioned that he and his parents were estranged. They'd never forgiven him for choosing to be a New York City cop instead of an attorney, like his father, in their upstate hometown. He'd made several attempts to reconcile, without success.

At her insistence, he'd written to them a few weeks ago, telling them of his engagement and forthcoming marriage. So far there'd been no response.

"You're their only son," she'd said. "Surely they'll come to the wedding."

"All we can do is send them an invitation," he'd replied.

When she compared this situation with the loving relationship she had with Pop and Mom, she felt both sad and angry. She'd written to Ike's parents a couple of days ago, expressing the hope that they'd attend the wedding. Since the letter was from her, not Ike, they might respond, she thought.

"You're a sweetheart to do that, but don't get your hopes up," he'd said when she asked him for his parents' address.

A voice penetrated her rambling thoughts. "Lizzie, I know you've been waiting to hear how the teacher was strangled." She looked up and saw Dan approaching.

Instantly, all thoughts other than those pertaining to Marva Malin's murder left her mind. "What did you find out?" she asked.

"First tests indicate that something hard, like a metal or wooden rod, was pressed against her throat," Dan replied. "Her trachea was crushed. When that happens, the airway is blocked, the victim loses consciousness almost immediately, the heart stops pumping, and death occurs within a couple of minutes." He paused, adding, "We'll know more as we go along, but this will give you something to think about. I'm on my way to a meeting, now. I'll see you later, Lizzie."

Something hard, like a metal or wooden rod. She tried to think of some items fitting the description—articles likely to have been in the stage area during the rehearsal yesterday. She remembered seeing instrument cases. Could the pressure of a violin bow crush a windpipe? She'd noticed drums, too. Could the murder weapon have been a drumstick? The killer didn't have to be a student violinist or drummer. Someone else could have taken either of these articles backstage during the break, after planning to follow Malin up to the balcony and use the implement to strangle her. But a violin bow couldn't have been slipped into a pocket or otherwise hidden. It would have been noticed by everyone else backstage. The killer would have to be pretty dumb to risk this being mentioned during a police interrogation. But anyone could have concealed something the size of a drumstick under a sweater or jacket.

Or a music teacher's baton! LoPresti might have planned to follow Malin up to the balcony and use his baton to throttle her. He could have taken it backstage without anyone seeing it.

A moment later, she realized this didn't jell. When Malin told everyone to take a break, nobody knew she'd decide to go up to the balcony. While on the break backstage, the killer had to have seen her going up there or heard her tell someone where she was going *before* deciding this would be a chance to murder her. Once the decision was made, the killer probably picked up the murder weapon somewhere in the backstage area during the break. That would eliminate a violin bow, a drumstick, or a baton, wouldn't it?

Liz shook her head. She shouldn't be concentrating on the case when she had work to do. Reluctantly, she put all thoughts of it on hold till lunchtime.

When she went out for lunch, she passed a newsstand. Headlines on the front pages of the *Daily News* and the *Post* caught her attention.

The *News* featured a photo of the victim below three-inch headlines.

TEACHER MURDERED
AT CHADWICK ACADEMY

The *Post's* coverage included a photo and headlines equally large but more creative:

GRIM FINALE
DRAMA TEACHER SLAIN
AT SCHOOL PLAY REHEARSAL

Even without the headlines, the photo would attract attention, Liz thought. Marva Malin was a beautiful woman, but her beauty did not deter her killer. Someone hated her enough to end her life in a vicious way. *Grim Finale*. A fitting description for a death connected to theatrics, Liz decided, as she bought a copy of the *Post*.

She read the paper while eating lunch in a nearby coffee shop. The coverage of the murder contained nothing she didn't already know. Ike wasn't providing hints to the news media—or maybe not to her, either, she thought, with a wry smile.

He couldn't go on withholding information indefinitely. He had to come out with a progress report soon, before Chadwick Academy parents began to fault NYPD Homicide for dragging its feet and pressured the DA for an arrest.

She recalled a previous case she'd followed, where a beleaguered DA had been driven to use weak circumstantial evidence to charge a man with first-degree murder. Certain that the wrong person had been accused, she'd done some snooping and stumbled on a possible clue. She'd let Ike in on it. He'd gone with it and apprehended the actual killer. That was the first case on which they'd worked together, and it formed the turning point in their relationship—*from adversaries to allies*.

The remembrance made her smile. If it hadn't been for that case, she might not be planning a February wedding.

She'd been back at her workstation for about an hour when Sophie phoned again from her patrol car. "The Chadwick Academy murder has the station house buzzing," she said. "The cops who were at the school say the victim was just as gorgeous as her picture on TV and in the papers. Was she?"

"There were too many people around the body for me to get a good look at her," Liz replied. "But I did see long, dark hair and a super shape."

"The cops found her handbag on the floor of the balcony. The script of the school play was in it and credit cards and money too, so robbery didn't enter into it. They said the bag had long strap handles. They'd be perfect for a strangling job."

"I thought of that, too, but straps are out. Dan told me something hard, like a metal or wooden rod, was pressed against her throat,"

"Too bad," Sophie said. "I thought I'd stumbled on the murder weapon. Oops, I gotta split. I'll see you at the restaurant tonight."

When Liz clicked off the phone, she realized she'd again forgotten to tell Sophie that Gram had offered her guestroom to accommodate Ralph's grandparents. Preoccupation with a homicide always took over her mind, leaving no space for anything else. Well, she'd let Sophie know tonight at the dinner party.

She reviewed her talk with Sophie. If Marva Malin's bag could contain a script, it must be large. Ike had called it a purse, but Sophie was going on what she got from the cops, and she'd called it a handbag. Maybe it was a tote bag. Was it leather or fabric? She wished she'd seen it. Sophie said it had shoulder-strap handles. But some bags had both shoulder straps *plus* a handle. Some handles were made of a hard material like plastic or wood. The killer might have sneaked from behind the victim, grabbed the bag and pressed the handle against her throat with enough force to crush her trachea.

After Dan let her know what else Forensics picked up, she could start figuring out connections between suspects and what was used as a murder weapon.

Later in the day, she phoned Gram.

"I've been following the school murder in the newspaper and on TV," Gram said. "It looks to me like it's not going to be any open and shut case. Did Dan tell you what the killer used to strangle the teacher?"

She reported what Dan had told her.

"A metal or wooden rod could be a lot of things," Gram said.

"I know. I'm trying to be patient while waiting for him to give me something more definite."

"A metal rod sounds like a gun barrel, but who'd be carrying a gun in a school like Chadwick Academy?" Gram said with a laugh. "Well, I'll say good-bye now, Dear. Let me know when you hear what was used, okay?"

Liz barely heard herself saying "Okay" and "Good-bye." Gram's joking remark about the gun barrel resounded in her mind. Excluding the guard, there was only one person she could think of who'd be carrying a gun in a school like Chadwick Academy: *Boris Tynkov's bodyguard.*

Chapter Five

The imagery formed in her mind of Big Tiny's bodyguard pressing his gun barrel against Marva Malin's throat, so suddenly and with such strength that she was unable to utter a sound. Just as she pictured the victim collapsing and the killer dragging her to her feet and pushing her over the balcony railing, she heard Dan's voice.

"I guess you thought I was never going to get back to you Lizzie."

The sight of his smiling face drove the ghastly picture from her mind. "I've had plenty of time to turn my imagination loose, and it got pretty wild," she admitted.

"Well, here's something else for your rampant imagination," he replied. "I just got word from the lab that the article used as the murder weapon was made of wood."

"Oh," she said. "You got here just in time. I was about to imagine the killer on trial for choking Marva Malin to death with his gun barrel."

"Did this gun-packing killer have an identity?" Dan asked with a teasing grin.

"Yes, but he's not a figment of my imagination. He's a member of the Russian Mob—one of Boris Tynkov's body-

56

guards. He came to the school the afternoon of the murder to drive Tynkov's daughter home."

Dan nodded. "I talked to Ike this morning at the autopsy. He mentioned the bodyguard."

"I didn't know Ike planned to attend the autopsy. I thought he was going over to the school for another search."

"He stopped in for a while, before going on to the school. Said he wanted to pin down the material the murder implement was made of. I got the feeling he was interested in something metal. I left word with Forensics to notify him when they found out."

Although Ike had told her Big Tiny would be more likely to order a beating than a killing, Liz thought this sounded as if he hadn't eliminated the bodyguard as a possible suspect. Ike, too, might have had a gun barrel in mind. "I guess he was hoping it would be something metal so he could pin down Tynkov's man as a suspect," she said.

"The bodyguard could still be a suspect," Dan replied. "Guns aren't the only weapons thugs keep on them. They carry billy clubs too."

A billy club. Why hadn't she thought of that herself? The bodyguard could have been ordered to give Malin a few whacks, maybe knock her out temporarily, but for some reason had to change tactics. Perhaps she'd turned around and gotten a good look at him and told him she knew he was the driver who always picked up Anna Tynkov after rehearsals. He couldn't risk implicating Big Tiny in the attack. The only way to shut her up was to silence her, permanently.

Her thoughts shifted to the discoloration found on Malin's neck. "That kind of club would have made quite a wide mark on the victim's throat, wouldn't it?" she asked.

Dan nodded. "You're wondering if the mark on her throat is as wide as a billy club. It's even wider, but that doesn't rule it out. Something less thick can't be ruled out, either.

When applied with strong pressure any size implement could shift, making a wider impression."

He chuckled as he turned to go into his office, adding, "I guess that gives you something to think about, Lizzie."

He was right. His remark about any size implement got her thinking about LoPresti's baton again. Though it would probably be only half as thick as a billy club, it couldn't be eliminated it as a possible murder weapon. Suppose LoPresti always kept it on him during school hours. That would mean he didn't have to find some other object, backstage, when he decided to go after Malin.

Now she had two potential suspects matched with two objects which might have been used to crush the victim's trachea. She found herself wishing that she and Ike weren't tied up with Ralph's and Sophie's parties tonight. The urge to go over this with him was almost overwhelming.

Ike phoned just before quitting time. True to his reluctance to discuss case developments on the phone, his first words were guarded. "I guess Dan told you the material in question is wood," he said.

He didn't sound disappointed that it couldn't have been a gun barrel. Most likely he'd thought of a billy club too. "Yes, he told me," she replied. "I wish we could discuss this tonight, but there's no telling what time the party for Ralph will break up."

"Yeah, it'll probably run a little late for me to drop by afterward. If the Moscarettis heard someone coming into the building after they turned in, Joe would be out of the sack like a shot to investigate."

"Brandishing his Marine corps gun," Liz added, laughing.

"Well, have a good time at Sophie's party."

"You have fun too."

"Right. See you tomorrow night. You want to eat out somewhere?"

If they went out to eat, they wouldn't be able to talk freely about the case during dinner, she thought. "I'll go food shopping on my way home from work and put something together," she said.

"Sounds good," he replied.

The time was going to drag until she saw him, she thought after they'd said good-bye. Needing to be with Ike was only half of it. Wanting to discuss her latest murder suspects with him was the other. Swapping ideas was a big part of their relationship.

She closed down her workstation, telling herself she should try to get her mind off billy clubs and batons for tonight and enjoy Sophie's party.

Chapter Six

Getting her mind off Marva Malin's murder had been easier conceived than accomplished, Liz thought when she reached to silence her alarm clock the next morning. Last night, her final waking thoughts had been about the case and this morning they were still there. It would be easy to blame Sophie for this. At the party they were seated next to each other, and several times during the festivities, Sophie had brought up the case with a whispered comment or question.

But the truth was, her own response made it equally her fault. Seventeen women attended the party, including Sophie's mother and younger sister, Staten Island friends, and friends from Sophie's NYPD station house. Almost all had something to say. In between the amusing speeches and the toasts, she'd managed to let Sophie in on her suspicions concerning the bodyguard's billy club and the music teacher's baton.

"I hope Ike pins down a prime suspect before Saturday," Sophie whispered. "I don't want to stand in front of the priest, thinking about murder weapons instead of wedding vows."

Liz knew she wasn't serious. Although Sophie's interest in homicides rivaled her own, when she and Ralph joined hands at the altar, Marva Malin's murder would be the furthest thing from her mind.

Just before the party broke up, Liz remembered Gram's offer of her guestroom for Ralph's grandparents. She told Sophie. "I've been so absorbed with this case I kept forgetting to tell you," she'd explained.

"Oh, that solves the problem. I'll phone your Gram tomorrow and thank her," Sophie replied. "And thanks to you, too, for taking the sewing room daybed." She paused, smiling. "Don't forget, my folks will have an extra bedroom after Saturday. When Ike's parents come for your wedding, they can stay in my old room if they want to."

The remark had stirred up the troublesome thought of Ike's estrangement from his parents. She hadn't mentioned this to Sophie. She'd been hoping Ike's mother and father would respond to her letter soon and assure her that they would attend their only son's wedding.

Now, as she brewed her morning coffee, she thought about this again. If only Ike's parents would decide to come to the wedding, the rift might be ended. The possibility cast a ray of hope onto the unhappy situation.

Before leaving for work, she switched on the TV to get the latest news about the murder. The newscaster reported that police were speculating on the possibility that the killer was an intruder who'd managed to slip out of the building after committing the murder. The implement used to strangle Marva Malin had not yet been identified. Nothing was said about it being a wooden object.

Ike and Lou were playing it cool, Liz thought as she left her apartment. But she had two solid leads that had nothing to do with an intruder—the billy club and the baton. She had a hunch there'd be more.

Dan came to her desk during the morning, saying he had a favor to ask of her.

"You know I'd do anything for you, Dan," she told him. "Just as long as it's not illegal," she teased.

"I swear there's nothing illegal about this," he replied with a smile. "I'm going to be tied up here, or I'd do this myself. Would you stop at Chadwick Academy on your way home and pick up my pen? It's the gold pen Edna gave me for our fortieth wedding anniversary, engraved with our initials and the date. When I couldn't find it yesterday, it occurred to me that I might have lost it Monday while I was at the school."

What luck! A chance to view the crime scene again! "Sure, Dan," she replied.

"Good. I appreciate this, Lizzie."

Not as much as she did! "I'm happy to do it," she said. "Did you phone the school today, and were you told someone found it?" she asked.

"Not exactly. I called there yesterday. The school was closed, but the janitor answered the phone. He said he'd look for the pen and get back to me. I thought it was gone for good, but I just heard from him a few minutes ago, and he said he found it on the gym floor."

"I'm so glad it turned up. I know it meant a lot to you."

He nodded. "I didn't know how I was going to tell Edna."

"Will I pick it up from the security guard?"

"Yes. The janitor said he gave it to the guard. I told him to let the guard know a young lady would be coming for it this afternoon. Leave work early, Lizzie, say four or so, and take a taxi to the school and to your apartment, too." He took out his wallet and handed her some bills. "And here's something for the janitor," he said, adding a twenty. "Lucky for me he's honest. That pen's eighteen-karat gold. He could have made a few bucks on it."

He turned to go to his office, pausing to look over his shoulder with a conspiratorial grin. "Don't tell Ike I said this, but while you're at the school you could have a look around."

She returned the smile. "Ike knows I couldn't pass up a chance like this."

At that moment Sophie phoned. She was in her squad car outside a doughnut shop. "Mike's gone in to get us coffee," she said. "Can you talk for a couple of minutes?"

"Sure." Sophie wanted to talk about last night's party, she thought. She was right.

"It was a huge success," Sophie said. "We had plenty of laughs, didn't we?"

"Yes, it was a lot of fun," Liz replied. "I hope the guys had a good time at Ralph's bash."

"Ralph phoned a little while ago. He said it was a good party."

"Any girls popping out of cakes?"

Sophie laughed. "I asked him about that. He said no, it was like a roast with him taking the heat. Sounded like they had a great time."

Liz told her about Dan's pen. "I'm leaving the office around four and going to the school to get it," she said.

"What a stroke of luck," Sophie replied. "This is your chance to get back to the scene of the crime."

"That's exactly what I've been thinking."

"Mike's coming out with the coffee," Sophie said. "Call me at home tonight, and let me know if you picked up anything new at the school."

"With your wedding coming up Saturday, how can you think of anything else but getting married?" Liz asked.

"Do you believe you'll be able to get a baffling homicide off *your* mind a few days before your own wedding?"

"Maybe not. But this is your last day of work before Saturday, isn't it? Starting tomorrow, I'll bet last-minute wedding details will shove Marva Malin's murder straight out of your mind."

"I guess it's possible," Sophie said with a laugh. "So long. Don't forget to call me tonight."

It was almost noon when her phone rang again. It was Ike. She knew he was going to be especially busy today, and she hadn't expected to hear his voice till he knocked on her door this evening. Her first thought was that he might have to work late on the case. "I hope you're not calling off our date tonight," she said.

"Nothing like that. I've just finished talking to Malin's parents. Her apartment is a few blocks from your building and since I'm in the vicinity I thought we could grab some lunch."

With her heart quickening, as it always did at the prospect of seeing him, she managed a flip reply. "I was going to have lunch with Donald Trump at the Waldorf, but I'll cancel."

They arranged to meet in a restaurant not far from her building. Ike was waiting when she got there, and he'd already asked for a table for two in a secluded alcove.

She had no illusions about this being a romantic gesture. He figured she'd want to discuss the case and wanted to make sure they wouldn't be overheard.

After they were seated and had looked at the menus, she told him he didn't need to waste time telling her about Ralph's party. "Sophie called and said Ralph told her all about it and of course she filled me in, so we can get right to the case," she said.

"Aren't you taking a lot for granted, assuming I was going to discuss the case with you?" he asked with a teasing grin.

"I don't think so," she replied. "Anything new?"

He held back his reply when a waiter approached the table. After they ordered, he gave a nod. "Yes. Lou and I were at the school yesterday, and we went over the balcony and the backstage area again. The school was closed, so we were able to search without any distractions."

"What were you looking for?"

"We thought we might find a possible murder weapon."

"And . . . ?"

"We found a hammer lying behind the backdrop on the stage."

The imagery of a large hammer with a wooden handle flashed into her mind. Her eyes widened. "Wow. That implicates the janitor, doesn't it?"

"It could. When we found it, we questioned him and he admitted it was his. He told us he'd loaned it to Greg Jensen on Monday afternoon to construct the backdrop, and Greg hadn't returned it."

"And the school was closed yesterday, so he couldn't ask Greg for it."

"Right. He said he hadn't seen Greg since he loaned him the hammer. He was pleased we'd found it. Of course we need to run tests on it to match it up with the marks on the victim's neck, but Duddy didn't seem concerned when we told him we had to hang onto it for a while."

Liz thought this over. If Duddy had used his hammer in the strangling, wouldn't he have gotten rid of it instead of stashing it behind the backdrop? Yes, she decided, until two more possibilities struck her in rapid succession. Duddy could have put the hammer behind the backdrop to implicate Greg, or Greg could be the killer. Although Ike had told her he believed Greg was too easygoing to commit murder, he'd also admitted he could be wrong and hadn't ruled him out.

But if Greg had done the strangling with the hammer, would he have brought it back to the stage and stashed it in the very place where everyone knew he'd been working? It wasn't the smartest thing for a killer to do, but maybe he planned to get rid of the hammer and tell Duddy he'd lost it. Meanwhile, he'd hidden it behind the backdrop.

Ike's laugh brought her out of her musing. "You were really sorting things out just now, weren't you? I like watching your face when you're doing that."

"Could you tell what I was thinking?"

"I'm not that good. How about letting me know?"

"Among other things, I was wondering if Greg Jensen could be the killer." She explained her reasoning.

Ike shook his head. "In our interviews with the kids, every one of them told us that Greg was backstage with Anna Tynkov during the entire break. But you didn't know that. Your thinking was good."

The waiter brought their lunch at that moment. She'd reminded Ike that she was going to cook a good dinner tonight, so they'd ordered just sandwiches and coffee. After the waiter left, he reached across the table and gave her hand a squeeze.

"You'd make one hell of a detective, Liz," he said.

"Must be Pop's genes."

He nodded. "I'm sure they're a factor. But another is your ability to perceive things from a woman's angle. That's something even Sherlock Holmes couldn't do."

Liz smiled. His respect for women's capabilities was one of the many things she loved about him.

"Did you do follow-up interviews today?" she asked.

"Yeah, besides the janitor, we talked to Bernice and the teachers and a couple of students. This time, the gym teacher admitted going to the rest room during the break. Said it slipped her mind before. We're gradually getting a fix on where each one of them was when the victim was pushed off the balcony, and we're trying to match up each suspect with other possible murder weapons. Duddy's hammer will be the first to be tested to see if it conforms to the marks on Malin's neck."

"When tests show a match, you'll have the murder weapon," Liz said.

"Right, and after that it shouldn't be difficult to find out who used it," Ike said.

Especially when the possible suspects didn't know that Forensics had identified the murder implement as wooden, Liz thought.

A question popped into her mind—something she should have asked Dan. "How could Forensics tell that the murder weapon was made of wood?"

"Dan told me that traces of properties used in wood finishing showed up on the skin. Also, marks on the victim's neck showed discoloration differences, indicating a variation in the shape or thickness of the murder weapon. Wood is the most likely material to have been shaped or carved or have a worn place. This will help in matching the murder implement with the neck marks."

"Every hammer handle I ever saw was shaped narrower down toward its head," Liz said. "And couldn't the handle get worn, over time, in the place where the user always gripped it? You told me Duddy is an ex-boxer. Wouldn't he have an extra strong grip?"

Ike nodded. "Good thinking."

Liz thought of Big Tiny's bodyguard. He'd probably wielded his billy club as often as Duddy used his hammer, and his hands had to be the size of hams. "A thug's billy club would have that kind of wear on it, too," she said. Then she remembered they hadn't discussed the possibility of a billy club or a baton, either.

She knew he'd picked up on this when he gave a teasing smile. "How many other ideas haven't you mentioned to me?" he asked.

"Only one more. The music teacher's baton."

His reply suggested he'd considered both possible suspects and both implements. "Again, good thinking. We'll talk about all that tonight. I'm looking into another possibility later today. We'll discuss that, too."

He eyed her empty plate. "How about some dessert?"

She shook her head. "No, thanks. I should be getting back to my desk. I have a lot of work to do, and I'm leaving the office early today. Dan left his pen over at the school Monday and . . ."

She'd barely finished explaining when Ike let out a groan. "Do I have to remind you there's probably a killer on the loose over there? Promise me you'll be careful."

"What possible danger could I get into, picking up a pen from the guard?"

"None, if that's all you do."

She had to be straight with him. "Well, I thought I might have a peek around backstage."

A fleeting frown crossed his face. "I guess that'll be okay. The play rehearsal will be going on. There'll be people backstage."

"They're going to put on the play anyway?"

"Yeah. They're only a couple of weeks away from opening, and the kids wanted to go on with it. Bernice Fripp has taken over as coach."

So Bernice was back working with the kids again. "I guess she's happy," Liz said. "This is what she wanted."

"We'll discuss her and the others tonight," Ike said as they left the table. "By the way, what are you cooking?"

"I haven't decided yet. I'm going to stop at the market on my way home from the school. Anything you're especially hungry for?"

He flashed a grin. "Yeah, *you*."

"That's on the menu," she said.

They walked from the restaurant to his car parked down the block, and he drove her to the building where she worked.

"You said you were stopping at the market after you pick up Dan's pen," he said. "What time do you think you'll be home?"

She did some quick calculating. "Oh, I think quarter of six at the latest."

He gave her a kiss. "Okay, I'll see you then. And Liz, please be careful while you're nosing around the school."

Chapter Seven

Liz left her desk shortly after four and hailed a cab in front of the building.

Chadwick Academy's reception hall was almost empty when she entered. A lone woman was signing in at the security guard's desk. But Ike had told her the homicide hadn't canceled the play and rehearsals were being held after school, as usual. People would soon start coming to pick up student actors and musicians. Big Tiny's bodyguard would be here. She imagined his billy club under his jacket, along with a gun, knife, and whatever else thugs carried around with them. Unfortunately, there'd be no chance of getting a glimpse of it and checking it for an irregular area.

"Will you sign in, please, Miss?" The security guard's voice came into her thoughts.

She signed her name on the register, including the time, 4:31. "I've come to pick up Dr. Switzer's pen," she said.

He nodded. "It's in the office safe. I'll have someone bring it out." He gestured toward a chair next to the desk. "Have a seat," he said, picking up his phone.

While she waited, more people came in. By the time the pen was brought to the guard's desk, the reception hall was filling up. As yet, Big Tiny's henchman had not arrived to pick up Anna Tynkov.

"Here you go, Miss," the guard said, handing her an envelope. "Better have a look and make sure it's the right pen."

There was no mistaking Dan's gold pen, engraved with his and his wife's initials and their wedding date. "This is it," she replied.

"I have to ask you to sign for it," the guard said.

As she signed the receipt, she remembered the twenty-dollar bill Dan had given her for the janitor. "Is Duddy around?" she asked. "I have something for him from Dr. Switzer."

"He should be sweeping the gym corridor or maybe backstage," the guard replied. "You can go have a look if you want to. If you don't find him, let me know and I'll try his quarters."

"Thanks." Liz headed for the gym corridor. There was no sign of Duddy, but it didn't matter. She'd already decided to do some snooping before she gave him the twenty.

In the corridor she noticed the stairway to the balcony was blocked by a large piece of plywood, with KEEP OUT hand-lettered on it. Recalling that Ike had told her the school would not be considered a crime scene beyond yesterday, she decided the sign had been a directive of Chadwick's headmaster. Did he believe anyone in the school would want to go up those stairs to the spot where a teacher had been so brutally attacked? Much as she loved investigating homicides, she wouldn't have gone up there herself, even for a quick look.

She walked along the corridor past the rest rooms and opened one of the doors to the gym. All the police barriers had been removed. On the stage, student actors were speaking their lines. Below it, the student orchestra was playing softly, sounding pretty good. LoPresti, neatly dressed in coat and tie, was waving his baton and Bernice Fripp, seated nearby, was nodding and smiling. Except for the sign at the foot of the balcony stairway, nothing remained as a reminder of what had taken place only two days ago. It was as if the murder of Marva Malin had never happened.

She closed the gym door and continued on her way along the corridor. Ahead she saw a short flight of steps. They led backstage, she decided. To the right, a stairway led downward, most likely to the basement. She recalled Ike mentioning Duddy's quarters were in the basement. If Duddy were the killer, could he have come down the balcony stairs, run the length of the corridor and into the basement stairway without anyone seeing him? With the number of people on their way to and from the rest rooms during the break, it seemed unlikely. Still, it was possible.

Voices sounded from the backstage area. Other cast members must be there—maybe the gym teacher and art teacher, too. She started up the steps. If anyone questioned her, she'd say she was looking for Duddy.

Looking through a doorway into the area behind the stage, she saw Julia Tulley in a corner with a group of little kids. The kids were sitting on the floor. Tulley, dressed in sweats and sneakers, was demonstrating a ballet step.

"We'll practice this tomorrow, children," she said after a final twirl. "It's almost time to go home."

This woman was light on her feet, Liz thought. It was easy to picture her making it from balcony to backstage within a couple of minutes. If she'd managed to clear the stairway area, anyone encountering her in the corridor might think she'd been in the restroom. But what would she have used for her murder weapon? Unlike Duddy's hammer, LoPresti's baton, and the billy club belonging to Big Tiny's bodyguard, there was nothing to be matched up with the gym teacher. But, something might turn up, Liz hoped.

Across the backstage area, she saw Cyril Gibbs and realized she hadn't matched *him* up with a possible murder weapon, either. Gibbs, along with Greg Jensen and several other boys, were clearing away what looked like materials used in some sort of project. She noticed rags, paint cans and brushes, scraps of wood, and short lengths of sawed-off two-by-fours—left over from the frame for the backdrop, she decided. With a twinge of excitement, she noticed some of the wood pieces weren't much bigger than a billy club or a large claw hammer.

Her excitement subsided when she realized the pieces were new, raw wood. There'd be no traces of the wood finish Forensics had picked up, nor would they have the indentation Forensics said caused the uneven discoloration on Marva Malin's neck.

At that moment, a voice from behind her startled her. "Excuse me, Miss." She turned and saw the janitor carrying a large trash can.

She stepped aside to let him by. If she gave him the twenty dollars now, she'd have no excuse for hanging out here any longer. She wanted to look around some more. When she drew closer to the pile of discarded material, Gibbs noticed her. "Something I can do for you, Miss?" he asked with a shy smile.

She couldn't say she was looking for the janitor when it was obvious he was right there helping with the cleanup. Instead, she returned the smile and made a couple of irrelevant remarks. "I'm so glad you're going on with the play. And by the way, the scenery looks great. I was told your art students painted it. Nice work."

The remarks had the desired effect. Gibbs' shy smile broadened. "Thanks, I think the kids did a pretty good job."

"They're doing a pretty good job cleaning up too," she said.

Gibbs turned to watch Greg and the other boys filling Duddy's trash can. He nodded. "They're hard workers."

During this exchange Liz had been looking carefully at the

debris. What else might there be in that pile of rubble that could have been used to strangle Marva Malin?

At that moment, Gibbs called out. "Hold it, Greg, don't throw away that big paintbrush! I thought I'd lost it. I've been looking all over for it."

Liz felt like yelling "Bingo!" when she saw Greg retrieve a paintbrush from the trash can. Its dark brown handle was long and thick and it had a slightly curved indentation toward the end of its length!

As she took a deep breath to quell her excitement, she heard Greg's voice. "Sorry, Mr. Gibbs."

"That's okay, Greg . . ." The art teacher took the brush from Greg's outstretched hand and thrust it, handle down, into his jeans pocket. He looked at Liz with a smile, shy again and almost apologetic. "I'm not surprised the boy thought this brush was a piece of junk. It's old, but it's my favorite. I've been using it to paint everything from houses to canvases, since I was in college."

With her eyes fixed on the brush protruding from his pocket, Liz was speechless for a few seconds. Her momentary look at the handle had put it squarely in her mind's eye. The top narrowed into a point, but between there and the indented curve toward the bottom, the handle was well over an inch thick.

"I guess we all have relics we can't part with," she managed to say. The art teacher's favorite paintbrush was right up there with the bodyguard's billy club, the music teacher's baton, and the janitor's hammer, she thought. Why hadn't Ike mentioned it? There seemed be only one reason for this. He and Lou had overlooked it during yesterday's search.

As if Gibbs suddenly remembered questioning her when she came backstage, he asked again. "Is there something I can do for you?"

Liz took another calming breath. "I was looking for Duddy.

My boss lost a valuable pen here on Monday, and Duddy found it. I came to pick it up and to give Duddy a reward."

A troubled expression crossed the art teacher's face, reminding her of how he'd looked while waiting to be interviewed. "Monday . . ." he said. She could sense his unspoken words—*the day of the murder.*

His brow furrowed as he scrutinized her. "You were here that day, weren't you?" he asked. "Now that I think about it, I seem to recall seeing you."

He'd noticed her when she was prowling around the gym, she decided. Or maybe he'd seen her talking to Ike. Unlike the music teacher, he hadn't attracted her attention by glaring at her.

"Yes, I was here," she replied.

His eyes took in her dark green pants suit and tan turtleneck sweater. "I guess you're a plainclothes cop, or maybe a detective," he said.

She would have set him straight if Music teacher LoPresti hadn't appeared at that moment. Evidently, the rehearsal had ended and he'd just come backstage and caught Gibbs' words. "*Who's* a plainclothes cop or a detective, Cy?" he asked.

His sudden appearance seemed to disturb the art teacher, Liz thought. A look of intimidation crossed Gibbs' face. *Was he afraid of LoPresti?* Before she could give more thought to this, her attention was diverted to LoPresti. Apparently, he'd just noticed her and fixed his dark eyes on her with an unmistakable glare. There was no doubt in her mind that he recognized her. His bushy, black eyebrows clashed in the same angry frown she'd seen before. He spat out a single word. "*You!*"

Obviously, LoPresti had taken a dislike to her. Why, when he'd only seen her for a few moments on Monday and even fewer today? Well, he wasn't the first man who once had a chip on his shoulder concerning her. If she could win over

Detective Sourpuss Eichle, she could at least coax a smile out of Mr. Scowlybrows LoPresti.

"Hello," she said, acting as if she hadn't picked up on the hostility. Extending her hand, she added, "I'm Liz Rooney, and you're the music teacher, aren't you? I heard your students playing when I came in . . ." She was about to say the band sounded great, but the words froze in her throat. His scowl deepened. He ignored her outstretched hand.

"Why are you here again today?" he asked in a demanding voice. "I thought the police were finished looking around."

Gibbs made the reply, somewhat timidly, Liz thought. "Vinny, she came to pick up a pen someone lost in the gym last Monday and to reward Duddy for finding it."

"Is that what she told you?" LoPresti asked. Suddenly, he gave Gibbs a friendly slap on the back, saying, "It's okay, Cy." He cast Liz a look that seemed to say *"You're lying."*

Liz glanced at the janitor, who was scooping the last of the rubble into the trash can, a few feet away. "Guess I'd better give him his reward now," she said.

Mindful of LoPresti's eyes scrutinizing her, she walked over to Duddy. "You're the one who found the gold pen, aren't you?" she asked.

The janitor gave a gap-toothed smile. "Yes, ma'am, that's me, Duddy Baca. Did you get it okay?"

"Yes. I have it." She opened her purse and took out the twenty. "Dr. Switzer asked me to give you this and tell you how much he appreciates your honesty."

A broad smile spread over the janitor's punch-flattened face. "My whole life I never took what I didn't have no right to," he said. "I didn't expect nothin'. Tell the doc thanks."

"I'll tell him." That should convince LoPresti she hadn't lied, she thought. But she noticed he was still staring at her with obvious dislike. Maybe a friendly remark would help. She walked back to Gibbs and LoPresti. "Before I leave, I want to wish you both the best of luck with the play," she said.

At that moment, a voice came from the wings. "The kids sounded good today, Vinny." Bernice Fripp, hobbling with her cane, appeared.

LoPresti ignored Liz and greeted Bernice with a sudden smile. "Thanks, Bern," he said. "I'll say the same for your coaching. This whole rehearsal went well today."

"It certainly did," another voice said. "All the actors and dancers were fantastic today. And Vinny, the band sounded great." Julia Tulley joined the group, probably back from delivering her little dancers to their mothers and nannies, Liz thought.

Liz sensed a warm feeling among the four of them. She introduced herself to both Julia and Bernice, explaining why she was there.

"Good old Duddy, he's as honest as the day is long," Bernice said.

"And did you notice how clean the corridor looks today?" Julia asked. "Duddy swept and mopped it."

Liz could almost feel what the four of them were thinking. Everything was looking up now that Marva Malin was out of the way. And they were all so relaxed—it was hard to believe one of them might have killed her. If one of them had, he or she must surely have been lulled into false security by police insinuations that the killer was an outsider.

Her thoughts returned to Gibbs' paintbrush, She could hardly wait to tell Ike she'd matched up another possible murder weapon with another possible suspect. A look at her watch told her she'd better head for home. After her stop at the market, she'd just about make it by the time Ike got there.

Turning to go, she said, "Well, so long, everybody. I know the play's going to be a huge success." They all voiced their good-byes except LoPresti who just stared at her. She heard someone remark, "It *will* be, now." Bernice's voice, she was certain.

Hearing the edifying comment, it occurred to Liz that Julia Tulley wasn't the only one she hadn't matched up with a possible murder weapon. She'd allowed Bernice Fripp's kind, gentle nature to divert her. Bernice's disability too was a factor. Hadn't Ike all but dismissed the idea that the murder could have been committed by an arthritic woman who walked with a cane?

The cane! With her instincts on the alert, Liz looked over her shoulder at Bernice. She'd always been aware of the cane, but she'd never really looked at it. Seconds later, she had the imagery fixed firmly in her mind of varnished oak, carved crook to bottom, in an ornate, undulating pattern!

Stumbling onto two possible murder weapons within a few minutes sent her spirits soaring. What a stroke of luck! And what a great discussion she and Ike would have tonight!

With the rehearsal over, the reception hall was crowded. While waiting in line to sign out, Liz continued to feel giddy with excitement. She loved being in on information the news media didn't have yet. She was one of only a handful of people who knew the police believed the murder was an inside job and that the murder weapon was made of wood. Fewer still knew that three objects were being considered as potential weapons, and now it looked as if there were five.

Out of all the possible suspects, only Julia Tulley had nothing that might possibly link her to the murder.

She thought, too, about Chadwick Academy's tight security. How long could the police keep the general public believing their investigation was following the concept that Marva Malin's killer was an outsider—an intruder who'd somehow managed to breach the school's elaborate system? That it had worked thus far was evident in the relaxed atmosphere she'd noticed among the four potential suspects.

After she signed out, she noticed Anna Tynkov sitting on a bench near the entrance. Her father's bodyguard would be here any minute to pick her up. She wished she could hang around and get another look at him, but she didn't have time for that. She wanted to be home when Ike arrived. Stopping at the market on the way meant she'd have to be lucky enough to get a taxi right away—not easy this time of day.

She left the building and made her way through a line of parked cars to hail a cab. After a few unsuccessful tries, she decided to walk to the end of the block where two-way traffic would give her a better chance.

She'd been standing on the corner for a couple of minutes when she heard a voice from behind her. "It's difficult to get a hack after five, isn't it?"

There was no mistaking the vaguely British accent of music teacher Vincent LoPresti.

Surprised. she turned around. Her surprise heightened when she saw a smile on his face.

"I regret that we got off on the wrong foot," he said. "I'd like to make up for my attitude by offering you a ride. A friend will be along any minute in his car to pick me up. We'll drive you wherever you're going."

She found herself thinking *why not?* The market was a short walk from her apartment. She could have them drop her off there. She'd buy the few things she needed for dinner and she'd make it to her place before Ike got there.

The thought of Ike reminded her of what he'd said before they said good-bye after lunch: ". . . please be careful while you're nosing around the school."

Well, she *had* been careful, and this wasn't the school, she rationalized. But her common sense countered the thought. What did she know about LoPresti except that he was Chadwick Academy's music teacher? Recalling his previous scowls and general hostility, she told herself she mustn't take a chance. He could be some kind of nut case. And now that he'd stepped closer to her, she noticed there was no warmth in his smile. It seemed forced.

"Thanks so much. I really appreciate the offer, but I'm sure it would be out of your way," she replied.

"Whereabouts are you going?" he asked.

She got the distinct feeling he wasn't going to take no for answer. She'd have to make up some destination a good distance from uptown Manhattan, yet not far enough away to make him suspect she was lying. "South Ferry," she replied. "I live on Staten Island." Manhattan's southernmost boundary ought to be out of range, she thought.

"No problem," LoPresti replied. "I want to make amends. We'll be glad to take you to the ferry."

Again her instincts warned her this guy might be bad news. She gave her head an emphatic shake. "No, really. Thanks a lot, but I'll just wait here for a taxi. There should be one coming along soon."

At that moment a car slowed a few feet from where they stood. Liz noted it was a large, maroon Mercedes SUV.

"There's my friend, Alvino," LoPresti said.

She was thinking his friend Alvino must have a well-paying job to be able to afford a car like that, when she felt LoPresti's hand on her arm. In the next instant, he tightened his grasp and guided her off the curb toward the waiting vehicle.

She felt a faint prickle of misgiving, and told herself she'd better get out of this situation as quickly as possible. "I guess I didn't make myself clear," she said. "I'll wait for a taxi." When she started to thank him again for offering her a ride, the look on his face sent a stab of fear into her heart. The forced smiled was gone, replaced by a dark and menacing scowl.

Chapter Eight

Liz's first instinct was to wrest free of his grasp and take off as fast as she could. But her attempts to pull away were useless—his hand on her arm had tightened to a vise-like grip. Just as she drew a breath to scream, his other hand firmed across her mouth and he shoved her toward the Mercedes.

With rising panic, she glanced about at the throngs of people hurrying along the sidewalk. It was still daylight. Didn't anyone notice she was in trouble? New Yorkers were notorious for telling themselves such incidents were none of their business.

But there was no way she'd let him get her into that car without a fight.

She began to struggle—trying to maneuver herself into a position to use the self-defense tactics Pop had taught her, like kneeing him in the groin, and kicking, hoping to land one on his shin. Realizing that her hands were free, while his were gripping her arm and covering her mouth, she slammed her hand hard onto his nose.

With a curse and a grunt, he uncovered her mouth and grabbed her wrist long enough to say, "Don't do that again, if you know what's good for you," before his hand went back over her mouth. She thought of shoving his fingers between her teeth and biting down as hard as she could, but decided not to. What a time to recall the germ warnings of her childhood: *You don't know where someone's hands have been!*

With a sinking heart, she saw that they were now alongside the Mercedes. The driver rolled down the window, leaned over and peered out at them. "What's this all about, Vinny?" he asked.

"Unlock the rear door," LoPresti said. Then, in a series of swift, sudden moves, he took his hand off her mouth, opened the SUV's back door, pushed her in, and climbed in after her.

Sheer fright choked off any words she might have spoken. She could only stare at LoPresti. He glowered back. "Fasten your seatbelt," he ordered.

This was his way of telling her he wasn't going to let her out of the car.

The driver turned around and looked at them in puzzlement. "What are you doing, Vinny? Who's this woman?" he asked. Liz noticed his hair and complexion were almost as dark as LoPresti's. And LoPresti had mentioned his name—Alvino. Another Italian, yet he spoke with the same slightly British accent.

"She's a police officer—most likely a detective," LoPresti replied. "I offered her a ride, but she refused. She thinks her position of authority makes her superior. I guess she thinks she's too important to ride with us."

Liz wasn't too overcome with fear to think this was a strange statement. It confirmed her idea that he had something against women in positions of authority. Would it do any good to convince him she wasn't a cop?

"I'm not a police officer," she said, opening her purse. She brought out her wallet. "Here, check my ID."

He didn't even glance at it. "I saw you in the school gym the day the teacher was murdered," he said. "You have a connection to the police, otherwise you would not have been allowed in there." He turned to the driver. "Get going, Al."

Liz had a moment of hope when Alvino shook his head. "I don't know about this, Vinny."

"Listen," LoPresti said. "You know we've been discussing various plans. Well, it's time we decided on one. I'll explain when we get home. You told me you were tired of waiting, same as me. This is our chance."

Tired of waiting . . . This is our chance . . . Liz turned the words over in her mind, trying to make some sense of them. And the plan—what was that all about?

She felt her heart sink when Alvino turned back to the wheel. "What about the others?" he asked.

"We're all tired of waiting," LoPresti replied. "Now let's get on with it."

Fear and despair closed in around Liz when Alvino started the car and pulled away. He'd been her one remaining hope of getting out of this. She tried to hearten herself by thinking he might still be reluctant to go along with whatever LoPresti had in mind and she might get through to him, somehow.

Of all the predicaments she'd been in, this was the worst, she thought. Though LoPresti's resentment of women in power seemed an unlikely force, she could think of no other reason why this music teacher had suddenly become an abductor.

She felt the pressure of his hands on her shoulders. "Slide down," he ordered. This was to prevent her from seeing where they were taking her, she thought. She couldn't slump down far with her seatbelt fastened, but apparently it was enough to satisfy LoPresti.

Her next thought brought on fresh fear and plunged her even deeper into despair. LoPresti was a hothead, but he was no dummy. He must know he was in this too far to turn around. From the moment he grabbed her arm and started pushing her toward the Mercedes, he must have known if he let her go she could have him arrested for assault. Was that why he wanted to go ahead with one of the plans he and Alvino had talked about? And forcing her into the car must be part of the plan he wanted to carry out. At that moment, she felt too afraid to think clearly.

Alvino spoke. Liz thought he sounded disturbed. "If this is the plan you told me about last night, Vinny, I . . ."

LoPresti shot a glance at Liz. "Not now, Al," he snapped.

"Whatever it is, are you sure the others will agree to it?" Alvino asked.

This seemed to enrage LoPresti. "Shut up!" he bellowed.

Suddenly, he broke into a volley of words in a language Liz could not understand. Strange, LoPresti was an Italian name. Her smattering of high school and college Spanish didn't ring the bell, either. The language sounded sort of guttural. Could it be German? Russian?

Alvino responded in the same language, further puzzling her. With his name, he, too, must have Italian roots. But Italy was a diverse country, stretching from the Alps to the Mediterranean. Maybe this was some kind of mountain dialect. Whatever it was, the two men continued to use it as they drove through Manhattan's early evening traffic.

With no way of knowing what they were talking about, Liz could only assume they were discussing "the others" and LoPresti was explaining his "plan." She tried to calm herself by thinking about what she'd heard them saying in English, just before LoPresti blew his top and launched into this foreign language. She recalled Alvino asking if the others would agree to the plan. That's when LoPresti got mad and yelled, "shut up." Right after that he'd started using the unfamiliar language.

She puzzled over this. Who were "the others" and why didn't LoPresti want to discuss them in English? And what was his plan? From what LoPresti said, she assumed they were taking her to the place where they lived. But, wherever that was, they'd have to get her out of the car and into a building. She could struggle and scream. Though it was getting dark, now, passers-by would notice. She'd be on the sidewalk, not off the curb, half-hidden by parked cars as she was earlier. Someone would surely come to her rescue. The hope comforted her.

She'd been so absorbed in her predicament; everything else had been relegated to the far corners of her mind. Now she remembered Ike was coming to her place for dinner. She pictured him arriving at her apartment, only to find she wasn't home yet. He'd probably wait for her at the Moscarettis', but when time passed, and she didn't show up, he'd probably think she was still snooping around the school.

The school . . . the murder . . . Like a streak of lightning, the Chadwick Academy homicide flashed into the forefront of her mind. How could she have stopped thinking about it, even for a little while? Close on this question, another came bursting into her mind. How could she have gone this long in LoPresti's clutches without realizing that anyone capable of his aberrant behavior could be capable of murder? His sudden swing from hostility to friendliness and back again, his use of force and his explosive temper, all added up. At that moment she was certain that, in a fit of rage, he'd crushed Marva Malin's trachea with his baton and thrown her off the balcony.

Just as she came to this frightening conclusion, she felt the car stop. She heard the two men exchange a few words in the foreign language before LoPresti spoke to her in English.

"We'll be getting out of the car in a few minutes. Just keep quiet and you won't get hurt."

With her heart pounding from the thought of being at the mercy of Marva Malin's killer, she managed to nod her head. Despite what he'd just said, she planned to cry out for help to passers by when he escorted her from car to building. This was her only hope.

But the hope was short-lived. When she unfastened her seat-belt, sat up, and looked out the car window she saw that they were in what appeared to be an underground parking garage with an elevator. Her heart sank further when she noticed it was almost deserted, except for a middle-age woman who'd just alighted from a Lexus in a parking spot a few yards away.

Liz felt sure her two captors wouldn't risk taking her onto an elevator with another person. She was right. The men made no move to get out of the car.

"We won't have to wait long, Vinny," Alvino said. "That woman lives on the third floor. The elevator will be down in five minutes."

Watching the woman board the elevator, Liz noticed she had a beautiful, standard-size, white French poodle on a leash. As the elevator doors closed, she was startled to hear LoPresti come out with a muttered oath. She would have recognized it even if it hadn't been spoken in English. His face bore the familiar, dark look.

"We'll have to get on the elevator right after that dog was on it," he snarled.

In a sudden flash of memory, Liz recalled his negative reaction when the other teachers were discussing Marva Malin's dogs. She'd thought, then, that a childhood dog bite might have given him a lifelong dislike of anything on four legs that barked. But objecting to boarding an elevator a dog had just been on was taking it to extremes. She noticed Alvino made no comment. He must be used to this quirk.

Recalling Alvino's initial reluctance to go along with Lo-Presti, she again hoped that he might help her. Or maybe the elevator would take them to a lobby. Most apartment buildings these days had security guards that screened everyone who came through. Maybe she could let the guard know, somehow, that she was in trouble.

The elevator came down a few minutes later. But when Alvino punched the button for the fifth floor, she realized that there was no mandatory stop at the lobby. Evidently the building security was set up with an underground garage key card system.

Despite her disappointment and increasing fear, she couldn't keep from noticing the highly polished brass, plush carpet, soft lights, and mirrors in the elevator. This was a swanky apartment building. LoPresti couldn't afford anything like this on a schoolteacher's salary. The apartment had to be Alvino's. He drove a Mercedes. He must have a lucrative job. Why had they brought her to his place when forcing her to go with them was LoPresti's idea? If she could have understood what they were jabbering about, she'd know. In a flash of wry humor, she told herself if she had to be in this predicament, at least she wouldn't be in some dingy, slum walk-up.

They got off the elevator and walked a few steps down a carpeted hall, where Alvino unlocked a door. This *was* his place, she decided. Maybe he and LoPresti shared it. She tried to see the apartment number, but LoPresti was blocking her view of the door. What good would it do her, anyway? She didn't know where this building was. It could be almost anywhere on Manhattan.

Entering the apartment, Alvino pushed a master switch that turned on all the lights. Liz held back a gasp of surprise. She'd expected it would be nice, but nice was not the right word for the marble-floored foyer with its elegant console table, gilded mirror, and porcelain base lamp that looked as if it had come straight out of a Ming Dynasty palace. The spacious room beyond the foyer gave an overall impression of richly upholstered sofas and chairs, gleaming mahogany tables, oil paintings, Persian rugs, and a wall of windows overlooking a panorama of twinkling city lights.

As she stepped toward the room for a closer look at all

that elegance, she felt a hand on her arm and heard Lo-Presti's voice, sounding almost friendly. "This way, Miss Police Detective."

He wouldn't let go of the notion that she was a cop, and he obviously had a strong resentment of women in positions of authority. But now that he was in control, his attitude had changed from threatening to patronizing. He must be confident that his plan, whatever it might be, was going to work, she thought. She knew she was part of the plan but couldn't imagine how she fit in.

He guided her into a hallway, where he opened the door to a luxuriously furnished room dominated by a massive, tester-top bed. "This is our guestroom," he said. "Make yourself comfortable."

At the risk of stirring up his anger again, she asked a flip question. "How long am I going to be your *guest*?"

The sarcasm didn't bother him. "As long as it takes," he replied. He glanced at his watch. "Are you hungry? Dinner will be in an hour or so. Someone will bring you a tray." He gave a grunty laugh. "Room service for our high and mighty woman guest."

What was this with him and women in authority? But now that he'd mentioned dinner, she realized she was hungry. She'd been too scared to think about eating or even to wonder what time it was. She checked her watch. It was almost six. Ike had arrived at her apartment and when she wasn't there he'd either gone to his car to wait for her, or to the Moscarettis'.

LoPresti opened a door and turned on a light. "Here's your bathroom," he said. She glimpsed marble, mirrors, and tile. "As I said, make yourself comfortable," he added with a smile so disarming that it was hard for her to believe he'd murdered a woman two days ago and kidnapped another today.

For one hopeful moment, she thought he was going to leave her alone in the room without going through her purse.

Her cell phone was in there. She could call Ike. Even though she didn't know where she was, at least he would know she was in trouble and he'd try everything possible to find her.

The hopeful moment passed when LoPresti took her purse away from her and opened it. The first object he removed was her cell phone, which he put in his pocket. Next, he took out her wallet and then the envelope containing Dan's gold pen. He slid her ID out, glanced at it, and pocketed it before giving her back the wallet. Then he opened the envelope, checked the contents, and returned it to her, along with her purse. She saw him give an appraising look at her diamond engagement ring.

She must have looked surprised when he didn't take the ring, her credit card, her money, and the obviously valuable pen, because he came out with a blunt statement as he turned to leave.

"We are not thieves."

Why hadn't he said, "*I* am not a thief?" She'd barely asked herself the question when she thought of an answer. The "we" meant Alvino and the "others" he'd mentioned previously. Who were these others, and how did they figure in this? And what did he intend to do with her ID?

With these questions whirling around in her head, she watched LoPresti leave. When the door closed behind him, she didn't hear the sound of it being locked. But before she got any serious ideas of leaving this room and getting out of the apartment, she told herself he wouldn't have made it that easy. He'd have made sure there was no way she could leave the apartment. Besides, any attempt she made to escape might throw him into one of his angry fits. She reminded herself that Marva Malin had been a victim of his enraged temper.

She walked over to the window. Although it was dark outside, maybe she'd recognize some landmark that would give her an idea where she was—a glimpse of lights on water, maybe, or the spire of the Empire State Building. But the view from the window held nothing recognizable.

She decided to search the room—go through the dresser and nightstand drawers, not solely on the chance she'd come across something to indicate where this building was located, but also something that would provide a clue as to who "the others" might be. The search turned up nothing.

Curiosity overcame her. What had LoPresti and Alvino been doing while she was searching the room? Maybe they were cooking dinner. She went to the door and opened it, first a crack in case someone might be standing guard, then wider to see if the entire hallway was empty. She didn't see anyone, but heard voices from the foyer—a bunch of male voices, talking in that same foreign language she couldn't identify. Were these "the others"? Had Alvino contacted them after LoPresti brought her to this room? Had he told them what LoPresti had done? She recalled Alvino asking LoPresti if "the others" would agree to his plan. LoPresti had seemed confident they would. What was it he'd said? She searched her mind and remembered it was something about everyone being tired of waiting. *Waiting for what?*

Just then, she recognized LoPresti's voice rising above the rest. Though she didn't understand what he was saying, evidently it met with approval. She heard the sound of cheers and hand clapping.

LoPresti said something, evidently a good-bye, because right after that she heard the apartment door close. He'd gone out somewhere. She checked her watch and guessed he wouldn't be gone long. More than twenty minutes had passed since he said that dinner would be in about an hour.

She closed the bedroom door and sank down among the soft pillows on a satin-covered chaise to think. How abruptly everything had changed. Less than two hours ago her mind was focused on possible objects used to strangle Marva Malin and matching them up with the killer. Now she was sure

LoPresti was the killer and his baton the murder weapon, but she was too scared to dwell on that now. All she wanted to do was get out of this predicament. She thought of Ike, waiting, wondering why she was so late. She thought of Sophie, wondering why she hadn't phoned, as promised. And Sophie's wedding was only three days away. Would she be released in time to stand up for Sophie? A terrible thought lurking in the back of her mind suddenly took over. *She might not be released, ever.* An icy chill clutched at her heart.

Until this moment she'd been scared, but she hadn't fully faced her dire situation. She'd managed to keep it at bay. Now it caught up to her. A feeling of hopelessness engulfed her. Tears flooded her eyes and coursed down her face. Uncontrollable sobs wracked her body and when they subsided she felt drained of all her energy, both physical and mental. She could only lie there, exhausted and immobilized by fear.

Chapter Nine

She didn't know how long she'd been lying there in a haze of fear and despair when a knock sounded on the door. She sat up and looked at her watch. Almost 7:15. Recalling Lo-Presti's remark about room service, she decided someone was at her door with dinner.

Some food might make her feel better, she thought. Calling "just a minute," she got up from the chaise and hurried into the bathroom to splash cold water on her face. Her weeping might have left her eyes red and swollen. Though it was unlikely that LoPresti had brought her dinner himself, if he had she didn't want to give him the satisfaction of knowing the woman detective had succumbed to feminine tears. She dabbed at her eyes with one of the plush, cream-colored washcloths in a small, gilded wicker basket on the countertop.

When she opened the bedroom door, she was surprised to see an elderly woman holding a tray laden with coffee service, a bowl of fresh fruit, a platter of cakes, and a large plate with a silver cover.

"Oh, hello," she said. "Thanks for bringing this."

The tray looked too heavy for an elderly woman to be

carrying around, she thought. She reached for it, saying, "Let me take that."

The woman ignored her. Without a word, she walked over to a table near the window and set the tray down.

"Thanks," Liz said, again.

The woman turned and was out of the room before Liz could get anything but a brief look at her. But in those few moments she'd noticed that the woman had dark eyes and gray hair, and was probably about seventy.

Liz hadn't noticed how the woman was dressed. But wouldn't a servant in this obviously affluent household be wearing a maid's uniform, and wouldn't Liz have noticed it? She decided the woman must have had on very plain, inconspicuous clothing. Since this was probably Alvino's apartment, maybe she was his mother. Come to think of it, she looked sort of Italian. But what kind of son would let his elderly mother lug a heavy dinner tray from kitchen to guestroom? A son like LoPresti, she decided. It wouldn't surprise her if LoPresti had *his* mother living here with him and Alvino and doing all the cooking, cleaning, and laundry. From his standpoint, that was probably the only kind of work women were meant to do.

During those few minutes of diversion, her despair had lifted slightly. She must try and ignore it and not give in to it again, she told herself. She needed to set her wits in action and figure out away to get out of here.

She sat down at the table and lifted the silver cover from the plate. A savory smell arose. Nestled amid an array of fresh asparagus, green beans, and tiny parsleyed potatoes, she saw what appeared to be roast duckling, garnished with red grapes and slices of orange. She stared at it in awed surprise. She'd been expecting something Italian, but this dinner looked as if might surpass even Rosa's cooking. It was right up there with the elegant food presentations she'd enjoyed on occasional dinner dates during her pre-Ike days, in places like the St. Regis, the Plaza, or Rockefeller Center's Rainbow Room. She had a lot of thinking to do and she could do it better while eating this delicious dinner.

When she unfolded the white cloth napkin and picked up her knife and fork, a disturbing thought struck her: *There could be drugs or poison in this food!*

She'd believed she had herself under control, but this possibility shattered her resolve to stay calm and think. Fresh feelings of fear and despair stabbed at her heart. Through rising tears she stared at the food, struggling to keep from going to pieces again.

"Get hold of yourself," she whispered.

It took a few minutes before her nerves calmed and she was able to think rationally. *Why would LoPresti want to drug or poison her?* Whatever his plan was, she knew she was part of it, maybe even the reason for it. It seemed logical that he needed her alive and well—at least at this stage of the game. She decided she could safely eat tonight's dinner.

While she ate, she thought of the time she'd put in, trying to match possible murder weapons with possible suspects? The last two, the art teacher's paintbrush and Bernice Fripp's cane, had seemed logical. But then, so had the billy club and the hammer. In retrospect, of all these implements, LoPresti's baton seemed the least likely to have been used in a strangulation. She'd seen him waving it and hadn't noticed any indentations. Still, it might have a worn spot where his hand constantly gripped it. While she thought this over, another thought came to her. She didn't have to wonder about a weapon for the gym teacher anymore.

The thought frustrated her. For a few moments, the feeling felt even stronger than her apprehension. She knew who killed Marva Malin, and there was no way she could let Ike know. Much of what he was doing was a waste of time. He'd told her that all the potential murder weapons would be tested for comparison to the irregular marking on Marva Malin's neck. The hammer was the first.

Meanwhile, LoPresti the strangler would be waving his baton around at Chadwick Academy by day, and LoPresti the kidnapper would be returning to this posh apartment every evening. How long would this continue? When would the baton be taken as possible evidence? What if LoPresti carried out his mysterious plan, resigned his job at Chadwick Academy and left for parts unknown before the baton was tested?

While she was asking herself these questions, the biggest question of all lurked in the back of her mind. She tried ignore it, but it came out, anyway: *What was going to happen to her?*

Perhaps from renewed fear or maybe because she'd almost finished the dinner anyway, her appetite dwindled. Thinking something sweet, with coffee, might comfort her, she ate one of the little cakes that looked like petits-fours. Then she poured coffee from the silver pot into a china cup and gave it a splash of heavy cream from a small china pitcher.

Ike would really go for this wonderful coffee, she thought with her first sip. With the thought, she felt a lump rising in her throat. She would have given anything to be sitting on the sofa with him in her apartment, drinking coffee nowhere near as good as this.

She couldn't imagine what Ike was thinking this moment. If he'd arrived at her place at quarter of 6:00, he'd probably given her another ten or fifteen minutes, deciding she'd phone him to explain. When it got to be after six and she still hadn't shown up, he might have tried to reach her on her cell phone, but by that time LoPresti had taken it.

Now it was past 7:30. Did Ike suspect she might be in trouble? She imagined him phoning Sophie on the chance that Sophie knew where she was, only to find out that Sophie had been expecting her to phone, but she hadn't. Maybe Sophie had tried to reach her too. She pictured the two of them growing more concerned every minute. Soon they'd both be frantic with worry, and there was nothing she could do about it.

Feeling herself on the brink of tears again, she shook her head and took a deep breath. Sitting here like a scared, helpless ninny wouldn't accomplish anything. She had to do *something*.

She went to the bedroom door and opened it. The hallway was empty, but from somewhere in the apartment she heard voices—the same hubbub of male talk she'd heard before, speaking that same unidentified language. LoPresti must have returned from wherever he'd gone and they were all eating dinner, she decided. There'd certainly be a dining room in this elegant apartment. She pictured a bunch of men seated around a huge table, and the elderly woman waiting on them.

What did she have to lose?

She took the dinner tray off the table and left the bedroom. If she encountered anyone it should be clear that she wasn't trying to escape—she was returning her tray to the kitchen. Even LoPresti wouldn't fly into rage about that. With a little luck, she'd get a look at the group of men, size them up and determine how many there were. She had no doubt they were "the others" Alvino and LoPresti had talked about.

When she stepped into the foyer, she was surprised to find it empty. She'd expected to see a guard posted near the entrance door to keep her from escaping. The sight of the unguarded door made her long to drop the tray and rush to get out, but common sense prevailed. As she'd figured earlier, LoPresti wouldn't have made it so easy. Either the door was locked from the inside or there was an alarm on it. She wasn't about to find out and have LoPresti strangle her now instead of later.

To make sure she wasn't passing up a chance to escape, she stepped closer to the door for a good look. Sure enough, it was dead-bolted and the key nowhere in sight. Across the foyer she saw a door she thought might lead to the kitchen. But off the foyer, the luxuriously furnished living room she'd seen before caught her eye, and through an archway she glimpsed the dining room and a group of men sitting at the table. From where she stood she couldn't quite see how many.

Again telling herself she had nothing to lose, she marched into the living room, across the Persian rugs, past the elegant sofas and chairs and mahogany grand piano, and through the archway into the dining room.

Apparently, they'd finished dinner. The table had been cleared of everything except coffee service, and the men were too deep in talk to notice her.

Raising her voice to be heard above the hum of voices, she spoke as calmly as her racing heart would allow. "Excuse me, but where's the kitchen?"

A sudden hush fell. Multiple dark eyes stared at her.

LoPresti's voice broke the silence. "You should have pushed the bell," he said. "Someone would have come to get your tray."

She noticed he'd changed out of his music teacher coat and tie into a tan sport shirt with a Ralph Lauren logo. Also, her sudden and unexpected appearance hadn't angered him. Again, she thought his ill humor was gone now that he was in control.

"I didn't notice a bell," she replied. She forced a smile. "The dinner was very tasty."

As she spoke, she counted the number of men around the table—six, including LoPresti and Alvino. Like LoPresti, all were casually but neatly dressed. She knew enough about men's clothing to recognize expensive merchandise. There wasn't a discount store item on any one of them. It looked as if Alvino wasn't the only member of the group with money to burn. They were all in their early to late twenties, she judged, all with swarthy complexions and dark hair and eyes. She noticed more than one set of eyebrows as black and bushy as LoPresti's.

As a native of Staten Island, where a great many nineteenth century Italian immigrants had settled, become citizens, started small businesses, and raised families, Liz had grown up among third-generation Italian-American kids. Although there were no flaxen blonds among them, many had lighter hair and complexions than LoPresti, Alvino, and the others around the table. And there were other differences. She thought of Joe Moscaretti's hazel eyes.

She puzzled over this for a moment. Assuming they were all of Italian descent, did they all have great grandparents who came from a part of Italy where the people were darker than the Italian-Americans she knew?

This train of thought was interrupted when Alvino spoke. "I'm pleased you enjoyed your dinner. There's no need for you to go to the kitchen. Just set the tray down on the table."

His manner of speaking reminded her, again, that his nature differed from LoPresti's. She still hoped he might help her.

She saw a door—the only one in the room. With a shake of her head, she walked quickly toward it, saying, "I'll take care of the tray."

The elderly woman was undoubtedly in the kitchen. Maybe she could get some information from her before Alvino or LoPresti came after her. It would only take a few seconds to ask the address of this building and get an answer.

The kitchen was straight out of *Architectural Digest*. As Liz set the tray down on a granite countertop, she saw a sink she could have taken a bath in, and a refrigerator that looked like a huge, stainless steel armoire.

She'd just caught sight of the elderly woman sitting at a table in a corner, reading a newspaper, when the door swung open and LoPresti came in. A smile, almost of amusement, played about his mouth.

"If you were thinking about asking our cook some questions, forget it," he said. "She is a deaf mute, and even if she were not, she would not understand English."

With that, he grasped her by the elbow, and guided her toward a door at the opposite end of the kitchen. He led her through the door into the foyer. Seconds later, she was back in her room, staring at the door and listening to LoPresti's retreating footsteps.

With her mind in a turmoil, she sat down on the chaise to think. It had all happened so quickly. Barely two minutes had passed from the instant she'd stepped into the kitchen till LoPresti whisked her away, but that was time enough for a startling realization.

In her brief look at the elderly cook, she'd noticed the woman wasn't bareheaded, as she was when she brought the dinner tray to the bedroom. Instead, a dark shawl covered her head and shoulders.

With her senses already alerted, she'd glanced at the newspaper the woman was reading, and felt her heart lurch. The headlines were not printed in any alphabet-lettered language, but in strange, bold characters!

Chapter Ten

Liz had it figured out in nothing flat. She told herself she'd have to be pretty dense not to recognize the cook's shawl as a Muslim woman's *khimar*, realize that the woman was reading an Arab language newspaper, and guess that the closest connection to Italy the men around the table had was probably a Manhattan pizza parlor.

With her heart palpitating in apprehension, she faced the situation head on. There was no doubt in her mind that Lo-Presti and the other men were Arabs or other Middle Easterners, and from all indications, terrorists. Racial profiling? You bet! This was no time to worry about being politically correct.

Why hadn't she figured it out sooner? Right from the start, she should have noticed the resemblance between Lo-Presti and the faces she'd seen, over and over, on TV news coverage of the Middle East. His Italian name had thrown her off.

That unfamiliar language should have given her a hint too, as well as some of what LoPresti and Alvino said before they stopped speaking in English. LoPresti had stated he had a plan, and when Alvino asked if the others would go along with it, LoPresti said they were all tired of waiting.

This sounded as if they were waiting for orders to carry out an act of terrorism!

There'd been other signs too—LoPresti's attitude toward women police officers, for one. She'd thought all along his deep resentment of women in authority didn't fit. Ralph had Italian roots, but it didn't bother him at all that Sophie was a cop. And LoPresti's intense dislike of dogs: Why hadn't she recalled her many talks with a Muslim college friend, who'd told her that in her culture, dogs were considered impure? Some people were radical about this, she'd said. Others kept dogs as pets but never allowed them inside their homes. This would account for LoPresti's almost violent reaction to the French poodle and Alvino's lack of concern.

But what about the Italian names and the flawless English spoken with the strong suggestion of a British accent? Her efforts to think of answers to these questions were interrupted by a knock at the door.

LoPresti? She hoped not. When she opened it, she was relieved to see Alvino.

"I came to show you where your TV is," he said. He stepped over to the wall opposite the bed and flipped a switch. Instantly, a panel slid aside, revealing a large-screen television set.

Under the circumstances, watching TV was the last thing on Liz's mind. "Oh, thanks," she replied. "I was afraid I was going to miss *Law and Order.*"

She didn't know how he'd react to the sarcasm, or if he'd even recognize it as such. His reply told her he got it.

"I regret this situation," he said. "I wish you had agreed to the ride Vinny offered you. If you hadn't refused, he would not have lost his temper, and perhaps this would not be happening."

Liz felt her own temper rising. Her redhead Irish temper, Ike called it. "So now it's *my* fault that your friend decided to kidnap me and you went along with it?"

A troubled look came to Alvino's face. "Vinny often doesn't handle rejection well."

"Well that's the understatement of the year!" Liz exclaimed. "And how about you? What's *your* excuse?"

He shook his head. "I have no excuse."

"Baloney," she said. "I know you didn't want to go along with this at first, but then your hot-headed friend said he had a plan. He said you were both tired of waiting and this was your chance, and you caved in. The plan—that's your excuse."

Alvino stood there looking at her, apparently at a loss for words. He was so different from LoPresti, she thought.

"I can only repeat what I first told you," he said after a few moments of silence.

"What? That it's my fault your friend lost his temper?" she asked, glaring at him. She knew she should let it go at that, but her anger was still boiling. "I suppose it was that teacher's fault too," she said. "Tell me. Alvino, what did *she* do to send Vinny into a homicidal rage?"

His astonished stare struck her as genuine. "You're talking about the teacher at Vinny's school. . . ."

"That's the one. Now I suppose you're going to tell me he didn't kill her."

Alvino's face paled. Shaking his head, he sat down on the edge of the bed. His voice faltered. "I've known Vinny for many years, I've seen him become violently angry many times, but I know he would never kill a defenseless woman."

Liz felt her temper start to cool, but she was still angry enough for one more jab. "Murder's out, but kidnapping's okay?"

She knew her remark bothered him when he started pacing around the room.

"Vinny didn't kill that teacher," he said. "He told me about her. He said he liked her, at first."

"*At first?* You mean something happened to make him dislike her?"

"Yes, but not right away. He told me he asked her to have coffee with him after school one day a few weeks ago, and she turned him down. But this wasn't enough to send him into a rage, if that's what you're thinking. He remained on good terms with her."

"You said he didn't handle rejection well. How come this didn't set him off?"

"He told me he wasn't strongly attracted to her. He liked her, but not enough for rejection to matter."

That sounded normal enough, Liz thought. But LoPresti didn't strike her as a normal kind of guy. Alvino had said LoPresti liked the teacher at first. "So what happened to make him dislike her?" she asked.

Alvino hesitated before answering. "I don't know."

Liz had no misgivings about expressing her thoughts to him. He wouldn't have told her this much if he were anything like LoPresti.

"I think you *do* know," she said. "And I think whatever happened didn't just make him dislike her—it made him angry enough to want to kill her."

She barely heard Alvino reply, "Vinny is not the killer." Her mind had started churning, trying to figure out why Lo-Presti would suddenly develop a strong dislike for Malin and how she could have enraged him to the point of homicide. The answer came in a flash of memory. Malin's real name was Malinbaum. Given the intense hatred between Israel and other Middle Eastern countries, it wasn't hard to imagine a hothead like LoPresti blowing his stack after finding out that he'd been spurned by a *Jewish* woman. Somehow, he must have found out about the name change.

She decided to be frank. "Alvino, I might as well tell you,

I've figured out you and LoPresti are not Italian-Americans," she said.

A long look passed between them. His dark eyes seemed troubled but held none of the menace she'd seen so often in LoPresti's. Again, she thought how different the two men were. Two individuals with opposite dispositions, bonded close by their radical ideology.

"You have guessed we are from the Middle East," he said.

She nodded. "Yes, and I also know you are . . ." She stopped short, reluctant to utter the word *terrorists*. "I know your friend Vinny has some sort of plan involving me," she continued, trying to keep her voice steady. "What does he intend to do with me?"

Alvino turned to the TV and switched it on to a news channel, saying, "Soon there will be a news bulletin that will tell you everything you want to know."

Her mind went to work. When LoPresti left the apartment earlier, he'd probably gone someplace where he could fax her ID to TV news channels. During the past few years, she'd seen enough TV terrorist kidnapping news from the Middle East to know her picture would be shown, along with a statement that she was being held hostage and demands for her release. Fresh fear struck her. If the demands involved political negotiations by the United States government, they would not be met.

She stared at the TV screen, where a commercial was in progress. When it was over, would the bulletin come on about her kidnapping? She sat down on the chaise, torn between wanting to see it and dreading it.

"Shall I go, or would you prefer that I remain here while you watch?" Alvino asked.

An empathic terrorist, Liz thought, not that this would do her any good. She'd almost given up hope that he'd help her escape. But maybe his presence during the newscast would keep her from going to pieces.

"Please stay," she replied. She glanced at the TV. The commercial was over, but a newscaster was announcing sports scores. "The bulletin might not come on for a while," she said. "I'm sure you can understand how anxious I am to know more about this. Can't you at least tell me *something?*"

He stopped pacing around. With a shake if his head, he sat down on a chair. "I should not tell you anything," he said.

She detected a note of uncertainty in his voice and decided to try again. "Surely there's something you let me know—like why I'm being held here."

He shook his head again. "Vinny said not to answer any questions. He said the news bulletin will tell you all you need to know."

Liz smiled. "I guess I should have known you have to follow his orders. He's the big boss, right?"

Apparently, the question struck a nerve. "No, I do not have to follow Vinny's orders and he is not my boss," Alvino replied. "However, he is the one who thought of this plan."

"So he's in charge," Liz said. "That's the same as being the boss."

Her statement had the desired effect. He frowned. "Very well," he replied. "You have already guessed we are all natives of Middle Eastern countries. We have known one another since we were in college. Our group was organized about four years ago."

"For what purpose?" she asked. *Would he admit the truth?*

"Our goal is to promote unity among Islamic nations and defend them against the influence of Israelis and Western capitalistic infidels," he replied.

Liz thought this sounded as if he'd been brainwashed. "How did you and LoPresti learn to speak such speak flawless English?" she asked.

"All of us were taught English as children and we were all fluent, but in order to lose our Middle Eastern accents, we spent many months in speech therapy."

"Why did you need to do that?" Liz asked,

For an instant, she thought he was going to clam up, but evidently she'd succeeded in getting him to talk. "It was necessary to achieve our goal," he replied. "About three years ago we came to New York together, got jobs, and assimilated into the population."

That was after 9/11, Liz thought. How could a group of men fitting this particular racial profile get into the United States so easily? How could they all get jobs and fit in with other New Yorkers? The answers came to her in a rush. These men had taken Italian names and obtained bogus American birth certificates and passports. With fake IDs completing the false identities and no trace of their former speech accent, they had become Americans of Italian descent. From what she'd picked up, she believed they'd come here to carry out some sort of terrorist scheme, but they'd never received their orders.

"Did you fly into the United States?" she asked. Even with forged passports identifying them as Americans, wouldn't six swarthy young men traveling together have raised red flags in airports?

"We came in by motor vehicle, from Canada," he replied.

She remembered his big SUV. "In your Mercedes?" she asked.

He nodded. "Yes, I purchased it there. But first, of course, we flew into Canada, two or three at one time. We stayed there for a while before crossing the border."

This must have taken a chunk of cash, she thought. A Middle Eastern terrorist organization must be financing them. "Who's paying for all this?" she asked.

"We receive no funding," he replied. "All of us have family wealth, and now we are all gainfully employed. I am a chemical engineer, and I am also fortunate to have more money than any of the others." He smiled and glanced around the room. "This apartment is mine. As you can see, I like my comforts."

"Do you all live here?" Liz asked.

"No. It would not have been wise for the six of us to live all in one place. Vinny and I and one other live here. The remaining three live in another building."

In other words, in the post-9/11 climate, six swarthy looking guys living together might have aroused suspicion. Liz thought.

She wanted to ask as many questions as possible before he clammed up. "Of course you and Vinny have other names," she said. "How come you call each other by your Italian names even here in your home?"

"In the beginning, it was decided that we must always speak our Italian names and never our real ones," he replied.

Liz thought it more likely that this was not decided but ordered by their parent terrorist organization, to avoid the risk of slipping up. She wanted to ask him what his real name was but decided to hold off for now. She must not overdo it.

She glanced at the TV, where a telecaster was covering the divorce of two Hollywood celebrities. "I wonder why the news bulletin hasn't come on yet," she said.

A moment afterward she thought she might have the answer to that. When the TV channels and networks got the fax about her kidnapping, they might have wanted to make sure it wasn't a hoax before putting it on the air. If they checked her home address, they'd find out from the Moscarettis and maybe from Ike too, if he was still there, that she hadn't come home from work at the expected time and hadn't been heard from. Once it was established that she was missing, the NYPD or the Manhattan division of the FBI probably would be contacted. All this would take time.

Her conversation with Alvino had diverted her. Now the enormity of her predicament came rushing back, along with imageries of Ike's reaction when the news of her kidnapping broke. She tried to lighten her despair by telling herself that at least Ike wouldn't need to check out all the hospitals, or even the city morgue, thinking she'd been in some dreadful accident. He'd know she was alive—at least for a while.

At that moment a newscaster began a report on Marva Malin's murder. Liz could only think that she and Ike should be sitting on her sofa now, watching this, discussing the various objects that could have been used to strangle her. She recalled he'd mentioned an additional possible murder weapon. He'd said he was going to look into it today and they'd talk about it tonight. What could it be? Gym teacher Julia Tulley was the only one to whom they hadn't linked a possible weapon. Had Ike found something that implicated her? She gave a deep sigh. It didn't matter anymore. LoPresti was the killer. She had no doubt that Ike would eventually figure this out. Meanwhile, it frustrated her to know he was following false leads.

At that moment, a knock sounded on the door, followed by LoPresti's voice. "Al, are you in there?"

Liz got the feeling that LoPresti thought Alvino wasn't into this plan wholeheartedly. Maybe he thought if she were alone with Alvino for any length of time, she might be able to talk him into letting her escape. If only that were true. Alvino was a different sort of man than LoPresti, but her conversation with him had convinced her that he was just as dedicated to "the plan" as LoPresti.

But exactly what was this plan? For what reason had she been kidnapped? It wasn't likely that these wealthy young men would demand ransom. What then? She closed her mind to a possible answer. Knowing would only make her feel worse.

"Alvino's here. Come in," she called.

LoPresti stepped into the room and immediately noticed the TV tuned to the news channel. "I see you've been waiting for the bulletin," he said. "So have I. I thought it would be on by this time."

"The FBI has to be notified before news like that is

broadcast," Liz said, pretending she knew what she was talking about.

LoPresti gave her a stare. "The FBI?" For a split second he looked uncertain, but then gave a grunty laugh. "If you are counting on the FBI to rescue you, forget it. They don't know where you are, and there's no way they can find out."

She found some solace in knowing her mention of the FBI had worried him, if only for a few moments. What a sleazeball! She felt a strong urge to tell him she knew he'd strangled Marva Malin. Perhaps she would have, if the long-awaited news bulletin about her kidnapping hadn't come on just then.

"And now, a shocking report of an act of terrorism in our city," the newscaster said. "According to a message received by this news channel from a radical, underground Middle Eastern organization, a young American woman was abducted here late this afternoon, apparently on her way home from her job."

A blow-up of Liz's ID with photo flashed onto the screen, as the newscaster continued. "The victim is Elizabeth Rooney, twenty-four years old . . ." The reporter gave her address and described the information on her ID. "Red hair, blue eyes, height five feet five, weight one hundred and fifteen pounds." She paused, adding, "When last seen she was wearing a green pants suit with a tan sweater."

The reporter concluded by asking anyone with possible information to contact the NYPD or the FBI.

Then came the announcement Liz had been dreading.

"The following message from the abductors was received by the State Department early this evening. *The American woman's fate is in the hands of her country's government, She will be released unharmed only after the United States military releases Zaki al Sarzai from prison in Iraq and he is escorted safely across the Syrian border.*"

Chapter Eleven

Zaki al Sarzai? The name penetrated Liz's mind. She'd never heard it in any news broadcast. He must be a Middle Eastern terrorist important to LoPresti and the others, but whoever he was, she knew the American government would not grant the demands for his release. She had to face what she knew was as unchangeable as the Declaration of Independence. The United States of America did not negotiate with terrorists. Trembling, she turned away from the television set.

"Well, now you know," LoPresti said with a mirthless laugh.

Her temper flared. She stared at him, wanting to double a fist and plant it squarely between his bushy, black eyebrows. "And now *you* know that I'm not a policewoman," she retorted. "If I were, it would have been mentioned on the news. If this Zaki what's-his-name is somebody important, you picked the wrong person to exchange for his release. I'm just a civilian nobody."

LoPresti answered with a smile that was almost a sneer. "Your FBI believes it is being clever, withholding the information that you are a law enforcement officer. It makes no difference whether Zaki is important or not. You are in law enforcement, and also a woman. Your government is soft where women are concerned."

This sounded as if he truly believed the United States government would depart from its steadfast policy and exchange a woman for any terrorist, important or obscure.

Her flaring temper receded. She felt despair closing in around her.

Alvino switched off the set. "I guess you have heard enough," he said. After a slight hesitation, he added. "Is there something I might do for you—perhaps get you a glass of water?"

She'd just nodded her head when LoPresti said, "When did you start waiting on women, Al? She can get her own water if she wants it."

"She has had a shock," Alvino replied on his way into the bathroom. "I don't consider it waiting on her to bring her some water."

"You've been in this country too long," LoPresti called after him.

The remark penetrated Liz's despair, diverting her for a few moments. What he'd said gave her something interesting to consider. This band of young terrorists had been living on Manhattan for three years, waiting for orders from some shadowy radical Islamic organization. As time passed, it would have been natural for them to seek out the company of young women. Liz's Muslim college friend had told her about the Islamic Society, located in Manhattan. That would have been a good place for these young men to meet Muslim women, but of course they couldn't risk blowing their cover. Thinking this over, Liz felt sure most if not all of these young Arab types with Italian names had American girlfriends or were looking for someone. Even LoPresti. He'd had his eye on Marva Malin before she turned him down for a coffee date. What would have happened if she'd accepted and they started dating seriously, and then he found out she was Jewish? Maybe he'd have discovered that he also had been too long in a country where ethnic differences were no big deal.

While her mind wandered, Alvino came out of the bathroom with a glass of water. As she thanked him, she wondered if he had an American girlfriend, and if her influence had altered his attitude toward women.

All these young terrorists must have grown restless during the past three years, she thought. They'd arrived here all fired up, ready to carry out whatever orders they received. As time went by without any word, their enthusiasm surely must have waned. They were probably all bored stiff. No wonder they went for LoPresti's plan. They were so desperate for action that they'd rushed into it. They hadn't taken time to think it through before they agreed to have LoPresti send the faxes. They didn't realize that, regardless of how it turned out, they couldn't get away with it. Did they think they could just pile into Alvino's Mercedes and head for Canada?

LoPresti's voice came into her thoughts. "Before we say good night, let me assure you that no harm will come to you. The United States government and the puppet government of Iraq will comply with our terms."

"Vinny is right," Alvino said. "Although your government has followed a policy of not negotiating with organizations such as ours, this situation is different. Never before have we taken an American hostage, especially a woman, in a United States city. This is happening, as you Americans say, too close to home. The citizens will not allow the government to turn its back."

"But you are doing this without authority from your leaders," Liz said. "What will happen to you when they find out you've acted without orders?"

LoPresti's triumphant smile told her he was positive that

his plan would be an overwhelming success. "With Zaki released, we will be heroes," he said. "I'll tell you something about him. He's the leader of our organization. If he had not been captured and imprisoned, our mission in the United States would have been accomplished and our cause would have been advanced, perhaps even won, by now."

Liz felt the clutch of a cold shudder. *Another 9/11—or worse?*

"As a result, the puppet Iraqi government would have been struck down and the former regime returned to power," Alvino added.

"The former regime!" Liz exclaimed. "Don't you want freedom for your country?"

The two men exchanged glances. LoPresti gave a shrug. "We are not Iraqis," he replied.

"We are all natives of other Middle Eastern countries, working to unite the Islamic world," Alvino added.

Knowing any kind of response would have been useless, Liz stared at them, one then the other, in silence. At some point during their formative years, perhaps while they were in college, they had come under the influence of radical clerics and professors. Now they were irrevocably bound to a skewed mindset.

"So, Policewoman or FBI Agent Elizabeth Rooney, whatever you are—now that you know why you are here, we'll leave you to your beauty sleep," LoPresti said. He walked toward the door, saying, "Come on, Al."

He'd never let go of the notion she was a cop Liz thought, but she knew he'd gone beyond that. She had become the certain means to a glorious end.

As Alvino followed LoPresti to the door, he looked over his shoulder. "You will need a sleeping garment," he said. "I will get one from our cook and bring it to you. You will find everything else you need in the bathroom cabinets."

When the door closed behind them. Liz took a deep

breath to dull the daggers of fear stabbing at her heart. She knew what would happen when the demand to release their leader was denied. Though Alvino and the others might possibly have some scruples, there was no telling how they would react. She had no illusions about LoPresti's reaction. He'd already committed a murder.

Thoughts of loved ones paraded across her mind. Ike . . . Mom and Pop . . . Gram . . . Sophie . . . Rosa and Joe . . . Dan . . . By now, they all knew she was being held hostage by terrorists. She felt tears in her heart, but she was beyond shedding them.

The NYPD and FBI must have started looking for her, but where would they begin? They had nothing to go on. They didn't even know if she was being held on Manhattan or if she'd been taken off the island.

She felt sure the State Department's rejection of the demand to release Zaki al Sarzai in exchange for her would be issued promptly. The firm policy of not negotiating with terrorists meant no time would be spent considering it. Most likely the statement would come tonight. The thought numbed her. She felt anesthetized by her own fear.

A knock at the door told her Alvino was back with one of the cook's nightgown. She called for him to enter.

He stepped into the room and handed her a folded, white cotton garment. "This will be somewhat large on you, but I guess it's better than nothing," he said.

Under the circumstances, sleeping in an oversized nightgown wasn't high on her list of inconveniences. She didn't give a damn whether she slept in it, or in her underwear, or in the nothing he'd mentioned.

"Thanks, Alvino," she said.

"Is there anything else I can do for you?" he asked.

Nothing ventured, nothing gained, she thought. At this stage of the game, anything was worth a try. "Yes, how about getting me out of here?" she asked.

He looked troubled. "I am sure you know I cannot do that."

"Why? This plan didn't come from your organization. It was Vinny's idea. I know you didn't want to go along with it at first. It's not too late to back out."

He shook his head. "This is our chance. With Zaki released, we will have taken a giant step toward ridding the Middle East of imperialistic infidels and unifying the Islamic world."

What a bunch of malarkey! She would have expressed the thought aloud if another hadn't popped into her mind. "I think you're afraid of Vinny," she said. "You're afraid if you help me get away he'll explode in one of his rages, and you'll end up like that teacher."

When his face clouded, she thought for a moment that she might have gone too far with this. She waited for an angry outburst, but he only shook his head again and spoke in his usual mild manner. "Vinny did not kill the teacher."

"How can you be so sure?" she asked.

His reply startled her. "Because he knows who did it."

She stared at him. "He told you that?"

Alvino hesitated. "Yes, but he didn't give a name."

This sounded phony, she thought. LoPresti was covering his own butt. "Was he an eye witness, or what?" she asked.

Alvino's reply seemed evasive. "He was not exactly an eye witness."

"Why didn't he tell the detectives what he knows?"

"He likes the person who did it, and he did not like the teacher."

Even if this whole thing wasn't a gigantic lie, the reasoning was crazy, she thought. "He should have told the police," she said. "By withholding information he was obstructing justice."

When Alvino made no reply, she got the distinct feeling that he knew more than he'd told her. Since he'd clammed up, she switched her thoughts to another angle.

She guessed that all six terrorists planned to continue their jobs while waiting for an answer to their demand. Though she thought the negative reply would come tonight, if it didn't, someone besides the deaf mute cook would have to be in the apartment till it did to make sure the hostage didn't escape.

She asked Alvino about this. His reply told her he truly believed the United States government would cave in. "We will take turns until negotiations have been finalized. This might take a few days. I have volunteered for tomorrow."

She spoke on an impulse. "Better you than Vinny."

A slight frown furrowed his brow. "Even after what I explained, you still think Vinny killed the teacher."

"His story about knowing who did it doesn't ring true," she replied.

"I have known Vinny most of my life," Alvino said. "He has always had strong likes and dislikes. With people he likes, he is extremely loyal. It did not surprise me at all that he would not want to implicate a friend in the murder of someone he disliked."

Again, she thought LoPresti was covering his own butt. She wondered why he'd told Alvino anything at all. Like some killers she'd heard about, did he feel the need to brag about what he'd done, but had sense enough to twist his story? That way he'd get some satisfaction without risk.

But what if there were some truth in what LoPresti told Alvino? The person LoPresti liked enough to protect would most likely be one of the other teachers or Bernice Fripp. She remembered the warm exchange between LoPresti and Bernice backstage today. Bernice could have followed Marva up to the balcony. LoPresti could have seen her coming down the balcony stairs a few seconds after Marva's body hit the gym floor.

But he'd seemed very friendly with Julia Tulley too, and she'd also sensed camaraderie between him and Cyril

Gibbs. But then, in a flash of recollection, she thought of the intimidated look on Gibbs' face when LoPresti came backstage. Was LoPresti's friendliness toward Gibbs a sham?

Did LoPresti know that Gibbs was the killer, and had he told Gibbs he knew? This would explain Gibbs' apparent fear of LoPresti.

Or could it be the other way around? Did Gibbs know LoPresti was the killer? This too would make Gibbs afraid of LoPresti.

She shook her head. Alvino had her believing LoPresti's cock-and-bull story. But again, if it were true, he knew more than he'd divulged.

His voice penetrated her thoughts. "I am sure you are tired after what you have been through today," he said. "I'll say good night to you now. I hope you sleep well. Your breakfast will be brought to you about eight o'clock in the morning."

Did he actually think she'd be able to sleep at all, or care what time breakfast was served? She noticed the door had an inside bolt and decided to use it. At least she'd be sure nobody could enter her room during the night, perhaps to inject her with a knockout drug and take her to some other location. Now she was getting paranoid. Why would they move her when nobody knew where she was? Besides, with the entire city on the alert, it would be too risky.

With thoughts alternating between her predicament and the Malin murder whirling around in her head, she took a shower in the lavishly marbled stall. She washed her hair with a pricey American cosmetic-brand shampoo from a bathroom cabinet. She wrapped one luxuriously soft, cream-colored towel around her head and dried herself off with another. She found a dryer and brush in another cabinet and worked on her hair.

Though LoPresti thought the demand for Zaki al Sarzai's release would be deliberated, perhaps for days, she knew better. Whatever the next few hours had in store for her, she'd face it freshly coiffed. Dark humor, she thought, slipping the cook's nightgown over her head. Alvino was right—it was too large. Also, it would never make the pages of the Victoria's Secret catalog.

Because she knew sleep would be impossible, she decided not to get into the huge bed. Instead, she'd lie on the chaise and watch a TV movie. She found a white terrycloth robe in the bathroom and put it on. It was nearer her size than the cook's nightgown. It and all the other amenities, plus the inside lock on the door, made her think that Alvino might often entertain female guests in his luxurious apartment. *And probably not a Muslim in the bunch!*

When she picked up the remote to get the movie channel, curiosity began to take over her feelings. Until this moment she had no desire to watch any more news. Hearing about her own kidnapping and listening to commentators' speculations would only add to her sense of hopelessness, she'd thought. But now a sudden urge to know what was happening made her start flipping through the news channels . . .

Her kidnapping dominated the news. Every channel carried it, but the coverage struck her as thin. Settling on one channel, she listened to her biography reported by a properly sober-sounding female commentator, followed by a rehash. Evidently, there had been no developments since the story first broke. But the way things stood, what developments could there possibly be? The only new angle to this story would come when the State Department released its statement rejecting the terrorists' demands. Why was it taking so long, when the issue was not subject to debate? But she knew it would come all too soon—maybe any minute now . . .

A dreadful feeling of desperation swept over her. She turned off the TV, burrowed her head in a pillow, and prayed more fervently than she'd ever prayed before—not for her own salvation; there was no hope of that now. Her prayers were for those she loved and who loved her in return. She asked that they be helped through what lay ahead and that they be comforted by knowing each one of them contributed to her life and made it as happy and fulfilling as anyone could have.

Sudden, loud noises made her raise her head from the pillow. From somewhere inside the apartment she heard a crashing sound, then a crescendo of voices. The thought struck her that the terrorists had been watching a TV news channel and something startling had come on—something that angered them. She pictured an enraged LoPresti, out of control, smashing things. She didn't have to wonder what could have set him off. It could only be the failure of his grandiose plan he was sure would have made them all heroes.

The State Department must have made the inevitable reply to the terrorists' demands. Though she had no doubt about the reply, she needed to hear it.

Taking a deep breath, she reached for the remote control, but before her trembling fingers could turn the TV on again, she heard the tread of multiple tramping feet in the hall outside the room. *They were coming for her.* In a few moments she'd hear someone try and open the door, and then LoPresti's infuriated voice, ordering her to unlock it. She felt sure he believed she'd been watching TV and she'd heard the State Department's rejection statement. LoPresti probably expected, even hoped, to find the female law enforcement officer cowering in fear, weeping, and begging for mercy.

What a time for her Irish temper to ignite! But here it was, coming to a boil, telling her not to give him this satisfaction. She'd show him what American women were made of! Before LoPresti tried the door, she'd fling it open, herself, and face him with her chin up.

She sprang from the chaise, rushed across the room, and slid the bolt.

Chapter Twelve

Although the men in the dimly lighted hallway were only a few steps away from the door when she opened it, the semidarkness kept their faces indistinct. With her temper still simmering, subduing her fear, she waited—ready to face LoPresti, when out of the shadows came a familiar voice, tinged with laughter asking a familiar question.

"What are you doing here, Rooney?"

Her heart went into a spin. Then she felt Ike's arms around, displacing her bravado and every shred of the terror that lurked behind it. She clung to him, feeling only joyous relief.

"Are you all right?" he asked.

Still speechless with joy and surprise, she could only nod her head.

He clasped her hand and led her back into the room. She saw him signal okay to the men in the hall and heard him say, "Give us a couple of minutes." When he closed the door and again took her into his arms, she felt safe for the first time since the moment LoPresti forced her into Alvino's SUV.

After a lingering kiss, she managed to speak. "How did you find me?" *Could Alvino have reconsidered, after all?*

Instead of replying, Ike went to the door and opened it. She caught a glimpse of three cops and another man—a FBI agent, maybe? No, she thought. She was familiar enough with relations between the NYPD and the FBI to know it wasn't likely that the two law enforcement agencies had carried out this rescue together.

A moment later, she stared in disbelief at the man Ike ushered into the room. The last person she'd expected to see was Russian mob leader Boris Tynkov!

His round face bore a faint smile as he fixed his deepset brown eyes on her. "Once more I show you thanks," he said. "And once more I tell you Big Tiny never forgets."

He'd never forget her testimony that saved him from a prison term, and evidently he'd played some part in her rescue, Liz thought. Maybe when she told him how grateful she was, he'd explain. But immediately after he'd spoken, and before she could put her thoughts into words, he gave a slight bow, quickly turned, and left.

"Wait . . ." she called, starting after him. Either he did not hear her or chose not to respond. He and the three cops disappeared down the hall.

She felt Ike's hand on her arm. "He doesn't want your thanks. He feels he's the one who'll never be done with thanking *you*. What he did this time is even better than the champagne."

Feelings of puzzlement and confusion swept over her. "How did Big Tiny help you find me?" she asked, "How could he have known where I was?" Before he could reply, another question flashed into her mind, demanding an immediate answer. "But first, please tell me what happened to the terrorists."

"Five men and a woman have been taken into custody," Ike replied.

Startled, she stared at him. "*Five* men? There should have been six!"

His face sobered. "Are you sure about that, Liz"?

"Positive. I saw them sitting around the dining room table and counted them. The owner of the Mercedes told me two of them lived here with him and three others I lived in a different building."

Ike pondered this. "There was no possible way one of them could have escaped after we broke in," he said. "The missing one must have gone out of the apartment before the raid."

He took a phone out of his pocket and gave her a long, serious look. "I'm calling the commissioner," he said. "This is classified information."

She nodded. He didn't have to say anything more. The public was still shocked about her kidnapping and reeling from the news of an al Qaeda cell on Manhattan. In the announcement of her rescue and round-up of the terrorists, it might be wise not to reveal, immediately, that one of terrorists had eluded capture. Reaction could lead to witch hunts all over the city.

By the time the missing terrorist became aware that his colleagues had been captured, his chances of getting off Manhattan might be slim, she thought. Ike would barely be off the phone before the NYPD and FBI would swing into action.

She found herself wondering if LoPresti might be the missing terrorist. He'd left the apartment earlier, to fax the messages to the news media. Had he gone out again before the raid? Having one of the terrorists missing was bad enough. For her, having him turn out to be LoPresti would be the worst. But if he'd been among those captured, wouldn't Ike have recognized him?

"One of the men who lived here is LoPresti, the music teacher at Chadwick Academy," she told him the minute he got off the phone.

She searched his face for a reaction. To her relief, he broke into a smile. "Yeah, I guess I don't have to tell you how surprised I was—but I was even more surprised when Tynkov told me he recognized him as the man who forced you into the SUV."

"How did Tynkov know that? And you haven't told me how he helped find me."

"I'll explain everything in the car. I want to get you out of here. I'll wait in the hall while you get dressed."

"Where are you taking me?" she asked, hoping she wouldn't have to go someplace for interrogation.

"The commissioner understands you've been through enough tonight," he said on his way out the door. "You're going home."

At first she felt as if she couldn't get out of her palatial prison fast enough, even if it meant departing while still wearing the cook's nightgown and the terrycloth robe. But she loved her Lord & Taylor pants suit. Besides, even on sale, it had set her back close to half a week's pay.

She'd never dressed as quickly in all her life, yet in those few minutes a variety of thoughts crowded into her mind. Besides her concern about the missing terrorist, she felt sure the TV news channels were carrying the story of her abduction nation-wide. She knew that Pop and Mom and everyone else she loved had heard about it. She must get word to them of her rescue, as soon as possible. If LoPresti hadn't taken her cell phone, she'd put in a call to Pop and Mom right now. But she'd marked the phone with her initials. If the cops found it, she'd get it back.

She recalled she'd been about to turn the TV on after she heard a loud, crashing noise and assumed the State Department's announcement was being broadcast. She'd believed the noise was LoPresti going berserk. Now she realized what she'd heard must have been Ike and the cops, and Big Tiny, breaking into the apartment. There'd been no government reply to the terrorists' demand. The State Department must have been informed of her imminent rescue, and now there was no need for a statement. The next news bulletin would be about her rescue.

While slipping her sweater over her head and reaching for her jacket, thoughts of Marva Malin's murder took over. How lucky that Alvino had told her about LoPresti covering for someone. It wasn't likely LoPresti would come out with this information. When things settled down, and she and Ike were able to talk without interruption, she'd let him know about it. She smiled. *She'd gone from terrorists' victim to amateur sleuth in record time.*

An aura of emptiness pervaded the apartment when she and Ike walked down the hall into the foyer. It hadn't taken long to herd the terrorists away. She thought of the cook. What would happen to her? She couldn't have known what was going on. She thought of Alvino—good-hearted but brainwashed by radicals—and found herself wondering if he might be the missing terrorist. She still felt that he had a lot of good in him. There must be many other misguided young Middle Easterners like him. Where would it all end?

They left the building through the lobby. In the street, Liz saw cops everywhere, and noticed a police van pulling away. *First a local jail for her captors, then Federal prison?* Whatever their fate, five fewer terrorists would be at large. She pictured a crestfallen LoPresti crammed in with the others— or had he burst out of control when he realized his dream of glory was shattered and been subdued with a straitjacket?

"Sorry, no TV cameras or news hounds, yet," Ike said, as they walked to his car. "This operation was carried out too quickly."

"Don't be sorry. Being bombarded by cameras and reporters is the last thing I need right now."

"You look so pretty, you should have your picture flashed around the world," he replied.

She smiled at him in pleased surprise. Ike wasn't the kind of guy who shelled out compliments like peanuts at the circus—and she without so much as a dash of lipstick! Good thing she'd washed her hair!

In his car, they lost themselves in a long embrace.

"I'd like to do this all night, but we need to get you home," Ike said.

Liz had to agree. "Oh, yes, I need to get home. I want to call my folks and Sophie and . . ."

"I would have called them all, but I thought it best to wait till I was one hundred percent sure you were safe," he said. He switched on the radio, saying, "The story of your rescue could break any time now." He paused, giving her another serious look. "There'll be no mention that one of the terrorists is on the loose."

Reaching into his pocket, he added, "By the way, here's your phone. One of the cops found it on LoPresti and turned it over to me. Good idea, putting your initials on it." He gave her a light kiss and started the car.

She decided to wait till she got to her apartment to call Pop and Mom. If news of her rescue came over the car radio, she didn't want to miss a word of it.

She was about to ask him, again, how Big Tiny got involved in her rescue, when she noticed the street signs. "We're not very far from my place," she said.

He nodded. "In a few minutes, the Moscarettis will be getting the surprise of their lives when they look out their door to see who's coming in."

She knew when Rosa and Joe saw her, home safe, Ike wouldn't get a chance for awhile to explain how Big Tiny figured in her rescue. "Will there be time for you to fill me in on Big Tiny before we get there?" she asked.

"Sure," he replied with an understanding grin. "Tynkov witnessed the incident between you and LoPresti outside the school."

"You mean he came with the driver to pick up his daughter today?"

"Yeah. He told us his driver had slowed the car, looking for a parking space, when you came out of the building and tried to get a cab. He said he recognized you and was going to offer you a ride, but you started walking down the block. He noticed a man following you, he said. He'd never met LoPresti. When the two of you started talking, he assumed you were friends."

"But surely he must have noticed him forcing me toward the SUV."

"Up till then, you and LoPresti had been talking amicably. He thought it was a lovers' quarrel."

"Some lover, with his hand over my mouth!"

"That's when he decided something was wrong. With other cars pulling up in front of the school, he said he couldn't get a good look at the plates, but he took down as much as he could see before the vehicle drove off. He was only able to get the first three digits and the make of the car, but a maroon Mercedes SUV is a standout vehicle, easy to trace. He said he would have followed it, but his daughter was waiting inside. The driver went in to get her and Tynkov called the police on his car phone and asked for me."

"I know he saw you at my apartment the night he brought the champagne, but how would he know your name and that you're a cop? Did you ever bust him?"

Ike shook his head. "I guess he made it his business to find out."

A man like Boris Tynkov would have ways of identifying anyone he chose to, Liz thought. For some reason, he wanted information about the man he'd seen in the apartment of the woman who'd saved him from a prison term.

A possible reason occurred to her. "Lucky for you, you always treated me right," she teased.

He flashed a sidelong grin. "Whatever he found out, he decided he wanted to talk to me and nobody else. Of course by the time he got through to the precinct, I was on my way over to your place. One of the men on night watch called me, and I contacted Tynkov."

Liz put it all together. When LoPresti left the apartment to send the faxes, Ike had already started tracing the Mercedes registration. No wonder they'd found her so quickly. It might have been even quicker if they'd had the complete license plate numbers.

"When we got the address of the Mercedes owner, I notified the commissioner and set up the rescue," Ike continued. "Tynkov insisted on coming along."

"I'm surprised the commissioner would allow that."

Ike faked a rueful smile. "I guess I forgot to run it by him."

No wonder he and Pop got to be such close friends, she thought. Before he retired from Homicide, Pop used to do the same kinds of unorthodox things. Bending the rules might have gotten them both in trouble with the higher-ups if they weren't two of the best detectives on the force.

"I hope Big Tiny's part in the rescue gets good coverage on the news," she said.

"I'm sure they'll play it up," Ike replied. "It isn't every day that a notorious racketeer does something worthwhile."

They'd reached Liz's street. Her building loomed ahead. When Ike braked the car in the nearest available parking spot, they could see lights shining from the windows of the Moscarettis' front room.

"Joe and Rosa are probably watching TV," Liz said, as she and Ike hurried toward the building. She found herself hoping the news of her rescue had been broadcast. That might cut down on the length of time they'd have to spend rejoicing with the Moscarettis and she could go up to her own place, make her phone calls, and then have her discussion with Ike. But don't count on it, she told herself. Joe and Rosa would probably insist that she make her calls to Pop and Mom, Gram, Sophie, and Dan from their apartment while Joe uncorked his best wine and Rosa brought forth whatever goodies she'd cooked that day. She was too fond of them to risk hurting their feelings.

News of her rescue had not yet broken. The Moscarettis were overcome with joyous surprise. But Ike handled everything. After hugs, laughter, a few tears, and a round of Joe's prized Ornellaia Le Volte, he announced that they must leave.

"I have to interrogate Liz," he told them.

"Sure," Joe said. "You gotta find out as much as possible about those terrorist bums."

Nodding agreement, Rosa scooped some anisette cookies and two cannolis into a plastic bag and handed it to Liz, saying, "We'll see you tomorrow, Dearie."

In her apartment, Liz switched on the TV to listen for the announcement of her rescue. Ike said he'd make coffee while she started in on her phone calls.

She'd just taken her phone out of her purse when the awaited announcement came on. Ike rushed out from behind the kitchenette screen and joined her.

As she'd hoped, Big Tiny was lauded as the person instrumental in effecting the rescue, but of course the media referred to him as "Russian mobster Boris Tynkov." In the file photo shown of him he looked more like the cruel, unrelenting loan shark he was than the temporary hero he'd become. But to her, he'd always be a kind of hero, she thought. *Big Tiny never forgets*. Well, neither would she.

Now that she was back in her apartment again, sitting on the sofa among Gram's needlepoint pillows, savoring the aroma of coffee and about to swap ideas with Ike, Liz got the strange feeling that the news program was all about somebody else.

"I can't believe I'm the one they're talking about," she said.

"You better believe it, and get on the phone with your folks," Ike replied. "They probably had their TV on and just got the news."

He was right. Pop picked up the phone on the first ring.

"Hello Pop, I'm home," she said.

His voice sounded happy and choked with emotion. "Lizzie, I was sure this would be you calling. We just got the wonderful news." He paused. She could hear what sounded somewhat like a scuffle before he came back on. "Your mother almost broke my arm trying to grab the phone. I better let her talk to you."

"Liz . . ." Mom's voice shook when she first came on, but soon she was firing questions. "Are you sure you're okay, Dear? They didn't harm you in any way? How did you get mixed up with such dreadful people? And speaking of dreadful people—is it true that awful Russian gangster helped find you? The news report said the NYPD rescued you. Was Ike there? Did he bring you home?"

When Pop came back on, he told her that they'd been planning to fly north and stay with Gram until she was found. "Now that we know you're safe, we'll stay put," he said. "Have you called your grandmother yet?"

"No. You and Mom came first. Gram's next, then Sophie and Dan."

"I'll say good-bye for now and we'll talk to you tomorrow," he said.

Liz phoned Gram. She too had heard the broadcast. "I just got home from lighting a candle for you at the church and turned on the TV," she said. The tone of her voice left no doubt of her faith in the power of prayers and candles.

When she called Sophie's cell phone, Sophie picked up with a squeal of delight. Her excited voice came next. "Liz? This better be you! The caller ID says it is. I don't want to talk to some terrorist."

"It's me," Liz replied. "I guess you didn't hear the news. I was rescued a little while ago. Ike just brought me home."

Sophie gave another squeal. "Ike rescued you? How cool is that? I didn't hear about it. I've been so upset I turned off the TV. I'm so happy! And now I won't have to postpone my wedding!"

"You were going to put off getting married?"

"Sure. Do you really think I'd walk down the aisle without my best friend at the altar to hold my bouquet? I was going to postpone it until you got back safe and sound."

"You took an awful chance. What if . . . ?"

"I knew you'd be rescued. You've been in and out of bad scrapes before. You've got the luck of the Irish with you, Liz Rooney!"

"It was with me today, that's for sure!"

"I know with Ike there you don't want to stay on the phone with me," Sophie said. "If you're working tomorrow, I'll call you there. I've taken the rest of the week off to get ready for the wedding. Any chance you'll have tomorrow off, and you could come over to the island? I'm dying to hear all the details of your latest kidnapping."

"No reason why I shouldn't go to work. I haven't been injured in any way, and I feel okay. I haven't called Dan yet, though. He might insist that I take tomorrow off."

"I'll bet he says don't come in. You feel okay now, but you could wake up tomorrow with a delayed reaction."

"Whatever happens, we'll be in touch tomorrow," Liz replied.

When she called Dan he'd heard the news of her rescue. "I guess you know how happy I was to know you're safe and sound," he said. "Thanks for calling, Lizzie. You sound like you're okay, but I don't want you in here tomorrow. I want you to take it easy. I'm sure the police commissioner will be sending someone over to question you in the morning, but after that maybe you could go over to Staten Island and visit your grandmother or Sophie and relax."

"Thanks, that's a good idea," she said. "And by the way, your pen managed to get through this, safe and sound too."

He laughed. "The pen was the last thing on my mind, Lizzie."

Hanging up the phone, she decided to go to Staten Island tomorrow.

"Everything squared away?" Ike asked, handing her a mug of coffee.

"Yes. Now we can talk about Marva Malin's murder."

Ike looked dubious. "Are you sure you feel up to a discussion? I thought I'd get going after we had our coffee and let you get some rest."

"I feel fine," she replied. "I have a lot to tell you and ask you." Before she went into what LoPresti had told Alvino, she wanted to hear what progress had been made. "First, how's the autopsy coming along?" she asked.

"They expect to complete it tomorrow or Friday."

"I guess the marks on her neck were photographed early on."

Ike nodded. "Each possible murder weapon we pick up will be matched against those marks. Since the object pressed against the throat might have shifted, they'll all be double-checked. It'll take a few days to complete the tests."

"For a while, I was sure LoPresti was the killer," she said. "But now I have my doubts." She related what Alvino told her. "It sounds like LoPresti's protecting someone," she said. "Could that someone be Gibbs? I don't know what to think."

Ike looked skeptical. "LoPresti could be protecting *himself*."

She told him about the camaraderie backstage and how Gibbs seemed intimidated by LoPresti. "At first I thought that was because Gibbs knows LoPresti found out he's the killer, but maybe it's the other way around. Gibbs knows LoPresti's the killer and he's scared."

"That bears looking into," Ike replied. "I'll get on it tomorrow. Meanwhile, we'll test the baton."

"Oh, you have the baton?"

"Not yet, but more than likely LoPresti put it in his locker before leaving the school today. Lou's going over there tomorrow and if we're lucky, he'll find it."

"Then you'll have two possible murder weapons being tested—the baton and Duddy's hammer."

As Ike started to reply, she remembered Gibbs' paintbrush and Bernice's cane. She couldn't wait to tell him about them. She interrupted. "Oh, I almost forgot, I have two more possible murder weapons. One is Bernice's carved wooden cane."

"We noticed the cane," Ike said. "That'll be tested as a last resort. We want to avoid letting anyone know what we're taking for evidence testing. We want to keep them all believing we're still going on the perp being an outsider. Duddy knows we have his hammer, but so far he hasn't figured out why we took it. We hope by the time he realizes it's being tested, we'll know whether or not he's the killer."

She should have known the cane wouldn't get by him, she thought. But evidently the paintbrush *had.* Somehow, he and Lou had missed it when they searched the school premises or it would have been sent to the evidence lab to be compared with photos of the marks on the victim's neck.

"The other possible weapon I happened to notice was the art teacher's paintbrush," she said. "The handle looked like dark brown wood and it was large—just about the right size for the killer to press against the victim's throat, and it had the curvy shape most paintbrush handles have, so it might match the discoloration differences on her neck."

Ike nodded. "Yeah, it had all the characteristics we were looking for except one. It's made of plastic."

"Oh," she said.

Ike set down his coffee mug and took her hands in his. "You were on the right track with that paintbrush," he said. "When we searched the trash pile yesterday and found the brush, we were sure at first we had something to connect art teacher Gibbs to the strangling."

He never downgraded anything she came up with, she thought, casting him an appreciative smile. "Too bad it wasn't wood," she said.

As she spoke, she recalled she'd interrupted him a few moments ago. "Sorry I broke in, before," she said. "What were you going to say?"

"Something else we can connect to Gibbs," he replied. "We continued looking through the trash and picked up an old wooden chair rung with dried green paint on one end of it. Evidently, Gibbs used it to stir paint with."

Liz felt a tingle of excitement. In her mind's eye she saw a curvy chair rung, exactly the right size to use as a strangling device.

But then another thought came. She voiced it to Ike. "What if the paint on the end of the chair rung was still tacky when the killer used it on the victim? Wouldn't some paint have come off on her neck or clothing? Or if the paint were dry, wouldn't there be flakes?"

He gave a smile of approval. "You're right in line with what we hope Forensics will find in the final analysis."

"So now you have the hammer and the chair rung being tested, and tomorrow you'll have the baton," she said. "But what about the billy club? How are you going to get hold of it, and when?"

"The billy club's out. We're dropping Tynkov's driver as a possible suspect."

This surprised her. "Why?"

"When I was with Tynkov tonight, he mentioned that his daughter played violin in the school orchestra. He seemed genuinely distressed about the murder. I got the firm impression he didn't know Malin had been picking on his daughter. Evidently, she never said a word to him about it. She must be a feisty little girl."

Liz remembered Pop saying damn little got by Detective

George Eichle. She knew if Big Tiny had been lying, Ike would have picked up on it.

"So, the billy club's scratched," she said. "And if nothing pans out with the baton and the hammer and the chair rung, you'll send in Bernice's cane."

"There's one more item that needs testing before we borrow Bernice's cane," he replied. "Do you remember my telling you I was going to look into another possible murder weapon today?"

"I remember now. You said we'd talk about it tonight. What is it?" She hoped this was something to implicate Julia Tulley. The gym teacher was the only one under suspicion without a link to the murder.

"It's something you put me onto," he said. "If it hadn't been for you, I wouldn't have thought there was any rush to have a look at this particular item."

While she stared at him in puzzlement, trying to recall what he could be talking about, he laughed and gathered her into a hug.

"It's Malin's handbag," he said.

Chapter Thirteen

Still puzzled, Liz tried to figure out what the victim's handbag had to do with the strangling.

"Do you remember I told you it was bagged for evidence after the first cop on the scene removed the ID and address book for me?" he asked.

She nodded. "Oh, now I remember. You said you hadn't seen it yet."

"Well now I've had a good look at it," he said. "The handbag definitely qualifies as a possible murder weapon."

"It does?" She wasn't too surprised to notice Ike was calling it a handbag now, instead of a purse. That meant it was large. It would have to be extra large to contain the script to the school play, she thought. Maybe it was a tote bag. Like most men, Ike wasn't too savvy when it came to women's accessories. But whatever it was, why did he believe it could possibly be the murder weapon?

"What's the bag made of?" she asked.

"Dark blue fabric—heavy, like canvas," he replied.

It sounded like a tote bag, she decided. She recalled the precinct cops had told Sophie the bag had long strap handles for wearing over the shoulder. But she'd seen tote bags made with an extra handle to be used when the straps were detached or tucked inside. Maybe this one had an extra handle made of wood. "Does it have a wooden handle?" she asked.

He shook his head. "Not a handle, but the way you'd get it to open or close—it doesn't have a flap or a zipper—it has two pieces of wood with an indentation to open it, and it snaps shut."

Ike's somewhat awkward description was enough to stir Liz's imagination. She could see those two strips of indented wood being pressed hard against Marva Malin's throat. "For me, this goes pretty high on the list," she said.

"Mine, too," he replied. "But until you asked me about styling, I didn't even consider wood on a purse. If the cops had described it as a bag, I would have given it prompt attention. If it turns out to be the murder weapon, we'll have your woman's point of view to credit."

She smiled, remembering he'd told her this was something even Sherlock Holmes couldn't have. "When will you know the results of the tests?" she asked.

"Tests on all the possible weapons should be completed in a couple of days."

"That brings us up to Sophie's wedding day. I hope there's a definite development before the ceremony. I'd like to be able to concentrate on something other than murder weapons."

"I'll do what I can to speed things along," he said. He finished his coffee and got to his feet. "You need to get some sleep, so I'm out of here."

She had to admit she was beginning to fade. The rescue had keyed her up, but now the tension of the past hours was taking its toll.

"I hope you're not going to work tomorrow," Ike said, at the door.

"No. Dan gave me the day off. I thought I'd go to see Gram and Sophie."

A frown came to his face. "With one of the terrorists still at large, that's not a good idea." But a moment afterward, the frown faded and he nodded his head. "On second thought, I guess it would be okay. The commissioner's sending someone over in the morning for information to pass on to the FBI, and the news media will be beating down your door, but after that you could take off for Staten Island."

He paused, adding, "Your picture will be running on TV all day. Better wear a hat and dark glasses when you leave for Staten Island so you won't be recognized and bothered."

"I know I should hide my hair," she said. "But a rain hat's all I have."

"Wear it, and be sure your hair's tucked up under it—no strands showing. And there's no need to prolong your questioning or your news interview by bringing up LoPresti. That story will break by itself." He kissed her good night. "I'll phone you during the day to see how you're doing," he said.

At that moment, they heard a commotion in the lower hall. Joe's voice floated up the stairs, loud enough to be heard through Liz's closed door. They couldn't catch what he was saying, but there was no doubt he was angry.

"What the . . . ?" Ike opened the door. They peered down the stairs and saw a pajama-clad Joe confronting a man and a woman in the vestibule.

"Take one step into this hall and you'll be sorry," Joe bellowed. "What kind of people are you, bothering her this time of night after what she went through today? I'm telling you again, come back tomorrow for your damn interview."

"Reporters," Ike said. He gave Liz a quick kiss. "Get inside and hit the sack. I'll help Joe handle this." He paused with a grin. "Not that Joe needs any help."

Liz wasn't about to close the door when she could relish the sight of Joe and Ike getting rid of two overzealous news hounds. Watching, she recognized the man as Yaker, a reporter for a sleazy tabloid. She'd never seen the woman, a young blond, before. Their press badges looked identical. Obviously, they were working together.

After they left, she heard Ike suggest to Joe that he should consider getting a buzzer entry system. Joe replied he'd look into having one installed tomorrow.

"Meanwhile, I'll keep the door locked and have keys made for Liz and Mr. Klein—and you too, Ike," he said.

She heard him add that since both she and Mr. Klein were in for the night, he'd lock the front door till morning. "In case some more reporters come sniffing around."

When Ike left, she closed her door. All she wanted to do now was get into her pajamas, pull out her sofa bed, and snuggle under Gram's patchwork quilt. There'd be no mulling over possible murder weapons before she fell asleep. Even speculations about Marva Malin's handbag would have to wait til tomorrow.

When she first awakened the next morning, yesterday's events seemed like fuzzy fragments of a fading dream, but after a few seconds everything came into focus. A glance at her wall clock told her it was almost 7:30. She grabbed the remote and turned on the TV. By now, the news channels would have full coverage of her kidnapping, her rescue, and the round-up of the terrorists.

Still in her pajamas, she brewed coffee and toasted a bagel while watching reruns of her photo and biography and listening to details of her abduction and the NYPD rescue. It didn't take long for her to notice the sparse information about the terrorists. No photos were shown, and no names were given. Last night's action had been too quick for complete media coverage. And of course, no mention was made that one of the terrorists had not been captured.

She found herself wondering if Alvino might be the missing one. But whether or not he was, with both the NYPD and the FBI on the job, she felt confident he'd soon be found. Ike must think so too, otherwise he wouldn't have changed his mind about her trip to Staten Island today.

LoPresti's involvement wasn't covered either. What a story that would have made! But it looked as if only she and Ike and Big Tiny knew, for now, that Chadwick Academy's Italian-American music teacher was actually a Middle Eastern terrorist.

She remembered Ike telling her not to inject LoPresti into her questioning by the commissioner's office or her news media interviews. The story of his part in the abduction would eventually break. But meanwhile, LoPresti wouldn't show up for work today or call in sick. Did any of his faculty friends know his phone number and where he lived? Would one of them call or go to the apartment? She decided that, under the circumstances, LoPresti would have kept his home address and phone number to himself. But the school office would have that information. When his unexplained absence continued beyond another day, someone, probably Bernice Fripp, would find out that LoPresti lived at the same address where the terrorist roundup had taken place. From that point on, speculation would run rife. Investigative journalists would get on it, resulting, at last, in glaring headlines and blaring bulletins containing the shocking truth about music teacher Vincent LoPresti.

Meanwhile, she guessed that as a security measure, specific whereabouts of the terrorists would not be announced. The investigation would proceed with little fanfare.

News of the rescue and the terrorist roundup all but crowded the Chadwick Academy murder out of the picture. A brief announcement was made that Marva Malin's body would be released to her family some time tomorrow, and a photo shot was shown of Mr. and and Mrs. Malinbaum walking the Pomeranians. The newscaster concluded the segment by quoting an unidentified NYPD spokesman.

"Progress has been made in apprehending the murderer. A break in the case is expected soon."

If this unidentified NYPD spokesman happened to be Ike, he hadn't let *her* in on any imminent break in the case, Liz thought. The murder weapon hadn't even been identified yet. But he *had* told her they'd all be tested within a couple of days. She went over them in her mind—LoPresti's baton, Duddy's hammer, Gibbs' paint-daubed chair rung, and Marva Malin's bag. And if none of these matched up with the marks on Marva's neck, he'd bring in Bernice's cane. The NYPD spokesman was right, she decided. Except for the bag—a tote bag, most likely, each possible murder weapon had a connection to a potential suspect. They were getting close to a neat wrap-up.

Seconds after this thought, others came. There was still no implement to link up with gym teacher Julia Tulley. Could the tote bag be that link? She imagined Julia following Marva up to the balcony during the break. Some of the kids had told Ike that the two teachers had a heated exchange earlier. Had Julia, still fuming, decided to have the last word? Had her anger flared out of control? Had she seized the tote bag, pressed the wooden closure against Marva's throat and held it there too long?

Ike had already thought of all this, Liz decided. They'd have another lively discussion when he came over tonight.

She'd just finished breakfast when someone introducing himself as Nelson Novak from the NYPD Commissioner's Office phoned. "I need to ask you some questions, Ms. Rooney," he said. "When would it be convenient for me to come to your residence?"

"As soon as you can get here," she told him. She didn't want to spend the entire day waiting. She wanted to call Gram and Sophie and tell them she'd be coming out to the island today.

Only today and tomorrow remained before the wedding, and tomorrow night was the rehearsal. Besides telling Sophie the details of her kidnapping, they had plenty to talk about.

In anticipation of Novak's arrival, she hurried to get dressed. To make sure she'd look inconspicuous on the subway and ferry, she put on a dark blue pants suit and white sweater. *As if a rain hat on a sunny day wouldn't attract attention.*

She folded up her sofa bed and made the place look like this was the living room and there was a real bedroom around, somewhere. If only that were true, she wouldn't have to move when she and Ike were married, she thought with a sigh.

Nelson Novak knocked on her apartment door about an hour later, after successfully running the Moscaretti blockade by showing his credentials. Liz was relieved and pleased when he turned out to be an affable, middle-age man who'd known Pop.

He told her the questioning would be taped but it wouldn't take long. He began by asking if she'd overheard any talk among the terrorists.

"Yes—mostly between the man who forced me into the SUV and the driver, before they began talking in a language I didn't understand," she replied. "I thought it sounded as if they'd been waiting for orders that never came—like they were tired of waiting and wanted some action." She filled him in on everything else she'd been able to pick up, including what LoPresti had told her about Zaki al Sarzai.

Besides recording the questioning, Novak took notes. "Sounds like al Sarzai's capture and imprisonment was the reason LoPresti and the others were left high and dry, without orders," he said. "Do you know if these men are Iraqis?"

"One of them told me they're not Iraqis," Liz replied. "He said they're all from various Middle Eastern countries, and their organization was formed to unite the Islamic world.

He's the one who drove the SUV and had the fancy apartment where I was held." She related everything else she could recall of her conversations with Alvino. "I believe this man might cooperate with you," she added.

Unless Alvino was the terrorist who got away.

"Do you know his name?" Novak asked.

"Only his first name. Alvino."

Novak made a note of it and got to his feet, saying, "We'll pass this information along to the FBI. Thanks, Ms. Rooney—you've been very helpful."

That was painless, and it was barely 10 o'clock. She phoned Sophie.

"How about if I come out to Staten Island today? I can look in on Gram, and then you and I can have one last hen fest before you're an old married woman."

"Great. But don't you have to meet with the FBI for questioning?"

"Someone from the police commissioner's office was just here, questioning me. He told me they'd give my information to the FBI."

"Oh, good. Then come as soon as you can. Come for lunch around noon."

"Okay. I want to phone Gram and then Pop and Mom, but I won't talk long, and then I'll drop in on Rosa and Joe, but I'll try and make the eleven o'clock boat."

She remembered Ike saying he'd call her during the day. If he didn't get her on her home phone, she knew he'd try her cell.

Next, she phoned Gram to make sure she hadn't gone on one of her church senior citizen bus trips to Atlantic City. There was no keeping Gram from going on these outings ever since she won $75 playing a casino slot machine.

After confirming that Gram would be home, she grabbed her purse, dark glasses and rain hat, locked her apartment, and started down the stairs to the Moscarettis'. She'd only stay long enough to say hello, then swipe her hair under the hat, put on her shades, and be on her way.

Rosa came to the door and quickly drew Liz inside. "I was about to phone you," she said. "I just looked out the window, and there's a crowd of people gathering out front, and TV trucks and cameras and heaven knows what else."

Joe came out of the kitchen. "You want me to run them off, Liz?"

Sooner or later she'd have to face the news media, she thought. And, after all, these people were only doing their jobs. "Thanks, Joe, but I should let them interview me and get a few camera shots," she replied.

Joe nodded. He went out into the hall and opened the front door. The unexpected appearance of a formidable figure over six feet tall, close to two hundred pounds with his Marine sergeant bearing still evident, must have made an impression. A hush fell over the assembled news people and onlookers.

"Okay, Miss Rooney will talk to you," Joe called. "But keep it cool. No crowding up the steps or that's it."

He went inside, holding the door open for Liz to come out. She stepped outside, hoping Joe's warning would do some good, and there would not be too great a surge of reporters and too noisy a barrage of queries. But what he'd said proved to be effective. Television commentators and other reporters kept their distance, staying at the foot of the steps, while newspaper photographers and TV equipment went into action. Questions came at her thick and fast. She answered them, giving as clear an account as possible of her experience, starting with being forced into the SUV. She was thankful Ike had advised her not to identify LoPresti. That might lead to further questions and prolong the interview.

A glance at her watch told her she wouldn't make the 11 o'clock boat if she didn't get going pretty soon. But the interview showed no signs of breaking up. She glanced toward the Moscarettis' front window where she felt sure Rosa and Joe were posted, watching. They must have sensed her distress. A few moments later, both Moscarettis came out onto the steps.

"Everything okay?" Joe wanted to know.

"I was planning to go out to Staten Island, but I'm afraid if this doesn't end soon I'll never get away," she replied.

"Joe—tell them she's had enough," Rosa said.

Joe nodded. "Sure, they won't mind. You already gave them a good interview, Liz, and they got plenty of pictures. After I tell them it's over, I'll walk you through the crowd and see that you get a taxi."

Taking a cab all the way to South Ferry would put a dent in her budget, Liz thought. On the other hand, walking to the subway would surely mean being pursued by reporters.

Joe had the solution. "You can take a taxi to a subway station and go the rest of the way from there," he said.

After bundling her hair under her rain hat and putting on her dark glasses, she was ready to go. Being escorted through the dense crowd by Joe was like being guided by Moses through the Red Sea. Soon she was in a cab, on her way to the Fourteenth Street subway station, asking herself how she could ever have handled this incident without Joe.

He and Rosa were two of the dearest people she'd ever known, she thought while waiting on the subway platform for a train to South Ferry. As she had many times before, she wished she didn't have to move when she and Ike were married.

She checked her watch. Sophie expected her for lunch around noon. If a train didn't come along in the next couple of minutes, she'd miss the ferry she wanted to make. That meant she wouldn't have time for much of a visit with Gram before going to Sophie's house.

Why was she fretting over this? She should put things in better perspective. Compared to what happened to her yesterday, missing a ferry was a triviality.

The rumble of an approaching train sounded. As Liz got ready to board, she noticed a man standing a few feet away from her, among the waiting riders. She caught him giving her a thorough visual check. But this wasn't why she first noticed him. It was his appearance—dark hair and eyes and a swarthy complexion. He would have fit right into the group of Middle Eastern men sitting around the dining room table last night. *Could he be the terrorist who got away?*

She told herself she was letting her imagination run loose. The missing terrorist wouldn't be roaming around Manhattan today. He'd be holed up somewhere.

Unless he thought the NYPD captors didn't know that there were six men in the group. There'd been nothing on the news about a missing terrorist. Did he assume that the raiders believed the five men they captured were all of them?

If he wasn't the missing terrorist, why had this man given her such a penetrating stare? The men gathered around the dining room table last night had only a brief look at her when she went through on her way to the kitchen. She would have been hard to identify today, even without her disguise, but the rain hat and glasses should have made her unrecognizable.

Unless he'd been in the crowd outside the house, and had seen her put on the hat and dark glasses.

She boarded. The car wasn't crowded and she found a seat. When she looked around for the man she spotted him sitting across the aisle, not directly opposite, but close enough for her to get a good look at him. Knowing the dark glasses concealed the direction of her gaze, she freely scrutinized him. The more she looked at him the more she suspected he was one of the young men she'd seen last night.

Was he following her? If so, why? Surely he didn't believe he could single-handedly kidnap her all over again. A frightening thought took hold of her. Maybe the captured terrorists had sympathizers on Manhattan. Maybe this terrorist-on-the-loose had contacted them and set up a plan to kidnap her again. Maybe they'd board the train, a few at a time, as it stopped at various stations, and when she got off at South Ferry, they'd make their move. They'd subdue her somehow, maybe with an injection, and get her into a waiting car. Again, she'd be held hostage in return for the release of their leader, Zaki al Sarzai.

She considered calling Ike on her cell phone, but wasn't sure it would work on the subway. Besides, if the man noticed her using it, he might suspect she was wise to him and this would only speed up the kidnapping. When his cohorts got on the train he'd signal them to grab her and get her off the car at the next stop.

Stop this nonsense—you're being ridiculous, she told herself. The silent directive was so emphatic, she almost thought she'd spoken it aloud. This was all her imagination. Her wildfire imagination, Pop called it. Both he and Ike liked to tease her about it. What a ragging she'd take if they knew what she'd been imagining just now.

At that moment, the train pulled into the Bleecker Street station. Doors opened. Some people got off; three got on. Despite her efforts to restrain her imagination she found herself studying those who got on, but the only passenger who fit the stereotype she was looking for was a woman. She watched her anyway. Couldn't terrorists be female? She made sure the woman didn't sit anywhere near the suspected terrorist and kept alert for any eye contact the two might have.

She continued this surveillance at all the stations. Several men who looked like natives of Middle Eastern countries boarded the car at various stops along the route. None of them gave her prime suspect or each other so much as a glance.

By the time the train stopped at Chambers Street, she began to feel foolish. Yesterday's ordeal must have worked on her nerves, she decided. This was New York, the nation's melting pot. She'd seen Middle Eastern men on the subway many times before. She'd been caught up in a fantasy resulting from frazzled nerves and vivid imagination.

While approaching the South Ferry station, she rose and stood by the doors. When the doors opened she glanced over her shoulder. The imagined terrorist was still seated, making no move to get off. He didn't even glance at her.

Ike would get a laugh if he knew what she'd been imagining, she thought. But of course she wasn't going to tell him. He'd never stop teasing her about it.

Chapter Fourteen

She barely made the 11 o'clock ferry. On this crisp, sunny October morning, not many people were aboard, which meant no competition for seats, especially those next to windows. Liz chose one on the starboard side where she could get a good view of the Statue of Liberty. While she was still living on Staten Island, she'd sailed past the statue countless times to and from work, but the sight of it never failed to touch her heart.

Today, a cloudless, blue sky formed the background for Lady Liberty. Autumn sunlight glanced over the verdigris robes and crown and upheld torch, symbol of a better life for the thousands who'd viewed it through joyful tears.

She thought of her forebears on Mom's side who'd been among those thousands—her great-great-grandfather Terrence McGowan and the red-haired colleen Mary Margaret Cosgrave whom he'd met in the steerage and married soon after clearing Ellis Island.

Liz didn't know which side of her ancestral Irish family she found more inspiring—the nineteenth-century immigrants from famine-wracked Ireland who'd fought their way

147

out of poverty and discrimination, or the eighteenth-century Rooneys and Sullivans who'd settled in colonial America and fought for freedom from the British. But one thing was certain, she decided. They all had Irish spunk, and they'd passed it along to her. Without it, she couldn't have faced up to the terrorists and endured the fearful hours without breaking down. Ike would have found her a quivering wreck. She wouldn't now be crossing the bay, contemplating the Statue of Liberty and thinking about her heritage. She'd be holed up in her apartment, afraid to set foot outside.

"Excuse me . . ." A voice came into her musing. An attractive young woman, blond, long-haired, thirtyish, slid onto the seat beside her. Liz got the feeling she'd seen her somewhere before.

"Didn't I see your picture on TV?" the woman asked. "Aren't you Elizabeth Rooney, who was kidnapped by terrorists and rescued last night by the police?"

The disguise hadn't worked. Liz held back a sigh and nodded.

"When I first heard about it, I got the shivers thinking of terrorists roaming the streets of New York," the young woman continued. "Do you have any idea why you were singled out to be kidnapped?"

"No," Liz replied. She wasn't about to go into the details. Anyway, this woman would eventually get the full story in the newspapers and on TV.

The woman went on with the questions. "Did the terrorists harm you in any way? I mean . . ."

"I know what you mean," Liz broke in. "No, I wasn't harmed."

"I guess that's because you were rescued so quickly. You were lucky."

"I know I was. The NYPD did a great job."

The woman's next comment and question put Liz on the alert. "I heard on the news that Russian mob racketeer Boris

Tynkov was involved in your rescue. How'd he get into it? Do you know him personally?"

It struck Liz that for someone who'd encountered her by chance, this babe was asking too many nosy questions. She must have been in the crowd when Joe escorted her to the taxi. She'd seen her put on the hat and shades. She'd followed them, hailed another cab, and tailed her to the subway and then to the ferry.

Déjà vu! She'd also imagined the missing terrorist was following her. But this time all her instincts told her it wasn't her imagination. Suddenly, she remembered where she'd seen this woman before—in the lower hallway last night, with Yaker, the tabloid reporter she'd clashed with during the Buford Doakes murder investigation.

"How come Boris Tynkov was in on your rescue?" the woman asked again.

Now Liz felt sure this woman was a tabloid reporter just as sleazy as Yaker. It looked as if they were working together on a story about her rescue. Maybe Yaker had sent her out to dig up something they could use to insinuate a relationship between the kidnap victim and the Russian loan shark rescuer. *Should she explain about Big Tiny witnessing the abduction and the rest of it?*

No, she decided. This scandal sheet reporter would twist everything around, anyway. She deserved to be lied to, Liz decided. "I guess only the police know the answer to that," she replied.

But to eliminate any shred of doubt about this woman, Liz launched some conversation. "It's a beautiful day to be crossing the bay, isn't it? Are you going to visit someone on the island?"

The woman hesitated for a moment before replying, "I'm going to visit an aunt. Whereabouts are you going?"

Liz chose an area in the opposite direction from New Dorp. "Port Richmond," she said. "Where does your aunt live?"

Again, a slight hesitation, then, "Grymes Hill."

Grymes Hill—location of Wagner College, and one of the few sections of the island many nonresidents would have heard of.

"Oh, that's a beautiful area," Liz said. "Does your aunt live on Forest Avenue by any chance? I think that's the prettiest street on the hill. All those big trees and the ocean view."

The woman nodded. "Yes, Forest Avenue."

Bingo! Forest Avenue was not on Grymes Hill, nor did it have a lot of big trees or a view of the ocean. She was right. This woman and Yaker must be collaborating on a story about the rescue. She'd dig up possible dirt, and he'd write the article. But so far she didn't have much to go on. She was probably planning on asking more questions and tailing her after the boat docked, hoping to uncover something titillating. When nothing turned up, she'd hint at it in the story anyway.

She was tempted to let the reporter follow her to Gram's house. It would be fun to witness her disappointment. But on second thought, she decided Ms. Tabloid would stalk her all day if she didn't get rid of her. She'd figure out a way to give this woman the slip before boarding the train for New Dorp. She couldn't let her know she was taking the SIRT. That would make tailing too easy.

"I guess you've visited your aunt before and you know which bus goes up to Grymes Hill," she said.

"Oh, yes, many times," came the glib reply.

Again, Liz suppressed a laugh. There was no bus route on Grymes Hill. Now she had no doubt in her mind that this woman was a scandal sheet reporter.

"Are you taking the bus?" the woman asked.

"No, I'm taking a taxi," Liz replied. If she could shake this babe after getting off the boat, the woman would head for the taxi stand while *she* boarded the train.

"That gives me an idea," the woman said. "I'll take a taxi to my aunt's house instead of the bus."

Ms. Tabloid had it all planned, Liz thought. They'd walk to the taxi stand together. They'd say good-bye and board their cabs. Ms. Tabloid would order her driver to follow the unsuspecting Elizabeth Rooney's taxi. Did she think it would lead her to a trysting place? *In Port Richmond, of all places? And with Boris Tynkov?* She suppressed another laugh.

When the ferry neared the Staten Island slip, Liz got to her feet. "I've enjoyed talking to you and I hope you have a nice visit with your aunt," she said. "I'm going up front early so I can avoid the crowd getting off the boat. I want to get off as soon as it docks because I'm going to stop for a cup of coffee before I take my cab. Can you find the taxi stand okay?"

She hoped the reporter wouldn't say she'd like a cup of coffee too. Luckily, she didn't. "I won't have any trouble finding the taxi stand," she replied. "I've enjoyed talking with you too, and I hope you have a good time with whoever it is you're visiting."

Something in her tone of voice suggested Ms. Tabloid believed the "whoever" might well be Boris Tynkov. Maybe it would be best to let her find out how far off base she was. Admit she'd lied about taking a taxi to Port Richmond. Tell her she was taking the train to visit her grandmother in New Dorp. Fake an apology. Pretend she did this because she'd become suspicious of everyone since her kidnapping and wanted to keep her destination secret. Then she'd be rid of Ms. Tabloid.

But would she? She'd had a previous brush with Cliff Yaker. Once a scandal sheet scribe latched onto an idea for a sensational story there was no letting go. True or not, a possible connection between kidnap victim Elizabeth Rooney and a notorious racketeer would be too titillating not to hang onto.

She decided to stick with her original plan to shake this dirt-digging dame off. She walked to the bow of the boat, glancing over her shoulder just once to make sure she wasn't being followed. Ms. Tabloid was still seated and hadn't shown any signs that she suspected her prey was on to her. If all went well, the newsmonger would soon be scanning the taxi stand in puzzlement while her subject would be on the train platform, boarding the SIRT for New Dorp.

Liz got off the train, crossed through New Dorp's business area, and walked to the tree-lined street where Gram lived. The sight of the old white clapboard house halfway up the block on the opposite side of the street brought back childhood memories. For a few moments, she felt like a kid again, skipping along the sidewalk after school was out, ready for milk and cookies in Gram's kitchen. There, she'd wait for Mom, who was still teaching at a North Shore school and couldn't make it home before Our Lady Queen of Peace dismissal time.

Crossing the street, she glimpsed Gram at the front window, watching for her. Moments later, she was inside and Gram was giving her a big hug.

"Take off your disguise and let me look at you. You look none the worse for your dreadful experience, Dear. Thank God Ike found you when he did."

"It was all over so quickly, I guess it didn't sink in," Liz replied. *No need to tell Gram how scared and desperate she'd felt during those few hours.*

"I know you said you were going to Sophie's for lunch," Gram said. "Do you have time to talk for a few minutes?"

"Sure." Liz followed Gram into the living room. They sat down on the old couch with the flowered slipcover.

"Do you feel like telling me what happened?" Gram asked.

Liz related her experience from the moment she'd been

forced into Alvino's Mercedes till her rescue, including a vivid description of Alvino's luxurious apartment.

"Well, at least you weren't thrown in some rat-infested cellar," Gram said. "But isn't it odd that this . . . what's his name? Alvino? . . . is so wealthy? Do you suppose he could be some sort of Arab prince?"

"I guess he could be." Liz hadn't thought of that angle. "Alvino told me all the men in the group have family money. Maybe they're all members of Middle Eastern royalty."

"Well there goes the poverty excuse for criminal behavior," Gram said. She peered at Liz over her bifocals. "Tell me about this Alvino. It sounds to me like the two of you got along."

Liz nodded. "We did. I sensed he's not all bad. For a while, I thought he might help me escape. I still think he would have tried to keep me from being killed."

"Thank the Lord it didn't come to that," Gram said with a shudder.

Liz cast her a grin. "Aren't you going to ask me how the Russian Mafia got involved in my rescue? Everyone else has."

"I figured it out for myself," Gram replied. "*Big Tiny never forgets.* You told me all about that. He must have seen you being forced into the car and recognized you."

"That's exactly what happened."

"Your kidnapping almost drove the Chadwick Academy murder out of the news," Gram said. "Are there any developments in the case?"

"Ike expects to have the murder weapon identified pretty soon."

"Last I heard, the police still believe the killer is someone who came in from the outside, but I've thought all along it was an inside job," Gram said. "Someone in the school had a grudge against that teacher."

Liz longed to tell Gram she was right on target—like Sophie. "Maybe Ike will have some news for me when he comes over tonight," she said.

"That reminds me—tomorrow night's Sophie's wedding rehearsal, and Ralph's grandparents will be arriving here some time during the afternoon. I have the guest room all ready for them, and the daybed's made up in the sewing room for you," Gram said. "Your gown's at Sophie's house, isn't it? And you're going over there Saturday morning to get ready?"

"Right. As maid of honor, I'll help the bride get dressed. But I'll be here after work tomorrow and drop off my overnight bag then walk over to the church for the rehearsal. Ralph's folks are taking the families and attendants to dinner afterward."

Gram gave a smiling sigh. "Such a happy time for Sophie. I'm glad she and Ralph are being sensible. No huge production with everything except circus elephants parading down the aisle, and a bachelor dinner and wedding reception for five hundred of their closest friends. Every time I go to one of those lavish weddings, I think all that money could be better spent."

Liz nodded. Gram already knew that she and Ike had planned a modest wedding too. Sophie and Ralph were to be their only attendants.

The thought of her own wedding reminded her of Ike's estrangement from his parents. He'd have good friends present, but no family. She was still hoping for a response to the letter she'd sent his parents a few days ago, telling them how much it would mean to both Ike and her to have them attend. Ike had advised her not to count on an answer. *How could parents be so unfeeling?*

She hadn't told Gram about the rift between Ike and his parents. She held back a regretful sigh and switched to a lighter subject. "What are you wearing to the wedding, Gram?"

"It depends on the weather," Gram replied. "It can turn

hot this time of year—Indian summer, you know—or it could get chilly. My tan silk jacket dress would do if it's a warm day, but if it's cool I could wear my dark blue wool suit. I want to look nice for Sophie. I've known her so long, she's almost like another granddaughter."

"You'll look great whatever you wear," Liz said. She got to her feet and gave her a hug and a kiss. "I should be getting over to Sophie's. I'll see you tomorrow night."

On their way to the door, Gram glanced out the window, saying, "I hope this nice weather holds for the wedding." Then suddenly she did a double-take. "That's strange," she said.

"What's strange?" Liz asked.

"That woman standing across the street," Gram replied. "I noticed her walking a few yards behind you when you came up the street. Why is she still hanging around here?"

Liz didn't have to look out the window to feel positive that the woman was Ms. Tabloid. Sure enough, when she looked, she saw the blond woman standing across the street, staring at Gram's house.

"She's a reporter for *The National Informer,*" Liz explained. "She tailed me from my place to the ferry. I thought I'd shaken her off when the boat docked but she's smarter than I gave her credit for." She related the incident on the ferry.

"A scandal sheet reporter?" Gram adjusted her glasses and took a good look. "I wonder what she expects to gain by hanging around here, watching my house."

"The way she questioned me about Boris Tynkov, I think she's working on a trumped up connection, with your house as a meeting place."

"What!" Gram burst out laughing.

"I know it sounds ridiculous, but those sleazy tabloids will make a story out of nothing to sell papers," Liz said. She glanced out the window again. "She must have figured I was on to her. She has it in for me now for lying to her trying to give her the slip. I have to get over to Sophie's house, but when I step outside, that woman will be across the street like a shot, and a confrontation will only make things worse."

"Phone Sophie and tell her what's happening." Gram said. "Ask her if she can come over here. Seeing another woman coming into my house might make that reporter think twice about writing a scandalous story."

"Oh, great idea, Gram." Liz went straight to the phone.

Sophie had a great idea of her own. "Give me a few minutes to change into my uniform, and I'll drive over in Ma's car," she said. "When that broad sees a cop going into the house and then coming out with you, she won't know what the hell is going on."

"Wonderful! She can't move fast enough on foot to follow a car. We'll be around the corner and into your street and inside your house before she can make it to the end of Gram's block."

Barely 15 minutes later, Liz and Gram looked out the front window and saw Sophie turn her mother's Buick into the gravel driveway alongside the house. Checking on Ms. Tabloid, they saw her dodge behind one of the big oak trees along the sidewalk across the street.

"She's peeking out from around that tree," Gram said. "She'll see the NYPD uniform any second now."

Just as she spoke Sophie got out of the car, slowly, Liz noticed, as if she were making sure the reporter would identify her as a cop. Then she cut across the small patch of lawn and came up the front walk onto the porch and rang the doorbell. She entered the house saying she'd gotten a glimpse of someone half-hidden behind a tree.

"But she got more than a glimpse of *you*," Liz said, as they hugged.

"I've never seen you in your uniform before, Sophie," Gram said. "Very impressive."

"Let's hope our stalking reporter was impressed," Sophie replied with a laugh.

She and Liz left the house and were about to cross the lawn and get into the car when Liz couldn't resist taking a furtive glance across the street. "Our stalker just stepped out from behind a tree," she told Sophie.

Sophie ventured a quick look. "I hope you were smiling," she said, a moment later. "We just had our picture taken!"

Chapter Fifteen

Wwe should have known she'd have a camera," Liz said as they scrambled into the car. "The photo of us will be in the next edition of that slime sheet she works for."

"So what?" Sophie keyed the ignition, hit the reverse, and peeled out of the driveway. Flooring it down the block and around the next corner, she added, "It was plain as day this wasn't a bust. Nothing sensational about you coming out of a house with a woman who happens to be a cop. When the reporter runs it by her editors, they might even consider it too tame to run."

"Not if the reporter suggests that the house might be a trysting place owned by Boris Tynkov," Liz said. She filled her in on Ms. Tabloid's questions about Big Tiny's role in the rescue. "I'm sure she's determined to write a scandalous story whether she believes I was there for a tryst or not. And you can bet she'll come up with something to explain why a cop came to the house."

"I'd bust out laughing if I didn't know those sleazy tabloids know exactly how to word headlines and articles so they don't get hit with slander suits," Sophie replied. "You're right, the story could have me a cop on the take. And

158

that reporter will dream up some reason why you left the house with me."

She pulled into her home driveway and drove the car into the backyard garage, saying, "Well, at least we know that scandalmonger couldn't have followed us here. You're rid of her for now. Meanwhile, maybe we can think of something to keep her from going ahead with her muckraking story."

They entered the house through the kitchen door. Sophie's mother greeted Liz with a big hug.

"It's so good to know you're okay, Liz. You gave us all a scare." She released Liz from her embrace and gave her a scrutinizing once-over. "I'd never guess you've been through such a terrible experience. You look good, doesn't she, Sophie?"

"Yeah. It takes more than being kidnapped by terrorists to get our Liz down," Sophie said with a laugh. "But wait till you hear what's happened now."

"Lunch is ready—tuna salad sandwiches," Mrs. Pulaski said. "You can tell me about it while we eat."

They sat down at the kitchen table. Liz gave a full account of her encounter with the tabloid reporter. "This woman plans to write a sensational story featuring a connection between racketeer Boris Tynkov and me," she explained.

Mrs. Pulaski gave a hearty laugh. "What in the world gave her that notion?"

"Tynkov being in on Liz's rescue, I guess," Sophie replied.

"Whether or not she thinks it's true, she knows it will sell papers," Liz added. "She'll write a story suggesting that came to New Dorp today for a rendezvous with Tynkov. She'll insinuate that he owns the house I went into."

"That's absurd," Mrs. Pulaski said with another laugh. "Would she write a story like that without finding out who actually owns the house?"

"She wouldn't give the actual address, of course," Liz

replied. "There are houses like Gram's all over New Dorp. All she needs is a photo, and we know she got at least one shot."

"How would she explain a cop coming to the house?"

"She could insinuate that the cop's in Tynkov's pocket," Sophie replied. "She could make it seen like Tynkov changed his mind about the meeting place and sent this corrupt cop over to escort Liz to another location."

"Dragging nice girls' names through the mud just to sell papers!" Mrs. Pulaski exclaimed. She paused. "But how would she know Sophie's name?"

"This is a long shot, Mrs. Pulaski, but that sleazy reporter might have connections in the DMV," Liz replied. "With you and Sophie having the same name, if she got a shot of the license plates on the car, she might be able to find out it's registered to a Sophie Pulaski, and . . ."

"And if she found out there's a NYPD cop named Sophie Pulaski, Sophie could be dragged through the mud too!"

Sophie nodded, frowning. "Whether or not she traces the car, I could come out looking like a rogue cop with ties to the Russian mob."

Mrs. Pulaski sighed. "This is a fine thing to be happening with your wedding coming up Saturday. If that story comes out before the wedding, it will ruin what should be the happiest day of a girl's life."

"Yeah, the bribed bride cop and her maid of dishonor," Sophie replied. She gave a sudden smile. "But don't worry about that story being published before the wedding, Ma. The *Staten Island Advance* will run a nice, proper article in Sunday's paper and the tabloid won't be out till Tuesday or Wednesday."

Mrs. Pulaski looked somewhat relieved. "At least the wedding will be over before people start gossiping about you two."

Liz nodded. "Sophie will be honeymooning in Bermuda when the story breaks."

Sophie's face saddened. "But you'll be here, facing it without me."

"I know it won't be any picnic, but I'll have Ike to lean on," Liz replied. *But this situation was the last thing Ike needed while he was concentrating on finding Marva Malin's killer.*

"Maybe by the time I get back, you and Ike will have the Chadwick Academy murder all sewed up," Sophie said.

Liz cast her a grin. "Thanks for making me part of the investigation." She recalled how she'd slipped up, mistaking the art teacher's plastic paintbrush for wood. She was about to add that she hadn't been much help so far, when she remembered Marva Malin's tote bag. Hadn't Ike told her that it was her woman's point of view that led him to examine its potential as a murder weapon?

Mrs. Pulaski's voice came into her thoughts. They'd finished eating, and she'd risen from her chair and started to clear the table. "You girls go have a good visit up in Sophie's room," she said. "This is your last chance for that. Once a girl gets married, things change."

"Okay, Ma," Sophie replied with a wink at Liz.

On their way up the stairs she said, "Things will never change between us."

"Not if I can help it," Liz replied. She thought of the many years they'd confided in one another, sharing everything from happiness to humiliation. Suddenly, she remembered the man she'd noticed on the subway platform. Sophie knew all about her best friend's runaway imagination. She'd get a big laugh out of this one if only she could be told about it, but of course she couldn't. The missing terrorist was classified information. Liz knew if she told Sophie she'd imagined being followed by one of the terrorists she'd seen in Alvino's dining room. Sophie would get the idea right away that one of them was on the loose.

Stepping into Sophie's bedroom was a little like stepping

back in time, she thought, even though the dolls and stuffed animals were gone from the four-poster bed and its frilly, ruffled spread replaced by a handsome quilt. The shelves which first held picture books, then children's classics and Nancy Drew mysteries, were now filled with good adult reading, old and new, including the series by Sophie's favorite mystery author, Ellen Elizabeth Hunter. In a corner stood the old desk where Sophie used to do her homework and write in her diary—secrets shared only with Liz.

They curled up on the bed and began to talk. Sophie wanted to know all the details about Liz's kidnapping. Although media information had been sketchy, news about the band of Middle Eastern terrorists posing as Italian-Americans was now common knowledge.

"I can't believe those creeps got away with pretending to be Italian-Americans all this time," Sophie said. "If Ralph had ever run into them he'd have figured it out in two seconds they should all be wearing dishtowels on their heads. Didn't that guy who forced you into the car look like one of Ali Baba's forty thieves?"

Sophie was anything but politically correct, Liz thought. "In retrospect, I guess so," she said. "But at the time I had no reason to think he was a Middle Easterner." She filled Sophie in on Vincent LoPresti's double life.

The revelation stunned Sophie. "You mean this faker who snatched you off the street is the music teacher at Chadwick Academy and you'd already met him?"

"Sure, otherwise I never would have started talking to him on the street."

Sophie gave an emphatic nod. "I never went along with police statements saying the murder at the school was committed by someone sneaking in and out, I've thought all along it was an inside job. I'll bet this phony Italian's the killer. Maybe this was the first in a series of murders and kidnappings intended to terrorize the city."

"I was sure, for a while, he was the killer," Liz replied. "But then one of the other terrorists changed my mind." She told Sophie about Alvino and what he'd said. "LoPresti knows who the murderer is. He's protecting whoever did it."

"Did you run this by Ike?"

"Yes."

"And . . . ?"

"He thinks LoPresti might be covering his own butt."

Sophie gave a wicked grin. "The interrogation will get to the *bottom* of it,"

Liz laughed and gave her a hug. "It's been so good talking like this. For a little while I forgot about the mess we're in."

"We've been in messes before and managed to get out of them," Sophie replied. "Anyway, let's not think about that now." She crossed the room and opened a closet door. "Let's try on our gowns. It wouldn't be bad luck for you to see me in my wedding gown before the ceremony, would it?"

Liz shook her head. "I think that only applies to the bridegroom. I don't believe in that old superstition anyway."

Sophie brought out the restyled white satin gown her mother had worn as a bride, and Liz's turquoise blue taffeta maid-of-honor dress. They helped each other get into them and surveyed themselves in the full-length mirror on the closet door.

"We look pretty good if I do say so myself," Sophie said.

"Yes we do. Especially you. Your mother's gown is lovely, and it looks great on you. You couldn't have found anything more beautiful in any store."

"I know you've been looking. Have you found anything you like yet?"

"Not really. I wish I could wear Mom's gown. In her wedding pictures it looks very pretty. She still has it packed away, but she says it's not in good enough shape."

"Hey, we used to borrow each other's clothes before I shot up to a size ten," Sophie said. "Why don't you wear this? It could be taken down a couple of sizes for you. And you could wear my veil too. It's supposed to be good luck to wear another bride's veil. How about it?"

"Oh, Sophie . . ." Liz answer was a big hug.

"Things don't have to change between best friends after they get married," Sophie said. "In a few years, we'll probably be borrowing each other's maternity clothes!"

They gave a final look in the mirror before getting out of their gowns. "Ma ordered yellow roses for you and Sis. They'll look perfect with your turquoise dresses," Sophie said, putting the wedding finery back in the closet.

The sight of her NYPD uniform on its hanger brought on a frown. "My brass buttons and blues did us more harm than good," she added, reaching for a tan pants suit.

Liz held back a sigh. This time together had diverted their worries about Ms. Tabloid's scandalous story. Now, as she started getting into her clothes, regretting all over again her inability to shake off the scandal sheet reporter, a knock sounded on the bedroom door, followed by Mrs. Pulaski's voice.

"Girls . . . I have something to tell you."

Sophie had started to put on the tan pants suit. "That's Ma's good news voice," she said. Half-dressed, she hurried to open the door.

It would take some really good news to offset Ms. Tabloid's scurrilous article with its sensational headlines, Liz thought.

Smiling broadly, Sophie's mother came into the room. "I just had a phone call from the society editor of the *Advance*," she said. "She was going over the details I sent her about Sophie's wedding, getting the article ready for Sunday's paper, when she noticed the maid-of-honor's name. She called me to find out if this could possibly be the same Elizabeth Rooney who was kidnapped by terrorists."

Why was Sophie's mother so pleased about this? A look exchanged with Sophie told Liz that Sophie didn't know either.

"When I told her yes and said you were born and raised on Staten Island and your grandmother lives in New Dorp, she was very interested," Mrs. Pulaski continued. "The first news of your kidnapping and rescue is in today's paper, of course, but she said they're running a follow-up article in tomorrow's edition, giving more details. She said the reporter who's writing the story might want to mention that the girl who was kidnapped by terrorists is a Staten Island native and she's going to be maid of honor in a Staten Island wedding on Saturday. She said she'd tell him about it right away."

Before Sophie's mother was halfway through, Liz started to get the significance of what she was saying. If the *Staten Island Advance* ran an article tomorrow mentioning that kidnap victim Elizabeth Rooney's grandmother lived in New Dorp, this might make Miss Tabloid think twice before writing a story about Elizabeth Rooney and Boris Tynkov and a New Dorp trysting place. She felt a surge of optimism.

Sophie apparently didn't feel as optimistic. "I doubt if a reporter for a New York slime sheet would be reading tomorrow's *Staten Island Advance*. And even if she did, she wouldn't scrap the story. She might decide to make some changes, like not mentioning the house is in New Dorp, but that's all. The fact that Tynkov was in on Liz's rescue suggests a connection that's too juicy for her to ignore. And then there's my role in this. She'd still ring in the corrupt cop."

"I guess you're right," Liz replied. "There'd have to be a lot more to have her kill the story."

There *is* a lot more," Mrs. Pulaski said. "I told the society editor woman that I know you're spending this afternoon with your grandmother, and . . ."

Sophie broke in. "Why did you say that when Liz is over here now, Ma?"

"I thought playing up Liz's Staten Island roots would make the *Advance* reporter more likely to mention it in the follow up article," Mrs. Pulaski replied.

Sophie shook her head. "Mentioning that Liz is a Staten Islander isn't going to keep the story out of the tabloid."

"I'm not anywhere near done yet," her mother said. "I was going to come up here and tell you about the society editor's phone call when I heard the buzzer on the clothes dryer, so I went down to the basement first. I wasn't down there longer than ten, maybe fifteen minutes, and when I came up the kitchen phone was ringing."

"Let me guess," Sophie said. "It was the reporter who's writing tomorrow's article. He's going to mention Liz's Staten Island background."

"More than that—he sounded very excited," Mrs. Pulaski continued. "He wants to interview you at your grandmother's this afternoon, Liz, and get pictures. I gave him your grandmother's address and phone number, and the minute he hung up I phoned her and filled her in on this new development. She said when the reporter phones she'll set up the interview."

Liz brightened. "An interview! And we were wondering if he'd even mention I'm a Staten Island native! This is wonderful! Sophie, you go with me to Gram's house. With you there too, don't you think the reporter will want to get a shot of the NYPD bride-to-be and her kidnap victim maid of honor?"

"Standing with your grandmother in front of her house," Sophie added with a big smile. "Liz, I think we're home free."

"I'm sure he'll ask me how Tynkov got in on my rescue," Liz said. "I'll tell him about Big Tiny owing me one." She threw her arms around Mrs. Pulaski. "Thanks to you, Sophie and I are out of this terrible mess."

"Yeah, nice going, Ma," Sophie said. "Liz is hot news. The *Advance* article and the photos will be picked up by all the other newspapers, including the *New York Times* and *The Washington Post* and featured on TV news channels and programs everywhere."

Sophie's mother nodded. "But you girls better hurry and get dressed so you'll make it over there before the reporter shows up," she said eyeing Sophie's tan pantsuit, and added, "and don't forget to change into your uniform, Officer Pulaski, for that shot of you and Liz and her grandmother in front of the house."

Chapter Sixteen

"Well, that should set things straight," Gram said, closing her front door behind the departing *Staten Island Advance* reporter.

He'd arrived barely 20 minutes after Liz and Sophie got there, thanking Liz for agreeing to the interview on short notice. "I had to move fast," he'd explained. "My deadline's coming up in a couple of hours."

He was pleased that Sophie was there. The upcoming wedding and Liz's participation in it would add extra interest to his article, he told them. Before he left, he shot a picture of Liz and Sophie standing with Gram in front of the house. "The photo will be on the front page, along with my story," he said.

"Do you think it's possible that the scandal sheet will go ahead with its story, anyway?" Liz asked after he'd gone.

Sophie shook her head. "Not a chance. He was taking notes while you were telling him how Tynkov happened to be in on your rescue. You can bet he's going to put it into his article. The New York papers covered that story at the time, so they'll pick it up again. With the *Advance* coming out with this tomorrow and every other news source picking up the article over the weekend, a sleazy tabloid story would fall flat."

Liz's cell phone buzzed at that moment.

This might be Ike, Liz thought, reaching into her purse.

It was. "I guess you're at Sophie's house," he said.

"No, I'm at Gram's. Sophie's here too; I'll explain when I see you tonight."

"I guess you and Sophie had plenty to talk about."

"You know we did, but there were a few things I wanted to tell her but didn't."

"If you mean about the Malin murder . . ."

"That's what I mean, She's already decided it was an inside job, and I've been dying to tell her she's right and let her know who the suspects are."

"Go ahead and fill her in. She's as good as you at keeping her mouth shut."

"Thanks. It's been hard for me not to tell Sophie the details. Now I'm happy."

"I like making you happy," he replied. "By the way, any idea what boat you'll be catching this afternoon? I've been putting in extra hours on this case, and I'm knocking off early today. I could pick you up at South Ferry."

"How about the three-thirty?"

"Great. I'll be at South Ferry around four. I have something to tell you."

She didn't press for more. Ike never divulged so much as a hint over the telephone. The crime lab must have come up with something on the possible murder weapons, she decided. Maybe he had the results on Duddy's hammer.

She thrust aside her need to know and gave him something of her own to think about. "I have things to tell you too," she said. "But nothing about the Malin case." The Ms. Tabloid incident would interest him, she thought, and even though he'd tease her about it, maybe she'd tell him about the imagined terrorist on the subway too.

"If it has nothing to do with the Malin murder, then it must be something about your kidnapping,"

"I guess you could say that."

He laughed. "I take it that's all you're going to tell me. Okay, we're even. See you at South Ferry, four o'clock."

Sophie had a question the moment Liz hung up the phone. "Did Ike say there's been a development in the school murder?"

"Not exactly, but I think there might be. All he'd say was he had something interesting to tell me, then he clammed up."

"You did some clamming up yourself," Sophie replied.

Sophie insisted on driving Liz to the ferry. "That tabloid dame might be hanging around the New Dorp train station, expecting you to show up on your return trip," she said. "Even though you know she's no threat anymore, you don't want her pouncing on you again. You don't need that aggravation."

"Thanks for offering the lift, but don't you think she'd figure Big Tiny would drive me back to Manhattan in his limo?" Liz asked.

"Possibly, but I'm going to take you to the three-thirty boat anyway. It will give us a little more time to talk."

On the drive from New Dorp to St. George their talk centered on the Malin murder.

"Do you have any idea what Ike's going to tell you?" Sophie asked, turning the Buick from New Dorp Lane onto Richmond Road.

"I think he might have the results on one or more of the possible murder weapons," Liz replied. She recalled she'd told Sophie only that Dan said the object used in the strangulation was something hard, like a wooden or metal rod, but now Ike had given her the go-ahead to fill Sophie in on suspects and possible murder weapons.

But, despite her limited knowledge about suspects and possible murder weapons, Sophie had drawn her own conclusions. "I'll bet the music teacher did it with his baton," Sophie said. "Maybe that's what Ike's going to tell you."

"I don't think LoPresti's the killer," Liz said. "But maybe Duddy's hammer tested negative for matching up with the marks on Malin's neck and Ike ordered LoPresti's baton tested next. The news that he's a terrorist will be breaking any time now, and Ike might have wanted to keep ahead of it."

"I know that other fake Italian terrorist made you decide the music teacher isn't the killer," Sophie went on. "But you told me Ike thinks he might be covering his own butt. Well, I agree with him."

"Sure, it's a possibility . . ." Now was the time to let Sophie in on all the other aspects and suspects. They'd have a good time weighing the pros and cons of the others and each possible murder weapon. They were halfway to the ferry. This was their last opportunity to delve into the case together. With the influx of relatives and the wedding rehearsal tomorrow, and the ceremony and reception on Saturday, they'd have no time for that. Besides, during the next two days the Malin murder would be the last thing on Sophie's mind. And at the rate Ike was progressing, chances were the killer would be nabbed before Sophie and Ralph got back from their weeklong honeymoon.

It was now or never.

She told Sophie everything she knew or suspected, giving as many details as she could recall.

"Wow, five possible suspects, and they all had it in for that teacher," Sophie exclaimed. "What a lineup—and a possible murder weapon to link up with each one! Who's number one on your list?"

"I can't make up my mind about that. The closest I came was when I thought LoPresti was the killer."

Sophie turned off Vanderbilt Avenue left onto Bay Street. "When you overheard the teachers and that other woman talking shortly after the murder, didn't you get any vibes?"

"Nothing to hang anything on. Tulley, the gym teacher said she was all shook up about it, but she didn't appear to be. She did more talking than the others. I remember she pointed out that the victim was always picking on the kids and suggested one of them could have done it."

"Sounds like she was trying to divert suspicion away from herself," Sophie said. "What about the others?"

"Gibbs the art teacher didn't say much. He seemed more dazed than upset by the murder, and music teacher LoPresti didn't show any emotion at all. He just made a few derogatory remarks about the victim."

"The art teacher could have been in a state of shock after committing murder," Sophie said. "As for that phony Italian music teacher terrorist—his lack of emotion might be a sign that he's a coldblooded killer. What about the other two?"

"Bernice the principal's assistant was very quiet. She said the murder had been upsetting for all of them, but like the others she didn't have anything kind to say about the victim."

"With her arthritis, I think she's the least likely," Sophie said. "How about the janitor?"

"I didn't see him close up until I went to the school to get Dan's pen. He's a friendly old guy—Ike said he's an ex-boxer. According to Ike, he wasn't at all concerned when they confiscated his hammer for the evidence lab."

"His lack of concern doesn't let him off the hook," Sophie said, braking at a red light. "He's an ex-prize fighter. Maybe he's punchy."

"That didn't occur to me, but I'll bet Ike zeroed in on it," Liz replied. "Maybe that's what he's going to tell me. Duddy's hammer tested positive as the murder weapon!"

"It's no wonder you can't decide which one to suspect," Sophie said. "They all had motive and opportunity, plus something they could use as a weapon."

"All except Julia Tulley," Liz reminded her.

"She could have picked something up," Sophie replied.

The imagery of Malin's handbag flashed into Liz's mind. "You're right! And it could have been Malin's bag." She related Ike's description of the bag's wooden closure.

Sophie nodded. "She could have grabbed hold of the closure and pressed it against Malin's throat. So now we have a weapon for everyone, but for me the music teacher and his baton come out on top."

She paused. "But let's suppose that the story the other terrorist told you is true and the music teacher is protecting the killer. Did you notice any particular one he seemed to be pals with?"

Liz recalled the general camaraderie among LoPresti. Gibbs, Tulley, and Bernice. "No. He was very friendly with all of them. In fact, they seemed like a close group. They all liked the janitor too."

"Hey," Sophie said. "Every one of them hated Malin's guts. Maybe they were all in on the murder together, like in that Agatha Christie mystery, I think it was *Murder on the Orient Express*,"

"A conspiracy?" Liz pondered the idea. "It's possible, but it seems to me only one of them would have followed Malin to the balcony."

"Right," Sophie replied. "And that person did the actual killing."

Liz pictured the suspects drawing lots to decide who should put Malin out of the way. Although they all disliked, perhaps even hated the slain teacher, it seemed farfetched that in every one of them these feelings would have become homicidal.

"Thumbs down on the conspiracy. I think the killer acted alone," she said.

They'd reached the passenger drop-off in the ferry terminal. Sophie braked and cast Liz a long look. "I have a hunch Ike will give you some answers tonight. Will you let me know what he told you?"

"Sure. You want to bet which one of us is on the mark?"

Sophie laughed. "No way. I'd love to have that fake Italian turn out to be the killer, but actually I'm almost as puzzled as you are."

Liz piled her hair under the rain hat and put on her dark glasses. They hugged good-bye.

"See you at the rehearsal tomorrow night," Sophie said.

Chapter Seventeen

She got off the ferry from the lower level, expecting she'd have to wait for Ike's car to show up in the haphazard line of cabs and other vehicles. Right away she saw it in a no parking zone a few steps away.

"I'm surprised at you, pulling NYPD rank, for nonpolice purposes," she said, getting into the car and taking off her hat and glasses.

He gave her a quick kiss. "I consider this a police matter," he replied. "I had to make sure you didn't get snatched again while you were getting off the boat."

She recalled the man on the subway. "I wasn't going to tell you this, but here goes," she said. "For a little while today I thought a man who looked like a Middle Easterner was following me and of course I thought he was the terrorist who's on the loose."

Ike's sudden frown faded into a suggestion of a smile. "Why weren't you going to tell me? Did you think I'd say it was your wildfire imagination?"

"Exactly, and you'd be right," she replied. "I doubt very much if the missing terrorist is roving around Manhattan looking for me. He's probably lying low til he can sneak out of the country." *And if he happened to be Alvino, hiding in the apartment of one of his lady friends.*

"When did you first notice this man and what made you think he was tailing you?" Ike asked.

"I noticed him on the subway platform. He seemed to be watching me. He got on the same train, but after I got off at South Ferry I didn't see him again so I forgot about it. Anyway, I had something else to think about."

She started to tell him about Ms. Tabloid. When she got to the part about the Tynkov tryst story she was sure the reporter planned to write, she noticed the twitch of a smile around Ike's mouth.

"What's so funny?" she asked. "Do you think I imagined *this*, too?"

He tried to quell the smile. "How can you be so sure she was a tabloid reporter, out to get a story on you and Tynkov? She could be working for a respectable paper."

"I recognized her from last night, when I saw you talking to those two reporters in the downstairs hall," Liz replied. "The man was Yaker, that sleazy reporter I had the run-in with during the Buford Doakes murder investigation. I figured he and the woman are cooking up a story, together. I believe she was in the crowd of reporters in front of Rosa and Joe's and followed me when I left. She must have seen me put on my disguise."

"Okay," Ike said. "Let's say it wasn't your imagination and this broad planned to write a story about you having a tryst with Big Tiny—but I don't think the editor of her tabloid would want to risk getting on the wrong side of someone like Boris Tynkov."

Liz pictured the tabloid's editor in a full body cast. "Much as I'd like to have Big Tiny send his goons to rough up anyone connected with that scandal sheet, I'd prefer that the story never appeared," she replied.

"With the coverage in the *Advance* and the tabloid editor's fear of retaliation by the Russian Mob, there's more than a ninety-nine percent chance it never will," Ike said.

At that moment Liz noticed they were heading for the West Side—a somewhat indirect route to her place. "Where are we going?" she asked.

"To look at an apartment," he replied. "One of the men on the squad is moving. He arranged for his wife to show it to us. Three rooms. Big kitchen. I thought we should check it out."

"Yes, we should. It sounds just right." Although Liz liked looking at possible places where she and Ike might live, the thought of moving saddened her.

"Getting back to the stalking tabloid reporter—I guess that's the long story you didn't want to tell me over the phone," Ike said.

"Yes, and now it's your turn," she replied. "What's the new development?"

He didn't keep her in suspense. "We have the results of the tests on the janitor's hammer. They were inconclusive."

"What exactly does that mean?"

"Irregularities on the wood didn't quite match the marks on Malin's neck, but we haven't ruled it out. We think the handle might have shifted during the strangulation."

Liz felt a pang of compassion for the aging pugilist. He hadn't seemed like a violent man. Had the relentless complaining to which Marva Malin had subjected him, plus her efforts to get him fired, pushed him over the edge?

"What's going to happen now?" she asked.

"After all the other tests are run, we'll compare the results."

"And the closest one will be the murder weapon?"

"Something like that."

"Why is it taking so long to run the tests?"

"The suspected objects are being tested as they turn up,

and they're not all turning up at once. Even so, it hasn't been very long."

She nodded. "Of course it hasn't. It just seems that way to me. I can't believe my kidnapping and rescue happened only yesterday."

The thought reminded her that the terrorists would not have shown up for their various jobs today. "All those men except possibly the one who wasn't captured were absent from work today, without explanation," she said. "Do you think the one who got away would have gone to work today, or would he have tried to get out of the country? And do the employers of the others know yet that these guys are terrorists?"

"The one who got away isn't aware that we know there were six in the group. I think he might have started making arrangements to get out of the country, but since he hasn't been identified as one of the terrorists, he might have gone to work as usual."

"And the others?"

"They've been under intensive FBI interrogation, but even if they revealed where they worked, their employers might not have been informed yet. When the location of the NYPD raid hits the news media, employers of anyone who lives there will make the connection. The same goes for the others when the FBI finds out where they lived."

LoPresti was absent without explanation this morning. Wouldn't someone, probably Bernice, have phoned his apartment? And what if the FBI was monitoring the line and answering with some sort of cryptic message, or the phone had been disconnected? Wouldn't that have aroused Bernice's suspicions? She imagined Bernice conferring with Cyril Gibbs and Julia Tully. Suppose they recalled meeting a young woman backstage yesterday. Suppose they recalled her name and realized it was the same as the terrorists' kidnap victim. They could have remembered she left the school building a few minutes before LoPresti and put it all together.

If LoPresti had been protecting one of them, wouldn't he or she be worried that this would come out during interrogation? But if it were true that Gibbs was intimidated by LoPresti because he knew LoPresti was a killer, how would he react?

She expressed her thoughts to Ike.

He nodded. "News that LoPresti's one of the terrorists might not be a bombshell to those three. And if Gibbs is afraid of him because he suspects or knows he killed Malin, he'll be relieved to know LoPresti's in prison."

"When do you think the news will break?"

"Any time now. The FBI should be well along in the interrogation." With a warm smile, he reached over and gave her hand a squeeze. "You're one of the few people outside of the FBI who knows one of the terrorists is still at large. I'm thankful you know when and how to keep your mouth shut. I guess your pop had something to do with that."

She smiled, nodding. The close friendship between her father and Ike was one of the joys of her life. Pop and Ike had been partners for a while before Pop retired from the force. They'd been close friends long before her relationship with Ike began to change from chilly to chummy.

Ike turned the car onto Twenty-third Street. "The apartment we're going to look at is only a couple of blocks from here," he said. "It's in London Terrace."

"Oh, I've heard that's a swanky place. Maybe the apartment has a view of the Hudson. That would be nice." *But not as nice as being able to stay with the Moscarettis.*

A few minutes later, Ike pulled into a parking space. "There's the London Terrace complex, across the street," he said.

Liz gazed at the impressive-looking red brick structure

that appeared to take up an entire city block. "I'll bet the rents are out of sight," she said. "Did your friend say how much he pays? Maybe that's why he's moving."

"It's a little steep, but if you like it we can swing it."

She was about to tell him she didn't like the idea of stretching their budget, but he seemed to be interested in this place. "Let's have a look," she said.

Half an hour later, they were back in the car. Going down on the elevator, they'd agreed they were tempted but turned off by the high rent. They decided to keep on looking.

As Ike started the car, Liz gave a last look at the handsome structure. "If the apartment had a view of the river I might have gone for it," she said.

"If it had even a peek at the Hudson, the rent would have been double," he replied.

His phone sounded at that moment. Seconds after he answered, Liz knew by the look on his face that something important had happened. *Had the news of LoPresti's double life been released but hadn't come on the radio yet?*

Ike's end of the conversation made her believe otherwise. "I just picked Liz up at South Ferry and we're heading for her place," he told the caller. "I'll get over there after I drop her off."

She felt sure the caller was his partner Lou. "Sounds like you won't be taking the rest of the evening off after all," she said.

He cast her a regretful look. "Yeah. I'll be tied up for a while. No telling for how long. I wanted to treat you to dinner someplace nice, but you'd better go ahead and eat. I'll grab something after we're done, and come over later."

Was he going to keep her in the dark about what happened? She'd barely asked herself the question when his look of regret gave way to a smile. "Here's something for you to think about while you're waiting for me," he said. "That was Lou on the phone. Missing Persons just called the squad room. Someone from Chadwick Academy notified them that their janitor, Dudley Baca, has disappeared."

"Duddy missing!" Liz exclaimed. "How long has he been gone?"

"I don't know yet. The caller said the woman who called Missing Persons is waiting for us at the school. She'll give us that information, and we'll probably pick something up when we search Duddy's room."

The woman who called Missing Persons was probably Bernice, Liz thought. "Everyone at the school knows you and Lou are handling the murder case. Why weren't you notified directly instead of going through Missing Persons?"

"Because everyone at the school was thinking exactly what we want them to think—an outsider committed the murder. They didn't make a connection between the murder and Duddy's disappearance."

Liz recalled Ike telling her that Duddy didn't object when he was told his hammer would be taken for a while. At first she'd thought this might indicate he had nothing to do with the murder. Now she wondered if his punch-battered brain had failed to grasp the significance at the time.

"Do you think Duddy suddenly caught on and realized his hammer was being tested in the police lab, and that's why he split?"

"Looks that way at the moment."

"That could mean he's the killer."

"It certainly keeps him in the line-up."

Liz thought of the others under suspicion. The police strategy had worked well. If one of them had killed Marva Malin, he or she might have fled for parts unknown rather than feeling secure. Instead, only poor, punchy Duddy had turned up missing. Was his disappearance at this crucial time a coincidence?

But whether Duddy or one of those lulled into false security was guilty, possible murder weapons were being tested at that very moment. Both the chair rung and the tote bag were already in the lab.

Ike's next statement surprised her. "LoPresti's baton is in the works too. We wanted to get it out of the way before news breaks that the Chadwick Academy music teacher is a terrorist and the guy who kidnapped you."

"Why?"

"On top of kidnapping and terrorism charges, we don't want to risk having to name LoPresti as the prime suspect in the Malin case. That could stir up accusations of racial bias from the usual sources and complicate the case."

Liz pondered this. It sounded as if Ike was pretty sure the baton would come out squeaky clean. "Have you decided he's protecting one of the others?" she asked.

"We haven't ruled that out, but here's the reason we don't believe he's our killer. As an undercover terrorist, LoPresti would keep a low profile. He wouldn't have risked calling attention to himself by committing a murder in the place where he worked."

"Then why do you suppose Gibbs seemed intimidated by him?"

Ike hesitated for a moment. "Maybe because LoPresti's a forceful character and Gibbs is somewhat of a wimp," he replied with a laugh.

"So after the baton's eliminated, what's next?" she asked.

"They're already testing the chair rung the art teacher stirred paint with."

Liz reviewed the situation. If nothing showed up with the chair rung, that left the handbag and Bernice's cane. She felt almost certain that Bernice was not the killer. That narrowed her own suspects down to three—art teacher Cyril Gibbs, gym teacher Julia Tully and, of course, Duddy.

"What if none of the possible murder weapons match?" she asked.

"We're not relying on that alone," he replied. "The lab is checking for fingerprints and residue too, like hair and clothing fibers."

Liz considered fingerprints the most likely evidence. *Duddy's wouldn't be the only ones on the hammer. Greg Jensen had handled it too.*

Of course, Ike would have remembered this. He would also have taken into consideration that others besides the art teacher might have used the paint-daubed chair rung. As for the wooden closure on the canvas tote bag, Ike was probably thinking that hadn't been handled by anyone except Malin, and any extra prints on it would have to be the killer's. Most likely the killer grabbed the bag before taking hold of the closure. *If only it were possible to lift fingerprints from cloth.*

Ike's' voice brought her out of her speculating. "You're very quiet all of a sudden. What's going on in that steel trap mind of yours?"

A compliment à la Ike! She smiled her appreciation. "I was just wishing the tote bag wasn't made of cloth," she replied. "If matching fingerprints other than Malin's were lifted from both the bag and its closure, and the indentations on the closure matched up with the marks on her neck, that would pretty well nail things down, wouldn't it?"

"It always helps when there's more than one piece of evidence in connection with the same item," he replied.

He steered the car around a corner onto Liz's street. A few minutes later, he pulled up near the Moscarettis' building.

"I'm surprised there are no reporters hanging around," he said.

"I guess they got enough of me this morning."

"Yeah, I heard you were on network news at noon, and I saw part of the interview on one of the cable channels. Didn't you catch it?"

"No, Sophie and I weren't watching TV."

"It's been running all day on the news channels. By the way, you looked very pretty."

He was getting quite good with the compliments. "Thanks," she said, kissing him.

They came out of a lingering hug. "Sorry I have to drop you off like this," he said. "Joe told me he was going to keep the main door locked after those reporters showed up last night. Did he give you a key?"

Liz glanced towards the Moscarettis' front window. "No, he didn't, but that's okay. I see Rosa looking out. She'll have the door open before I'm halfway up the steps."

"I'll wait till I know you're in before I take off," he said. Moments later, with a tap of the car horn, he pulled away.

Rosa opened the door before Liz reached the top of the steps and proudly announced that the buzzer entry system had been put in that day. She also pointed out the mail slot Joe had put in the vestibule. Prior to this, the postal carrier came inside and put letters for the Moscarettis, Liz, and the other tenant, Mr. Klein, in a big box in the hall.

"Now the postman can just drop the mail in the slot, and Joe or I will put it in the box," Rosa said. "And by the way, all you got today was your credit card bill."

It didn't bother Liz that Rosa knew the identity of all her correspondents, business and social. It was almost like living with her parents again and having Mom announce, "You got another letter from that boy at Boston College." Even though she was eagerly anticipating sharing an apartment with Ike, she was going to miss this homey atmosphere.

"Is Ike coming back?" Rosa asked.

Liz paused on her way to the stairway. "Not until later on. Something came up and he had to meet his partner some-where."

"When he comes back, are you going out to eat?"

"No. He didn't know how long he'd be tied up. I'll microwave a frozen dinner."

The instant Liz mentioned *frozen dinner* she knew how Rosa would respond.

"Come eat with us, Dearie. I'm making spinach raviolis and meatballs."

Chapter Eighteen

Rosa's kitchen was steeped in the redolence of true Italian cooking. Breathing in the savory aromas that so often drifted up to her apartment, Liz was struck with her familiar sense of impending loss. Another part of living here that she'd sorely miss.

Joe greeted her with a big smile. "Before we eat, I want to show you how to work the buzzer in your apartment," he said.

The buzzer had been installed near her entrance door. It took only a minute for her to become familiar with it. "I'm glad you had this put in, Joe," she said as they went back to the Moscarettis' apartment. "Ike will like it too."

"Everything will be ready soon," Rosa said, bustling around the kitchen, putting a gaily-flowered vinyl cloth on the table and setting a third place. "Meanwhile, have a glass of wine, Dearie."

She raised her voice to be heard in what the Moscarettis called "the front room," where Joe had gone to watch TV. "Joe—open a bottle of chianti."

"Wait a minute," he called back. "A bulletin's coming on about the terrorists."

News revealing LoPresti's double life? Liz rushed to join

186

him. Rosa was close behind her. Seconds later the news-caster was telling viewers that Vincent LoPresti, the music teacher in a prestigious Manhattan private school, had been identified as one of the Middle Eastern terrorists rounded up last night by the NYPD.

"LoPresti has also been identified as the man who forced Elizabeth Rooney into a car yesterday and kidnapped her," the newscaster continued. "Until her rescue, she was held hostage in a Manhattan luxury apartment, believed to be headquarters for an al Qaeda cell.

A photo of LoPresti, neatly dressed in coat and tie, was shown. Liz decided it had come out of the school files.

Rosa bristled with indignation. "Look at that Arab all dressed up like an American schoolteacher."

"Yeah," Joe said. "What's he doing with a name like Lo-Presti?"

The newscaster touched briefly on Big Tiny's role in the rescue but went on to explain how the terrorists had man-aged to pass as Italian-Americans.

Rosa shook her head. "It makes me sick just thinking about that bunch sneaking into our country with fake pass-ports and living here all this time, fooling everybody with Italian names."

When the newscaster announced she'd be right back with more about the terrorists after a commercial break. Joe turned off the TV and got out of his faux leather recliner. "I've had enough of this," he said. "I'll open the wine now. After seeing that faker's picture, I could use a couple belts."

They all went into the kitchen. Joe took three goblets from a cabinet, opened a bottle of chianti, and poured it. He and Liz sat down at the table.

Rosa, hovering over the stove, turned to look at Liz. "You're very quiet, Dearie. We haven't heard a peep out of you since news about the Arab music teacher came on."

"Maybe seeing his picture got her upset," Joe suggested.

Rosa looked concerned. "Is that it, Dearie? Did looking at the picture of that bum who kidnapped you scare you all over again?"

"Nothing like that," Liz assured them. "I was wondering if Ike heard the bulletin."

That and much more. She'd been thinking Ike must have been in the school when news about LoPresti broke. By that time almost everyone would have left. The only persons she could think of who'd still be there were the security guard and headmaster's assistant Bernice. She recalled the guard kept a transistor radio on his desk. Most likely he'd have had it on when the bulletin was broadcast. If Bernice didn't have a radio or TV on in her office, she'd have gotten the news from him.

Poor Bernice—first Marva Malin's body had come hurtling down from the balcony, landing a few feet from her. Next, the school janitor had disappeared. Now she'd been hit with the news that someone she considered a friend was a terrorist and a kidnapper. Two shocks and then a bombshell. Unless, as she and Ike thought possible, LoPresti's masquerade might not have come as a bombshell to Bernice.

And what if it were true that LoPresti knew the killer's identity and was protecting him or her? If the killer knew this, wouldn't LoPresti's arrest greatly disturb the killer? Wouldn't the killer fear that the truth might come out during LoPresti's interrogation? When Chadwick Academy opened tomorrow, would someone else turn up missing?

The need to talk this over with Ike was almost overwhelming.

"Well, I'm ready to dish up," Rosa said putting pasta bowls on the table. "Let's not talk about the terrorists while we're eating. Liz needs to get her mind off her kidnapping."

Rosa might be surprised to know the kidnapping wasn't as much on her mind as the murder, Liz thought. But when they sat down at the table she decided she'd turn to a pleasant topic—Sophie's wedding. The Moscarettis had met both Sophie and Ralph several times when they came to visit.

"She's a beautiful girl and she's lucky to be getting a fine man, a cop and all," Rosa said.

The "and all" meant Italian too. In Rosa's estimation, any bride was lucky to be getting a groom with this extra advantage.

"Do you know where they're going on their honeymoon?" Rosa asked.

"Bermuda."

"Oh, I hear it's lovely there. How long will they be gone?"

"Six days."

Rosa pressed on. "And where are they going to live?"

"In Ralph's place. He has a three-room apartment in this area."

If only she didn't have to move, she and Sophie would be neighbors.

Rosa fell silent. Liz guessed she was thinking about the move too.

Joe had been too busy quaffing his wine and putting away his raviolis and meatballs to join in the talk. Now he spoke up. "How are you and Ike doing, looking for an apartment?"

Before Liz could reply, Rosa did. "I don't even want to think about that. I'm going to miss you something terrible, Dearie. Isn't there some way the two of you could manage living upstairs? What if Joe built a closet for Ike's things?"

Joe nodded. "Yeah, I could do that. On the wall next to the refrigerator would be a good place."

Jutting out into the room that served as her living, dining, and sleeping quarters, diminishing the already cramped space, Liz thought.

Rosa gave a deep sigh. "Let's not kid ourselves. Another closet isn't going to solve the problem. What Liz and Ike need is a real bedroom, maybe even a spare room too, for when her folks come to visit, and a real kitchen big enough to eat in."

"We got all that, Rosa, and a dining room too—we could swap apartments with her," Joe suggested with a playful grin.

Liz knew he was teasing. Rosa would be like a fish out of water in the tiny, makeshift kitchenette, separated from the living/dining/sleeping area by a three-panel bamboo screen.

Rosa was not about to assume sole blame for turning thumbs down on the suggestion.

"You want to sleep on a hide-a-bed, Joe?"

Liz ended this exchange. "I hope we can find a place in this vicinity," she said. "That way I can see you often."

"That would be nice," Rosa replied.

Liz sensed what she left unsaid. Things would never be the same.

"What's for dessert?" Joe asked.

With the change of subject, Rosa brightened. "Apple pie with spumoni."

"I'm taking mine into the front room," Joe said "I'm ready to watch some more TV. Maybe there'll be something on about the school murder for a change. It's been crowded off the news ever since Liz's kidnapping and the terrorists' arrest."

"Liz probably wants to watch TV too," Rosa said. "We'll all have dessert in the front room."

She arranged three plates—wedges of apple pie topped with generous dollops of spumoni. "I know you like coffee after dinner, Dearie," she said to Liz. "Joe and I don't drink it at night, but I made some for you."

"Thanks, Rosa." Liz watched her fill a mug from the coffeemaker. Rosa also remembered the splash of half-and-half Liz liked.

Rosa put everything on a tray and carried it into the front room. Joe had already switched on a news channel and was watching a good-looking, dark-haired female deliver a rehash. The school photo of LoPresti was shown again. A segment of Liz's interview that morning was rerun.

"They're playing the same stuff over and over," Joe grumbled.

Like the coverage of Marva Malin's murder, Liz thought. Before her kidnapping took over the news, she'd seen the photo of Malin and of Chadwick Academy's façade on TV more times than she could recall. She looked away from the screen and began to eat her dessert, aware of the newscaster's voice but not paying attention to the words.

"Hey, something new for a change," Joe said suddenly.

Liz snapped to attention. just as a photo flashed onto the screen. There was no mistaking the elderly woman she'd seen in Alvino's apartment.

"The FBI has announced the release and planned deportation of a woman picked up with the Middle Eastern terrorists in last night's raid," the newscaster said. "Interrogation has revealed that the woman, Hava Shukri, seventy-three, a deaf mute, entered the United States from Canada with the terrorists to serve as their housekeeper. Due to her age and handicaps, Federal authorities have ascertained she poses no threat."

"That woman brought me my dinner last night," Liz said. "I'm thankful she isn't being held in prison. She couldn't have known what was going on."

Rosa looked dubious. "Personally, I'm thankful she's being sent back where she came from."

"Yeah," Joe added. "But I'd bet my last buck Canada's not where she came from. The terrorists brought her there straight out of one of those Arab countries."

Liz preferred to believe the Muslim housekeeper had been in Canada legally and had family, or at least connections there. She felt sure the FBI had checked this out.

When the news became repetitive again, Rosa suggested switching to a movie channel. "You don't have to leave yet, do you, Dearie?" she asked. "Stay till Ike gets here."

"Okay," Liz said. Rosa was probably thinking, as she was, that visits like this soon would be few and far between.

They watched an old Clint Eastwood Western. It was winding down when Liz heard her cell phone. Probably Ike, letting her know he was running late, she thought.

She was right. "I'll be stuck here for a while," he said. "There's no telling what time it'll be before I can get away. I want to stop by your place, but maybe you'd rather not wait up for me."

"I don't care how late it is, I want to see you and continue our discussion."

"Okay. Joe said he's keeping the doors locked and he didn't give me a key yet. I'll phone you when I pull up outside the building so you can come down and let me in."

"Oh, you don't need a key. Joe had a buzzer system put in today."

"Good. It's time he stopped playing watchdog. This will be much better for everyone."

"I'll be waiting for your buzz," she said.

While she'd been talking to Ike, Joe had switched back to a news channel, where a photo of LoPresti was again being shown. "I see red every time this guy's picture comes on," he said. "I wouldn't be surprised if it turns out he's the school murderer."

"Joe, you're getting forgetful." Rosa said. "The police think the killer was an intruder—someone who didn't have anything to do with the school."

"I remember as good as you, Rosa," Joe retorted. "But maybe they'll change their minds now that they know a terrorist was right there in the school the whole time."

At that moment a knock sounded on the apartment door.

"That's gotta be Mr. Klein," Rosa said, rising from her chair. "I saw him this morning, and he said he'd be stopping by tonight."

"He must be going to visit his daughter in New Jersey over the first of the month, and he's paying his rent early," Joe replied.

Rosa went to answer the knock. They heard her open the door and greet the caller. "Oh, good evening, Mr. Klein."

A few minutes of barely audible conversation followed. Liz was sure Rosa had invited him to come in, but he'd probably declined. He didn't have the sociable relationship with the Moscarettis that she had.

Joe muted the TV during a series of commercials. "It shouldn't be taking this long for the old guy to hand over his rent check," he said. "He's probably trying to talk Rosa into something. Last time he stayed more than a couple minutes he wanted his apartment repainted."

They heard the door close. Seconds later, Rosa appeared with an envelope in her hand and a big smile on her face.

"So Mr. Klein's going to visit his daughter and he gave us the rent early," Joe said.

"That's not all he gave us," Rosa replied, her smile broadening. "He's moving to a retirement place near his daughter in New Jersey, and he gave us sixty days' notice."

She swooped down on Liz with a hearty hug. "Living room, bedroom, and kitchen with a small room off it, could be a dining room or another bedroom. If you and Ike want it, it's all yours, Dearie!"

Chapter Nineteen

Speculations about Marva Malin's murder retreated to the far corners of Liz's mind. The wonderful reality of being able to stay with the Moscarettis took over. After the joyous excitement with Rosa and Joe subsided and she went upstairs to her apartment, she wanted only to be in Ike's arms, to savor their happiness alone, together.

She'd tell him the instant he stepped inside her door. She imagined his reaction. "What a lucky break," he'd say, hugging her. And then they'd agree that they'd always feel a special attachment to this small apartment where their romance had blossomed. "We'll always have fond memories of this place," she'd tell him as they sat down on the sofa. "Here's where it all began for us." It would probably take a while for them to get around to discussing the Malin murder, she thought with a smile.

She turned on the TV and curled up on the sofa to wait for him. He'd be ready for coffee when he arrived. She'd put it on as soon as he got here. Meanwhile, she'd see what she could find on television.

After watching the last half of an old movie, and then an hour-long sitcom, she turned to a news channel. Her kidnapping and the capture of the terrorists still dominated. No mention that one of the terrorists was on the loose. Evidently, Ike had guessed right—it was classified information. When coverage of the Malin murder came on, it was a rehash, but she watched it anyway.

During a commercial her thoughts wandered. What a day this had been! With her news media interview, the imagined terrorist in the subway, and the very real Ms. Tabloid, it would have been full enough, but now Duddy's disappearance and the news about Mr. Klein's apartment topped it off.

And hurray for the new buzzer entry system! Joe should have had it put in long before this, she thought. All three apartments had double dead-bolts on the insides, but anyone could walk right into the building. Even though intruders couldn't get into the apartments, Joe and Rosa were ever on the alert in the daytime, and late at night any sound in the hallway would awaken Joe. He attributed this to his experience as a Marine in Vietnam. Now, if he heard footsteps in the hall and on the stair, he wouldn't have to investigate. He'd know it was Ike. Tonight, when Ike came in, Joe would roll right over and go back to sleep.

She was getting drowsy. She decided to make coffee and drink a mugful while waiting for Ike. She didn't usually drink coffee this late, but maybe it would keep her from dozing off. When Ike got here she wanted to be alert and ready to hear what happened at the school tonight.

Ike was putting in a lot of extra time on this case, she thought, taking her coffee mug to the sofa and settling herself among Gram's needlepoint pillows. She hoped that meant he'd have plenty of time off for a honeymoon. They hadn't decided yet where they wanted to go. Maybe Sophie and Ralph would come back from Bermuda and tell them they absolutely had to go there.

A small sip of her coffee told her it was still much too hot to drink. She was about to set the mug down and wait for the coffee to cool when the buzzer sounded. With the mug still in her hand, she rushed to push the button and let Ike in. An instant afterward, she remembered she could have spoken to him first, but in her intense need to see him she'd forgotten about this.

She opened her door, ready to greet him, but she'd barely heard footsteps coming up the stairway when she sensed something was wrong. It sounded as if more than one person were coming up the stairs.

Seconds later, she knew her instincts were right. Her heart lurched with fear when two young men appeared at the top of the stairway. In the glow of the overhead hallway light she could plainly see two swarthy faces and two sets of deep, dark eyes similar to those she'd seen staring at her in Alvino's dining room.

Quickly, she moved to get back inside her apartment and lock the door, but it was too late. A hand gripped her arm. Another firmed across her mouth to keep her from screaming. She felt herself being shoved inside and heard the door shut behind her.

She realized she was still holding the coffee mug when a few drops of the scalding hot liquid spilled onto her hand. Without a moment's hesitation, she dashed the rest of it into the face of the man who had her in his grip and flung the empty mug at the other.

With a howl and a volley of foreign words she was sure were oaths, the scalded man let go of her. Before the other man could grab her, she darted behind the screen, seized the coffeepot and stood there, trembling but ready to use its boiling-hot contents to defend herself.

Now she had a chance to scream, before the men came after her. Would Joe hear her? She drew a deep breath, but before the scream materialized she heard her apartment door burst open and a voice she couldn't identify bark an order.

"Police! Get your hands up!"

Relief washed over her, along with puzzlement. From that voice, she knew it wasn't Ike who'd come bursting into her apartment. She set the coffeepot down and peered around the screen. To her surprise, she saw Joe. That voice hadn't sounded anything like his, either. Then she saw another man frisking her two assailants, while Joe stood by, gun poised. She did a double-take when she got a good look at the other man. There was no mistaking the imagined terrorist she'd seen on the subway.

Now puzzlement and confusion joined her relief. *Three men who looked like Middle Eastern natives—two bad guys and one apparently a cop.* Was the man she'd seen on the subway really a cop, she wondered, or was he an imposter in cahoots with the other two and this was part of some bizarre plan to kidnap her again? And how did Joe get into it?

She watched the frisking and wasn't surprised when the man who might be a cop found a gun on each of the two men. He also took what looked like car keys from one of them and, from the man who'd shoved her into the apartment, a small bottle and a piece of cloth. After removing the cap, he very briefly held the bottle under his nose.

"Looks like they were going to chloroform Ms. Rooney and take her away," he said. He put keys, bottle, and cloth on a table; handcuffed the two intruders; and ordered them to sit on the floor. Liz noticed red blotches on the face of the one she'd splashed with the coffee. She hoped it hurt. Anyone who'd douse a rag with chloroform, hold it over a woman's face till she passed out, then drag her off deserved to be in pain. She wished she could have scalded the other one too.

With the assailants cuffed and sitting on the floor, Liz saw Joe lower his gun and look toward the kitchenette screen. His eyes met hers. "It's okay now, Liz," he said.

But was it? Still unsure, she stepped out from behind the screen.

Her apprehension dissolved when she saw the possible cop on his phone and heard him calling for backup and then a few moments later phoning the FBI. He was a cop, all right. But her puzzlement grew more intense. How had all this come about?

Keeping a wary eye on the two handcuffed men, Joe gave her arm a gentle pat. "You okay, Liz?"

She glanced at the two men and then at her imagined terrorist from the subway, who she now knew was a police officer. "Yes, but I'm confused . . ."

The officer had just clicked off after talking to someone at Manhattan FBI headquarters and heard her. "I know you're confused," he said with a grin. "You noticed me on the subway today, didn't you?"

She nodded. *Would he be insulted if she told him she'd suspected he was the missing terrorist?* She decided not to. With this information so hush-hush, it might not have been divulged to every cop on the force. This officer might not know that only five of the six terrorists had been captured in last night's raid.

His next statement proved her wrong. "With a terrorist on the loose, the department thought it wise to provide you with some protection." He extended his hand. "I'm painclothes officer Howard Musab. I was with you from the time you left your house for the subway till you got off the boat on your return trip to Manhattan."

This explained why Ike was willing for her to go to Staten Island, even though the sixth terrorist might be roaming around the city, she thought. He knew there'd be an officer keeping an eye on her.

"Sounds like you've been following me around all day," she replied, shaking his hand. "But I never saw you again after I got off the subway."

"I made sure of that after you spotted me on the train platform," he said. "Most people aren't as observant as you. I'll bet you noticed a woman tailing you—a reporter, I figured."

She laughed. "Yes, I was on to her."

She glanced at the two handcuffed men, shackled and sitting on the floor under Joe's watchful eye. The one with the coffee scalds was holding his hands against his face. The other looked sullen.

"One if them must be the sixth terrorist, but who's the other one?" she asked.

"A sympathizer, most likely," Officer Musab replied.

Liz recalled her imaginings on the subway. Maybe her imagination wasn't so wild after all. "There actually are people willing to help terrorists?" she asked.

He nodded. "But the department and the FBI are on top of it. Without an active al Qaeda cell, they're no threat. They don't do anything on their own, and now that we've nabbed this one, the whole sympathy movement could be busted wide open."

Liz hoped this terrorist sympathizer would undergo a lengthy interrogation, minus any courtesy or respect. Individuals such as he were as despicable as the terrorists themselves.

Another thought came to her. "I'm not clear on something, Officer," she said. "You were on foot when you followed me to the subway and onto the boat and train, and when you were hanging around my grandmother's and my friend's houses. But when you saw me drive off with my friend, how did you follow me to the ferry? Besides, how could you have known where we were going?"

"I was in touch with an NYPD detective by phone the entire time," he replied. "He told me you were making the three-thirty boat. I got a lift to the ferry in a squad car from the New Dorp precinct."

Who else could this NYPD detective be but Ike?

"You must be talking about Detective George Eichle," she said.

"Right. He told me you two are getting married soon. Congratulations."

"Thanks. I guess he also told you he'd meet me at South Ferry and you could take some time off."

"Yeah. First he told me he'd cover you for the rest of the evening and he'd call me when it was time for me to take over again, but later he phoned to say he had to work on a case, and . . ."

"And needed you to keep watch on my place till he could get here?"

"Exactly. I picked up my car and Eichle waited till I got there before he left. I was parked outside your building from the time he drove off till I saw these two men go in."

Liz gave a puzzled frown. "But I saw Ike drive off only a couple of minutes after he dropped me off."

"He phoned me after you went in, and we worked it out. He drove down the block and parked till I pulled up near your building. Lucky I found a space close enough to get a good look at the men when they passed under the outside light."

Liz wanted to ask him if he noticed the two men fit the racial profile for terrorists. He was as American as she, but with his looks and his name he must have roots in the Middle East. Would the question offend him?

She didn't need to ask it. "One look at those Arab faces was all it took," he said. "I knew one of them had to be the missing terrorist. I didn't take time to call for backup. I knew I had to get to you as fast as I could. Eichle told me your place was upstairs, so I pushed the button for the downstairs apartment." He gave Joe an appreciative smile. "When your landlord came to the door I flashed my badge and filled him in."

"Rosa was asleep but I was still up, watching TV," Joe said. "I knew he'd need help till he could get backup, so I grabbed my gun and the key to Liz's door and we both took the stairs on the double."

At that moment two NYPD officers came into the apartment. After consulting with Musab for a few minutes, they read the intruders their rights and placed them under arrest. Then they pocketed the car keys and bagged the chloroform bottle and cloth.

A few minutes later, two more men appeared, identifying themselves as FBI agents. They conferred with Musab and Joe and the backup cops, then introduced themselves to Liz and told her they'd try to keep this second assault out of the news.

"With a police van and squad car out front, word will get around that something happened at this address," one agent said. "But we'll handle it."

She thanked him. She could do without another round of media attention, she thought, as she watched the backup cops get the prisoners to their feet. While the joint escort of NYPD and FBI marched them out of the apartment, one of the agents suddenly halted and glared, first at Musab, then at the other officers.

"One of these men looks like he's been roughed up," he said. "Don't you cops ever learn? If the news media gets wind of this, we'll be up against every bleeding heart organization in existence."

Liz took a good look at the scalded man. His reddened cheeks made him look as if he'd been slapped around. She started to tell the agent she was responsible, but he was still talking, saying he wanted it on record that the FBI had nothing to do with this.

Liz wasn't surprised that Officer Musab and Joe both looked confused. How could they know she'd thrown a mugful of searing hot coffee into that man's face?

"None of our officers touched the man," Musab said.

"I can vouch for that," Joe added. "And neither did I—not that I wasn't tempted."

"Well, somebody did," the agent snarled. Suddenly, his eyes rested on Liz. "You must have witnessed the incident, Ms. Rooney," he said. "I want your statement that this is a case of New York police brutality and the Bureau agents had nothing to do with it."

Liz saw Joe and Officer Musab exchange puzzled looks.

The agent, an Arnold Schwarzenegger type, looked as if he'd smacked around a few prisoners himself, Liz thought. She'd heard enough out of him. When he went on with his tirade, she interrupted.

"Excuse me, but I'm responsible for the red marks on the prisoner's face. He grabbed me and pushed me, so I threw a mugful of hot coffee at him."

All three men stared at her. The agent was the first to burst out laughing.

"A clear case of self-defense," he said as he turned to catch up with the others. At the door he paused, looking over his shoulder at Joe and Musab, saying, "Sorry, my mistake." Then as he was closing the door behind him, he said, "and nice going, Ms. Rooney."

Several minutes passed before Musab and Joe could stop chuckling.

"Good thing you're not a policewoman, Liz," Joe said. "You'd be in big trouble."

"She should be a cop," Musab added. "She'd make a first-rate detective."

The door had opened while he was speaking, and now a voice sounded from the threshold. "That's what I keep telling her."

Ike strode in and caught her up into his arms.

Chapter Twenty

Liz, I guess I owe you an explanation," he said.

"Good guess," she replied. "Why didn't you tell me I had police protection?"

"I knew you wouldn't go for having someone following you around, but after what just happened, you have to admit it was a good idea."

He said he'd pulled up in front of the building while the two terrorists were being loaded into the NYPD van and their car impounded. "I was stunned when I found out you'd almost been kidnapped again," he said. He turned to Musab, adding, "Let's have a full rundown."

Musab and Joe described everything—even the scalding coffee episode, which Ike seemed to get a kick out of. Liz realized that Ike wanted all the details, but she only wanted to be alone with him, to feel his arms around her. She needed to tell him the good news about Mr. Klein's apartment too, and to find out about Duddy.

"What would have happened to me if Officer Musab and Joe hadn't arrived in time?" she asked when she and Ike were alone at last.

He drew her onto the sofa and into a hug. "You'd have

been knocked out with chloroform and taken away," he said. "Looks like they planned to use you as a pawn to free the men rounded up last night. It will all come out when FBI and CIA interrogators go to work on them." He paused, firming his arms around her. "Thank God for Joe. It would have been tough for Musab to handle this alone."

She nodded. "They were wonderful. I'm very grateful to both of them, but . . ."

"But you thought they'd never leave?" Ike asked with a grin.

"I sound like an unappreciative wretch, but we have so much to talk about," she replied. "And I have something absolutely fantastic to tell you," she added, thinking of Mr. Klein's apartment.

"Is there any coffee left or did you throw it all in that guy's face?" he asked.

She tossed one of Gram's needlepoint pillows at him. "It was only a mugful."

"Yeah, I know. I was just being funny, trying to pretend this hasn't knocked me for a loop. I love you so much, Liz. There'd be damn little in my life if I lost you."

His rare, tender words touched her heart. She kissed him and told him she loved him too. "With the missing terrorist hauled away, it's all over," she said. "Now, how about some coffee?"

He followed her behind the screen. "Do you have any doughnuts?" he asked.

"Sorry. How about some of Rosa's cookies?"

"Great," he said. "I know your attachment to the Moscarettis goes beyond Rosa's kitchen, but I hope we can find a place not too far from her oven."

"We already have," she said, putting coffee mugs and a plate of cookies on a tray. She told him about Mr. Klein's apartment.

"That's the best news I've had in a long time," he said

with a broad smile. "I guess we should start shopping for more furniture."

"Yes, we'll need a bedroom set."

"But between this place and mine, we have enough for our living room. One of our TVs could go in the bedroom, but what are we going to do with two sleeper sofas?"

"Rosa said there was a small spare room."

"Good. One of the sleepers could go in there for when your folks come up from Florida."

If Ike were not estranged from his parents, they too would make use of the spare room when they visited.

She thought of the letter she'd sent them a few days ago. They must have received it by now. Ike had told her not to expect a reply, but she was hoping. Answering her letter, even if they said they would not attend the wedding, would be a tiny olive branch.

"So what happened while you were at Chadwick Academy tonight?" she asked when they'd settled themselves on the sofa with their coffee and cookies.

Ike took a swallow of coffee. "I'm sure you know the news about LoPresti is out, but before we go into that, I'll report on Duddy's disappearance. Bernice was the one who reported him missing. She told me he'd promised to adjust the thermostat in her office yesterday and when he didn't show up to do it by the time play rehearsal was over and everyone was getting ready to leave, she went down to his quarters to remind him. He wasn't there. Turns out nobody remembered seeing him all day. The last time anyone saw him was yesterday around five."

"Isn't it strange that nobody noticed he wasn't around?"

"You'd think so, but apparently the old guy wasn't what you'd call a stickler for routine. Bernice told me he'd often knock off work early—sometimes in the middle of the day— and retire to his room with a six-pack."

"So, when Bernice didn't find him in his room, that's when she reported him missing?"

"She and the security guard searched the building first, to make sure he didn't have a heart attack in the boiler room or somewhere. When they didn't find him, Bernice called Missing Persons."

"Doesn't a person have to be missing a lot longer than Duddy was for the police to take action?"

"Yeah, but when Missing Persons got the call reporting the Chadwick Academy janitor missing it must have rung a bell. Somebody thought of the murder and decided that Homicide should be notified."

"Do you think Duddy left the building some time last night?"

"Most likely, but when we searched his quarters, it didn't look like he took off permanently. Toothbrush still in his bathroom. No empty spaces in his clothes closet or bureau drawers. Even his tools were there."

"Maybe he met with an accident—hit by a car or something."

"Yeah, the hospitals are being checked."

And if Duddy didn't turn up in any of them, the morgue would be next, Liz thought. Poor old Duddy. He'd probably gone out to a bar, had one too many, and got into trouble on his way back to the school.

"The teachers involved in the school play seemed to like Duddy," she said. "Were they still in the building when you got there?"

"Gibbs the art teacher and the gym teacher, Julia Tulley? Yeah, they hung around. They both seemed concerned. And here's something interesting. Tulley cornered me and whispered didn't it look suspicious, Duddy suddenly taking off."

Interesting and significant, Liz thought. "What did you tell her?" she asked.

"Same as I told you. We don't believe he intended to be gone permanently."

A macabre thought stole into Liz's mind. Julia Tulley might be hoping that Duddy would turn up in the morgue and Malin's murder would be pinned on him. She wouldn't be hoping for this unless she was the killer.

Ike's voice penetrated her thoughts. "We've covered Duddy. Now let's get to the news bulletin about LoPresti."

Hearing about reactions to the bulletin took priority over her idea about Tulley. It was a wild idea, anyway. "Okay," she said.

"We were all getting ready to leave Duddy's quarters when the security guard came rushing down the stairs saying he'd just heard something on his radio about LoPresti. We turned on Duddy's TV and caught a bulletin."

Liz wished she'd been there to see how Bernice, Tulley, and Gibbs reacted to the news about their friend and colleague. Ike's next words told her he was on top of this.

"I watched all three of them when they heard the bulletin," he said. "Gibbs and Tulley were both very startled, but Bernice didn't seem surprised. Later, she told me she'd tried to phone LoPresti when he didn't show up at the school this morning and didn't call to explain why. She sensed something fishy when she was told the phone was disconnected. If he didn't come in tomorrow she'd planned to follow up on it, she said.

"If LoPresti knows who killed Malin, do you think the killer is aware of this?" Liz asked.

Ike shook his head. "None of the three showed any signs of worry that LoPresti might let this out during interrogation."

"So where do things stand?"

"We'll have a good idea when we get results of the tests on the last two possible murder weapons."

Liz did some quick calculating. "The last two? Did you get the results on LoPresti's baton?"

"Yeah, I forget to tell you. The baton didn't come anywhere near close."

"So that leaves the chair rung with the green paint on it, and Malin's bag."

"Right." He took a drink of his coffee. From the tilt of the mug it looked as if he'd almost finished it.

"Looks like you need a refill," she said, extending her hand for the mug.

"Yeah, thanks," he replied, handing it over.

Like many cops, Ike put away a lot of coffee, she thought. "We're going to need a larger coffeemaker after we're married," she called from behind the kitchenette screen.

"Maybe someone will give us one for a wedding present," he called back.

Wedding presents. The pleasant thought occupied her mind for a few moments. Like sugarplums in the old night-before-Christmas poem, visions of a big, state-of-the-art coffeemaker, plus other beautiful gifts, danced in her head.

But the dancing visions faded as quickly as they'd begun. "When do you think you'll get the results on the chair rung?" she asked, returning to the sofa with Ike's coffee.

"We can't say for sure. Unlike the baton, the chair rung has a distinct curved area. It'll take time to compare it with photos of the marks on Malin's throat. Like Duddy's hammer, there might have been some shifting."

Again, Liz thought about the paint on the end of the chair rung. "Did the autopsy pick up any signs of paint on Malin's body or on her clothing?"

Ike shook his head. "None were found on the body, and tests on the clothing she wore at the time of the murder are still incomplete."

"If traces of paint are found on the clothing, and the photos of the marks on Malin's neck match up with the chair rung, wouldn't that pretty much pin down the chair rung as the murder weapon?" she asked.

"Sure. More than one positive result would be solid evidence that the killer used the chair rung as a strangling device."

"And if the art teacher's fingerprints are the only ones on the chair rung, that would make him the killer," Liz said. She felt sorry for Cyril Gibbs. If it turned out that this quiet, mild-mannered man was the killer, she felt sure Malin must have said or done something to drive him into a blind rage. *Temporary insanity.* She'd followed enough murder cases to know about that.

Ike nodded. "The fingerprints will tell all." He finished his coffee and checked his watch. "If you're going to work tomorrow, I'd better hit the road. You've had quite a day."

"Yes, it was a full one, all right. I'll admit I'm getting sleepy, and I *am* going to work tomorrow."

Ike got to his feet. "With the wedding rehearsal at seven tomorrow night, I guess you'll go to Staten Island directly from work."

"Yes—I'll go to Gram's and drop off my overnight bag, and walk to the church from there."

"I should make it to New Dorp shortly before seven. I'll pick you up at your grandmother's."

"Thanks, that will be great." In the car they'd have a few minutes to discuss the case. Once they got caught up in the rehearsal and dinner afterward, there'd be no more opportunity for this until much later in the evening.

Now she thought about what had happened tonight, and hoped that this second attempt to take her as a hostage could be kept out of the news. She wanted to spare Gram and her other loved ones needless worry, but they'd be shocked if she didn't tell them and they heard it on the news. Should she keep mum about it and hope the FBI could prevent the story from making headlines or bulletins? She asked Ike what she should do.

"Don't tell anyone," he said. "Remember, it's classified information that a terrorist has been on the loose. If his capture made the news, this would all come out. Chances are the police report will be toned down—maybe scrubbed."

"Oh, I hope so, and I'll keep my mouth shut. Meanwhile, if you hear anything about Duddy tomorrow, will you give me a call?"

"Sure. The hospitals and morgue checks should have been completed by now."

At the door, they lingered for a few minutes before a final kiss. "I wish it was *our* wedding rehearsal tomorrow night," he said.

"Me too," she replied. Ike had never been big on verbal expression of romantic thoughts. This, plus the tender words he'd spoken earlier, added up to a heart warming fact. Something good had come out of her ordeal with the terrorists.

Chapter Twenty-one

The following morning, as she did every weekday, Liz turned her alarm clock off and her TV on to a news channel, and allowed herself a few more minutes before getting up.

Reviewing last night's harrowing experience, she was surprised that she felt no after-effects. Was being the target of terrorists getting to be routine?

There was nothing on TV news about last night. Her kidnapping and rescue still dominated. LoPresti's terrorist connection was a close second. Interviews with several Chadwick Academy parents came on. Their comments ranged from concern to outrage.

"I can't express how shocked and disappointed we are. This is worse than having your child in a public school."

"You'd think for the tuition they're charging we wouldn't have to worry about terrorists on the teaching staff."

"This is unacceptable. We're taking our son out of Chadwick Academy immediately."

Liz stared at the irate faces on the screen. "You mommas and poppas haven't seen anything yet," she said aloud. "Wait till the news breaks that Malin's killer wasn't an outsider and

211

you realize your kids have been exposed to a murderer on a daily basis!"

She continued listening as she got up and started the coffeemaker. On her way to shower, a bulletin came on, halting her midway between kitchenette and bathroom. Duddy's disappearance had made the news.

Her first thought was that Bernice, Gibbs, or Tulley had reported this to the media. If one of them was Malin's killer, he or she might have believed this would throw suspicion on Duddy.

On second thought, it seemed more likely that an alert news reporter had picked up on the police check of hospitals and the morgue. If the school name had been included, it would have been a red flag. However it happened, this development would surely start rumors that the Chadwick Academy janitor had something to do with the murder at the school.

Chadwick parents might not be so gullible from now on, she thought. The possibility that Malin's killer was connected with the school might overshadow police insinuations to the contrary.

She showered and dressed. She decided to wear the tan wool jacket and brown, knee-length skirt she'd bought last payday. With her favorite creamy-white silk blouse, it would make a nice outfit for dinner after the rehearsal. Ike hadn't seen it yet. When he did, she was sure he'd like it and give her an approving smile—maybe even a compliment.

Being in love with a man who wasn't lavish with flattery was sometimes disappointing, but at least she knew when he did drop a compliment, he meant it.

After coffee and a bagel, she packed her bag for her overnight stay with Gram. Thoughts crowded her mind. Around this time tomorrow she'd be on her way over to Sophie's house to get ready for the wedding. Mr. Nicky, owner of Nick's Crowning Glory and a classmate of theirs at New Dorp High, was coming over at 8 AM to do their hair.

After the church bells rang at noon, Sophie would be married in the same church where they both used to go to Saturday confession when they were kids. She recalled once asking Sophie what she'd confessed to. Sophie's reply still made her laugh.

"I couldn't think of anything bad enough, so I made something up."

En route to the subway she passed a newsstand and paused to check out the newspapers. Even though the scandal sheets wouldn't come out today, and Ike had almost convinced her there wouldn't be any story anyway, she wanted to make sure Ms. Tabloid hadn't pulled a fast one. Satisfied that she hadn't, Liz turned her attention to headlines in the dailies:

TERRORIST MUSIC TEACHER STRIKES SOUR NOTE

TEACHER TRADES AL QAEDA CELL FOR PRISON CELL

The Staten Island paper wouldn't be out till later. She'd have to wait until she got to the ferry this evening to read the story that would bring Ms. Tabloid down in flames.

When she entered the subway her bag was subjected to search. Watching the cop go through the few things she needed for an overnight stay, she imagined how it might have been if terrorist leader Zaki al Sarzai had not been imprisoned. The Manhattan al Qaeda cell might have received those orders that never came. Perhaps by now there'd have been bombings in the New York subway system.

Before going to her desk, she stopped at Dan's office to

give him his gold pen. Mindful of Ike's reminder, she didn't tell him about last night. With nothing about it on the news yet, she hoped the story had been squashed or pulled.

Dan greeted her with a big hug. "Did they take this away from you and the cops got it back?" he asked when she gave him the pen.

"No—and they didn't take my engagement ring either."

"They kidnap and kill but they don't steal," Dan said with a wry smile.

"I wonder where they're being held," she said. "Except for the buzz about LoPresti, there's been almost nothing on the news about them."

"They're still under FBI interrogation," Dan replied. "But it's possible the CIA has stepped in. They might be in one of the CIA's secret prisons."

Liz was about to go her desk when he said, "I heard about the missing janitor. I called the morgue this morning. The only body they have of an elderly white male came in during the predawn hours. He had no ID on him."

"Oh, that could be Duddy! Maybe he was mugged and his wallet stolen."

Dan shook his head. "The description I was given didn't fit. I only saw him once—the day of the murder, but I noticed he had a badly broken nose. The old guy in the morgue doesn't. Would you like to view the body and make sure?"

"I'll pass on that. No broken nose is proof enough he's not Duddy."

"He'll probably turn up in a hospital," Dan said.

Unless his body washed up from one of the rivers, Liz thought. She fervently hoped he didn't—not only for Duddy's sake, but for Ike's too. Ike and his partner had put in many hours on this case. They were on the verge of determining the murder weapon. They were getting close to matching up a weapon with the killer. She didn't want the

DA's office to conclude that Duddy was the killer and he'd committed suicide.

Her mind eased when Ike phoned during the morning. "Duddy's in Bellevue," he said. "Evidently he got into a fight outside a bar last night and was knocked out cold. He was found in the bar alley this morning."

"Thanks for letting me know."

"How are you feeling after last night. Any delayed reaction?"

"None whatever. Can you tell me what's going on in the evidence lab?"

"There's been a new development. I'll let you in on it when I see you tonight. I'm on my way over to the lab right now."

Something important was in the works, she thought. "See you on the island, later," she said.

"Before we hang up, there's something else on my mind." he said. "The missing terrorist is behind bars and you don't need Musab anymore, but with the constant news coverage, the number of people who've seen you on TV has probably doubled since yesterday. When you leave work I want you to take a cab. Even with your hat and glasses, you could be recognized on the subway. You could be mobbed."

She knew he was right. Her coworkers had almost mobbed her when she got to her desk this morning.

"All right," she said. "I'll take a taxi to the ferry."

"Good. You'll probably go unnoticed on the boat if you get a newspaper and hide behind it, but the rush hour train's a different story."

"I'll be fine on the train."

"Well, okay . . ." Ike never ended his phone conversations with "I love you," and this one was no exception. Saying it to him would have been a sure fire way of getting a similar response, but she wanted him to think of it himself.

A few minutes later, Gram phoned to tell her the *Advance*

had come out earlier than usual because of the big story featuring the Island girl who'd been rescued after being kidnapped by terrorists. "It's a good article, and the picture turned out great," Gram said. "You'll see when you get a copy at the ferry terminal."

"I can't wait to see it. I wonder if that scandal sheet babe knows about it yet."

"If she hasn't, she soon will," Gram said. "The reporter did a superb job of explaining why Tynkov was in on your rescue. I'd like to see that woman's face when she reads about Tynkov being grateful to you for testifying on his behalf and how he saw you being kidnapped and notified Ike. The reporter even mentioned that Ike's your fiancé."

"Oh, Gram, that's wonderful!" *Any lingering fears concerning the Tynkov tryst story were laid to rest once and for all.*

"What boat are you making?" Gram asked.

"The five-thirty."

"I'll pick you up."

"Thanks, but you don't need to do that, Gram. I'll hop the train."

Gram's reply was firm. "No, I'm meeting you. Your kidnapping has made you a kind of celebrity. On the ferry you can find a seat and huddle behind your copy of the *Advance,* but it would be different on the rush hour SIRT."

Liz still wasn't convinced. "I know it can be very crowded, but . . ."

"But nothing," Gram retorted. "You'd be nose-to-nose with people getting suspicious about you wearing dark glasses on the train and in the crush, your hat could be jostled right off your red head. Next thing you know you'd be mobbed by autograph hounds. You probably wouldn't be able to get off the train at New Dorp. You'd be jammed in all the way to Great Kills."

This had a familiar ring to it, Liz thought. "Gram, have you by any chance been talking to Ike?" she asked.

Gram's answer warmed her heart. "Well, as a matter of fact, he called me a few minutes ago."

Who needed to hear "I love you" at the end of a phone conversation?

Chapter Twenty-two

Gram pulled her aging Chevy into the passenger pickup area and braked. "That's a pretty good disguise," she said as Liz climbed in. "Even though I've seen it before, I had to look twice to be sure it was you."

"I probably could have taken the SIRT without anyone giving me a second glance," Liz replied. "But thanks for sparing me from the six o'clock sardine special."

She longed to tell Gram about last night, but knew she had to keep quiet. Gram would be shocked if it made the news. But If the news media *did* get hold of the story, wouldn't it have broken by now?

Gram had just started the car when she was overcome with a sudden coughing and sneezing spell.

"Your allergy, Gram?" Liz asked.

Gram nodded, dabbing at her nose with a tissue. "Those darn chrysanthemums," she said with a final cough. "They're everywhere this time of year, but who'd think they'd bother me in the ferry terminal, of all places? I hope I don't start hacking and wheezing at Sophie's wedding."

"Oh, Gram—Sophie told me there'll be vases of big white mums around the altar."

"I'll sit in the last pew," Gram said. "In that big church with that small crowd, everyone will be way down front. If I start coughing, nobody will notice if I have to get up and go outside."

She turned the car into the stream of traffic exiting the viaduct. "What did you think of the article in the *Advance?*" she asked.

Liz patted the newspaper rolled up under her arm. "It was great. Everyone on the boat was reading it. Nobody even noticed my rain hat on a day without a cloud in the sky." She took the hat off and shook her hair free.

Commercials blared from the car radio. Gram reached over and turned down the volume. "A bulletin was on a few minutes ago," she said. "The FBI found maps of Manhattan and materials for making bombs in that apartment where you were."

Bomb-manufacturing paraphernalia in Alvino's apartment? Liz's feelings of disbelief were shortlived. Sure, Alvino had seemed less threatening than LoPresti and for a while she'd hoped he'd help her. But this seemed to indicate he was no different from the others. In a flash of recollection, she heard him telling her he was a chemical engineer. He might have been top operator in a deadly plan that never materialized.

"It was a huge apartment," she replied. "Plenty of space to store all kinds of chemicals and wires and whatever, but there was no sign of anything in the room where I was held."

Again, she described the room and the bathroom to Gram, adding, "They were unbelievably luxurious—definitely designed for female guests."

Gram stopped the car at a traffic light on Bay Street. "I don't care how luxurious it was—with terrorists roaming around the place, a woman guest wouldn't be safe," she stated emphatically. "You were lucky nothing happened to you while you were there."

Liz recalled the bolt on the inside of the bedroom door. She'd assumed that Alvino wanted to ensure a lady guest complete privacy. Now she thought he wanted to ensure her safety too. Gram was right. With a group of young men on the lookout for female companionship constantly in and out of the apartment, this was a wise move.

"I was never in that sort of danger, Gram," she said. "The door could be bolted on the inside. Alvino wasn't taking any chances with his lady friends."

Braking for a traffic light on Bay Street, Gram cast Liz a curious look. "Alvino? The Arab prince? The one you thought might help you escape?"

"Yes. I thought I sensed something different about him. I even told the man who came to question me from the NYPD that Alvino might cooperate." She shook her head. "But after hearing about the maps and the bomb making material in his apartment, I guess I was wrong."

The light changed to green. Gram got moving. Seconds later, the commercials ended and a male news commentator came on.

"Just in—new coverage concerning kidnap victim Liz Rooney, who was held hostage by al Qaeda terrorists for several hours last Wednesday before being rescued by the NYPD," he announced.

News about last night? Liz held her breath but breathed a sigh of relief when the newscaster continued. "According to the *Staten Island Advance,* Ms. Rooney is to be maid of honor at the wedding of NYPD Officers Sophie Pulaski and Ralph Perillo, tomorrow in Our Lady Queen of Peace Church on Staten Island."

"That article in the *Advance* has attracted attention," Gram said. "Most likely all the newspapers and TV news channels have picked it up by now. There'll be a crowd of news media people outside the church tomorrow."

Liz frowned. "Tomorrow is Sophie's special day. I hope

hordes of TV cameramen and reporters won't try to crash her wedding to get shots of me."

"I'm sure all the news paraphernalia will be camped outside the church," Gram replied.

"Well—as long as they don't disrupt the ceremony," Liz said.

At that moment, the radio commentator announced a news bulletin.

"The Manhattan division of the Federal Bureau of Investigation has stated that one of the al Qaeda terrorists being detained and interrogated for the kidnapping of Elizabeth Rooney, has shown signs of cooperation. Stand by for breaking coverage."

The cooperating terrorist might be Alvino! It would be a safe bet it wasn't LoPresti, Liz decided. But among the others she'd seen at the dining room table there'd been two who looked barely out of their teens. One of those young men might have broken down under the intensive interrogation.

Gram must have thought of Alvino too. "Maybe the terrorist who's cooperating is the one with the fancy apartment," she said.

They listened expectantly for more details, but the promised "breaking coverage" didn't come on. Instead, the commentator reported on the indictment of a crooked corporate executive, the death of a foreign political leader, a plane crash, and a messy Hollywood divorce. Details of the divorce were still being described when Gram turned her car into her driveway.

"I forgot to tell you, Ralph's grandparents are here," she said as they stepped onto the porch. "Ralph's father dropped them off about an hour ago. I got their bags up to the guest room and left them watching TV with a pot of tea in the living room."

By the time Liz had greeted the grandparents and visited with them for a while, Ike arrived. She made introductions and after telling them they'd meet again at the rehearsal dinner, she and Ike took off for the church.

She didn't want to waste even one minute of the only time she and Ike would have alone together until much later in the evening. She didn't ask him if he'd heard the FBI's announcements about the bomb manufacturing material in Alvino's apartment or the cooperative terrorist, or even mention that there'd been nothing on the news about a second attempt to kidnap her. She wanted to get right to the new development he'd mentioned concerning the Malin murder.

She settled herself in his car. "What do you have to tell me?" she asked.

"First, the final tests on Duddy's hammer showed no match with the marks on Malin's neck."

"So Duddy's off the hook?"

"It looks that way."

"You said that was the first development—so what's second?"

"The chair rung's out too," he replied. "It didn't come anywhere close to a match. Not only that—final tests on Malin's clothing didn't show any traces of paint."

Until that moment Liz hadn't realized how strong her feeling had been that the paint-daubed chair rung would turn out to be the murder weapon and art teacher Gibbs the killer. "Does this mean the art teacher's off the suspect list too?" she asked.

"Not one hundred percent. We can't rule him out till everything's been tested."

She turned the remaining possible murder weapons over in her mind. *Malin's tote bag and Bernice's cane.*

"They'll be running tests on the bag today and tomorrow," Ike said. "We should get the results by tomorrow afternoon."

And if the bag didn't show the evidence, that would leave the cane.

"Bernice impressed me as a calm, level-headed woman. I can't picture her getting steamed up to the point of killing someone," she said.

"There's no predicting what a person can be capable of in a blind rage," Ike replied. "But I agree with you. I'd like to scratch Bernice and her cane right now, but we can't do that till the bag's been tested."

Liz recalled Ike's description of Malin's tote bag. He'd said it had lengths of wood, grooved in the center where it snapped together for closing or apart for opening. She thought of fingerprints on the wood. It seemed logical that Malin would have handled only the grooved middle part when opening or closing the bag. The two ends wouldn't have been touched.

The realization struck her that in the process of eliminating possible murder weapons she hadn't given much thought to gym teacher Julia Tulley. Tulley was the only one not linked to something which could have been used to strangle Malin. Now, imageries whirled in her mind of Tulley following Malin to the balcony, of heated words and flaring rage, and Tulley's hands grabbing Malin's bag by each end of the wooden closure . . .

Ike's voice penetrated her mental picture of the gym teacher slamming the wooden strips against Malin's throat, crushing her trachea. "If you hadn't asked me about the styling of Malin's handbag, I might not have gotten around to taking a look at it right away, and we wouldn't be on the brink of solving the case."

Liz nodded. "You said the cop who bagged it referred to it as a purse. I guess you pictured a small handbag. Then Dan told you the killer used an object made of wood. It's easy to see why you didn't make a connection."

"Yeah, you're right. The word *purse* threw me off. The idea that it might be a large bag with wood on it never entered my mind until you asked me how it was styled. The minute I saw it I knew we had another potential murder weapon."

She got the feeling they were waltzing around the obvious. Although Ike hadn't come right out and said it, she felt sure he'd reached the same conclusion as she. The tote bag wasn't just a potential murder weapon—it *was* the murder weapon.

Ike pulled his car into a parking space a few steps away from the church entrance. "Thanks to your woman's point of view, we're damn close to wrapping this one up," he said. Flashing a grin, he added, "Remember what I said about Sherlock Holmes?"

She nodded, "I wonder if old Sherlock realized he was at such a disadvantage."

"With his ego—no way," Ike replied as they went up the church steps. "The possibility of a female counterpart would never have entered his mind."

"Are you saying I'm a female counterpart to Sherlock?"

"You're close enough to qualify. I think I'll start calling you Redlocks."

She laughed, but any clever retort she might have thought of was stopped cold. They were inside the church now, surrounded by members of the wedding party. From now on they'd be caught up in the flurry. Little time for discussing Redlocks Rooney's part in solving the Malin case. How could she get in her ideas concerning Julia Tulley during the short ride from the church to the rehearsal dinner, or later, on the way to Gram's house from the restaurant? She wanted to let it all out, without interruption. Maybe she should postpone it till they got to Gram's house.

But she'd discussed enough murder cases with Ike to know if they started swapping ideas after they got to Gram's, they'd be up all night. She had to get over to Sophie's house very early tomorrow morning. That meant no lingering in Gram's living room. A quick good night and Ike would be on his way, and she'd be into the daybed in Gram's sewing room.

By this time tomorrow they'd know for sure that the tote bag was the murder weapon. After that, it wouldn't be long before they knew who'd used it to kill Marva Malin.

Chapter Twenty-three

Sophie's wedding and reception were over. Watching Ralph's brother turn his Toyota out of The Staaten's parking area. Liz exchanged a wave with Sophie and Ralph and gave Sophie a lingering smile. This was one of her life's milestones. Her best friend since first grade was now married and on her way to New Dorp to change into traveling clothes, then on to the airport and a Bermuda honeymoon.

She listened to the typical comments voiced by others gathered to see the newlyweds off. "It was a beautiful wedding." "They make a handsome couple." "Sophie looked like she should be on the cover of *Bride's* magazine."

Everything had gone smoothly after the news media invasion had been quelled. It was almost as if had never occurred. Even Ike seemed to have forgotten about it.

"As weddings go, this one went pretty smoothly," he said.

She stared at him in surprise. "How can you say that when you had to call the New Dorp cops to keep those news hounds from ruining Sophie's big day?"

"I've attended weddings with worse glitches than this," he replied. "The groom passing out at the altar from hyperventilation, the bride's former boyfriend showing up drunk and disorderly, a fire in the church . . ." He flashed a grin. "Your grandmother probably could have handled this one all by herself."

They both laughed, recalling what had happened.

Ralph's father drove the two mothers to the church a few minutes before noon. Liz and the other bridal attendant, Sophie's younger sister, Debbie, were driven by Uncle Stan Pulaski just ahead of Sophie and her father. As Uncle Stan's car approached the corner where the church stood, Liz was surprised to see TV camera trucks and other paraphernalia clogging the street in front and a crowd of news media people crowding around the entrance and onto the side street.

Sophie's modest wedding wouldn't have drawn this much media attention. With growing dismay, Liz realized she was the focus of it.

She could see that the church doors were closed, indicating that all the wedding guests were seated, waiting for the bridal procession to begin. A sense of foreboding gripped her. She and Debbie should be out of the car and into the church within the next few minutes. Sophie and her father, who'd be arriving at any moment, would follow. But, from the looks of things, trying to get to the church door through this mob of reporters, photographers, and TV equipment operators would be worse than running a gauntlet. She'd be surrounded the instant she was recognized, and with her red hair, that wouldn't take more than a few seconds. The way to the door was blocked. Neither she nor Debbie nor Sophie and her father would be able to get through.

Her uneasiness dissolved into a feeling close to despair. *Sophie's wedding was going to be held up, and it was all her fault.*

Uncle Stan hadn't grasped the potential trouble. "They've taken up the whole street out front," he grumbled. "I'll have to let you girls out around the corner."

He pulled into a space on the side street. Before Liz

thought of telling him how apprehensive she felt, he was out of the car and opening the rear door to assist her and Debbie. Evidently, the news hounds had been watching for the maid-of-honor-kidnap-victim to arrive. Whether it was her gown and flowers or her red hair, someone must have spotted her.

A loud shout went up. "There she is!"

Quickly, Liz pulled the door shut, but it was too late. Photographers and reporters swarmed around the car like bees around a hive, tapping on the windows, calling her name, aiming cameras at her through the glass.

She tried to decide what to do. The longer she stayed in the car, the more demanding the crowd would get. If she got out of the car and let this frenzied mob shoot pictures and interview her, there was no predicting how long they'd keep her from going into the church. Whatever she did, when Sophie and her father arrived, they'd find a mob blocking their way to the church door.

If only Ike were out here, she thought, he'd know how to handle this, But she knew he and one of Ralph's brothers would have already escorted the bride's and the groom's mothers to their seats. Like everyone else, he was inside, near the altar, waiting for the bridal procession to begin.

As she peered out the car window, watching for Sophie, she noticed that Sophie's Uncle Stan had started arguing with one of the reporters. Uncle Stan tried to push him away from the car. With mounting alarm, she saw the reporter swing at him. Uncle Stan ducked and landed a punch on the reporter's jaw. The reporter countered with another swing, just as Sophie and her father arrived and parked nearby.

Mr. Pulaski saw it all and was out of his Pontiac in a flash. He socked the reporter squarely on the nose, knocking him to the ground. Two more newsmen rushed to the scene, taking on Sophie's father and Uncle Stan. Liz hoped it would be over when several men stepped in and tried to stop the fracas. Instead they too were drawn into it by others joining the fray. On the verge of panic, she pictured this developing into a free-for-all comparable to something out of an old John Wayne movie.

Through it all, she could see Sophie looking out of the car window, close to tears.

When Sophie's sister Debbie started to cry, Liz decided she must get out of the car and surrender herself. She had no illusions that this unruly mob would get what they wanted over with in a quick, orderly way, allowing them all to enter the church and start the procession, but she had to try *something* to keep this from marring Sophie's big day.

Hoping she wouldn't get caught between two lunging fists, she reached to open the car door. At that moment, through the milling throng, she saw the church door open. Gram, in her tan silk jacket dress with pumps to match and her hair freshly coiffed and auburned, stepped outside, closing the door behind her. After two loud sneezes into a tissue, she became aware of the fracas.

"What's going on out here?" she demanded of the crowd around the door. She didn't wait for an answer. Her voice pealed, loud and clear, above the commotion. "Stop! Stop this minute! Can't you see there's a wedding about to start? You're acting like a bunch of ruffians, attacking members of the bride's family. You're spoiling everything. Shame on you!"

The sound of her voice didn't break up the crowd around the car or the church door, but it *did* stop the fighting. Fists halted in midair. Arms slowly slid downward. After the exchange of some unflattering phrases, the combatants walked away from one another.

Sophie's father returned to his Pontiac. Liz saw him trying to comfort Sophie.

Uncle Stan got into his Ford Escort, looking contrite. "I'm sorry," he said.

"He swung at you first," Liz replied. She noticed both men looked disheveled, but nothing that some attention to their hair, shirts, and ties wouldn't fix.

Gram was still addressing the mob. "Suppose it was *your* sister or *your* daughter getting married?" she called out. "How would you feel if something like this happened on her special day?"

A voice from the crowd called back to Gram. "Lady, we only want to interview the girl who was kidnapped by the terrorists and get some shots of her."

"Well, you're going about it the wrong way," Gram retorted. "You should have the decency to wait until the wedding's over."

A murmur of dissent, mingled with jeers, swept through the crowd. Liz felt her heart plummet. Nobody was going to leave anytime soon, she thought. They were all determined to get their pictures and interviews, whenever and however they could. She might as well get out of the car and give herself up to the mob.

But at that moment she felt her sinking heart rebound. The church door opened and Ike stepped out. After he'd spoken briefly to Gram, Liz saw her go back inside. Then Ike looked around, saw Uncle Stan's car, and made his way toward it.

Reporters and photographers were still surrounding the car. When they let Ike through, Liz was sure he'd flashed his badge. With a wonderful feeling of relief, she opened the car door.

"Stay put," he said, leaning in and giving her a kiss. "I've called the New Dorp station house."

She smiled. The police station was only a few blocks away. She imagined the reaction when a NYPD detective reported that the marriage of two NYPD officers in Our Lady Queen of Peace Church was being disrupted by a mob of out-of-control newshounds.

"There was only a handful of photographers hanging

around out here when we went in about fifteen minutes ago," Ike said. "I assumed they were waiting to take shots of the bridal party coming out of the church. If I'd had any idea there was going to be a mob buildup like this, I'd have called the cops right away."

Sophie's sister had stopped crying, but her voice was still tearful. "Will Sophie be able to get married?" she asked.

"Sure she will, Debbie," Ike replied. "In a few minutes you and Liz will be walking down that aisle, and Sophie and your dad will be right behind you."

As if on cue, three squad cars and a police van came racing up New Dorp Lane, sirens wailing. It didn't take long to disperse the mob. Most of the news people packed their gear and left peaceably. Only a few had to be herded into the van.

From then on everything had gone off without a hitch. Uncle Stan made sure his hair, shirt, and tie looked okay. before going into the church. Sophie brushed at her father's coat, straightened his tie and shirt and smoothed his hair before they started down the aisle. Liz doubted if anyone would have noticed anything amiss, anyway. All eyes were on Sophie.

Liz's only worry now was the possibility of the same unruly media mob showing up at the catering hall where the bridal luncheon was to be held. "You know we'll find news hounds waiting at The Staaten," Liz said to Ike after the ceremony. "I hope they've gotten themselves under control."

"Don't worry—I've arranged for police presence," Ike replied.

By the time everyone arrived at The Staaten, a squad car was parked in front and the news media with its TV trucks and other equipment congregated down the block.

"They can get as many shots of me as they want to after the reception's over," Liz told Ike.

"Nothing doing," Ike had replied. "I'll give them twenty minutes and then I'm taking you home."

After the luncheon, Ike went outside and signaled the okay to the waiting news media. There were fewer of them than before. "I'm surprised the whole mob didn't show up over here," he said as he and Liz watched them approach. He grinned, adding, "I guess some of them were afraid they'd run into your grandmother again."

"Very funny, but you and Gram saved the day. I know she was sitting in the last pew because she was afraid she'd have a sneezing and coughing spell from the flowers in the church. If she did, she wanted to be able to step outside without disturbing anyone. But how come you saw her go out? Weren't you down near the altar with Ralph and his brother?"

"Yeah, but I didn't have my back to the door and I saw her leave. During the few seconds the door was open I thought I heard what sounded like a commotion outside, so I went to investigate."

"And that's when you called the New Dorp precinct."

"Yeah—one look at what was going on out there was all it took."

A polite voice broke into their talk. "May we take some shots of you, now, Ms. Rooney?" The speaker was a male photographer. Several more stood by,

"And do you mind answering a few questions?" a woman asked. Liz assumed she was one of the reporters.

If they'd been in the mob scene outside the church, they'd learned their lesson. "I'm ready," she replied. "Make the first shot one of the bride and me together."

Thanks to the article in the *Advance,* photographers and reporters knew that the NYPD detective who seemed to be in charge was both her rescuer and fiancé. After Sophie and Ralph left, photographers wanted shots of the kidnap victim and her rescuer together. One female reporter seemed caught up in the romantic angle. Other pictures of them were taken with Gram and with Sophie's family and Ralph's.

Reporters asked questions such as "While the terrorists had you, did you think you wouldn't make it to your friend's wedding?"

She lied and told them the thought hadn't crossed her mind. How could she possibly express the despair and anguish she'd felt?

Less than an hour later they were finished. One cameraman told them the coverage would be on his network news that evening. Liz couldn't help contrasting this to the bedlam outside the church. It must have been caused by a few overzealous newshounds, she decided.

Ike drove Liz and Gram back to Gram's house, where Liz changed out of her maid of honor gown and packed her bag. With a big hug and kiss for Gram, and praise for her role in breaking up the mob that could have spoiled Sophie's wedding, she and Ike took off for Manhattan.

"Alone at last," Ike joked, backing his Taurus out of Gram's driveway. "I didn't even get a chance to tell you how beautiful you looked in your gown. I've never seen you looking so . . ." He paused. "Not that you don't always look good whatever you wear, but . . ." Pausing again, he cast her a rueful glance. "I guess I blew that, didn't I?"

She smiled. "Not at all. I know what you meant. Thank you." However misspoken, it qualified as one of his rare compliments.

His cell phone sounded at that moment. He glanced at the caller ID, saying, "It's Lou."

Liz heart began to race. *Hadn't Ike told her the tests on the tote bag would be completed this afternoon? Was Lou phoning with the results?*

She waited in suspense, listening to Ike's monosyllabic part of the conversation with his partner. "Good . . . Yeah? . . . When? . . . Okay." And then, "Liz and I are just leaving New Dorp on our way to her place. I'll drop her off and meet you at the lab."

She didn't even wait for him to click off. "So, did any prints other than Malin's show up on the tote bag?"

"They did," he said, heading the car toward Richmond Road. "Two beautiful sets of a thumb and index finger, one on each end of the wooden part. Partials from the other fingers and the palms showed up too."

Again, Liz pictured Julia Tulley's hands grabbing the canvas tote bag at each end of its wooden closure. "This definitely establishes the tote bag as the murder weapon, doesn't it?" she asked, resisting the urge to tell him she thought Tulley was the killer.

"I would say so. But we don't have to go on the prints alone. The tests picked up some more evidence—some light brown hairs showed up on the canvas."

She felt a surge of excitement. *Julia Tulley had light brown hair!*

"What's your next move? DNA tests?" she asked.

"We'll go into that if we have to, but the prints are so clear they'll be enough to make an arrest."

"When are you going to get fingerprints for comparison?"

"We already have the art teacher's prints, all good ones, from the chair rung and a couple of paint cans, and we got a beautiful set of Tulley's prints from some instruction sheets of ballet steps she left backstage. Paper is one of the best materials for lifting fingerprints."

Liz felt confident of a match between the prints on Julia Tulley's instruction sheets and those on the tote bag's closure. After that, if there should be any doubt that the gym teacher was the killer, DNA tests on those light brown hairs would wrap it up.

She was about to tell Ike she was sure of Tulley's guilt, when another thought flashed into her mind. *Art teacher Gibbs had light brown hair too!*

Chapter Twenty-four

"**Y**ou've been very quiet," Ike said as they exited the Verrazano Bridge. "I thought the news about the tote bag would get you chattering nonstop. Aren't you excited, knowing how close we are to solving the case? And aren't you pleased, knowing your woman's viewpoint sped things up?"

"Sure I'm excited and pleased, but I'm confused too. I was close to being sure that art teacher Gibbs is the killer, and then you told me the chair rung isn't the murder weapon. Then I decided that the tote bag had to be it, and I started considering Julia Tulley because she's the only one we couldn't link up with some object that might have been used to kill Malin."

Ike smiled. "Good thinking. Go on."

"I thought she could have followed Malin to the balcony to continue the argument they'd had earlier. I thought maybe she didn't intend to kill her. Maybe Malin said something that set her off and she just wanted to shut her up. So, in a fit of rage, she grabbed the only available object, the bag, and pressed the wooden part against Malin's neck."

"Everything you're saying makes sense," Ike said. "Why are you confused?"

"Because of the light brown hairs on the bag. My first thought after you told me about them was *Tulley has light brown hair*, but then I realized *so has Gibbs.*"

"Cheer up. You won't be confused much longer," Ike said. "After I get you home I'm heading straight for the lab."

Would fingerprints on the bag's wooden closure match Gibbs' prints on the chair rung and paint cans? Or would they match those lifted from Tulley's ballet instruction sheets? However it went, they'd soon have enough evidence for an arrest, she thought.

Ike's next statement echoed her thoughts. "This is it, Liz. I'm 99% sure one of those two teachers will be taken into custody as soon as we can clear it with the DA."

"No DNA test on the light brown hairs before the arrest?" she asked.

"The prints are so conclusive, there's no immediate need for a DNA, but we can do it later if we have to."

"Will you phone me when you know how the fingerprinting tests turned out?" she asked, hoping he'd bend his rule about not discussing case developments on the phone with civilians.

"After we have the results I'll get back to your place as soon as I can," he replied.

She suppressed a sigh. Unable to think of anything more to discuss concerning Cyril Gibbs or Julia Tulley, she let her thoughts take over.

She reviewed her impressions of the art and gym teachers when she'd seen them in the school last Monday, shortly after Malin's body hit the gym floor.

She remembered art teacher Gibbs had been very quiet, and there'd been a dazed expression on his face. She'd seen that dazed expression again, the day she went to the school to get Dan's pen. It had crossed his face when he mentioned he'd seen her in the gym on *Monday*, as if he were recalling that Monday was the day of the murder. Ike said some of the kids told him Malin had made insulting remarks about the backdrop Gibbs and his students had painted. But surely that wouldn't have driven him to kill her. If it turned out he was the killer there had to be something else. Maybe he had a sensitive point—something Malin delighted in jeering at him about. *Had she jeered at him once too often? Did his dazed look indicate he was in shock after committing murder?*

As for Tulley—she'd remarked that she was "all shook up" about Malin's murder, but she didn't act like someone shocked and saddened. In fact, she'd made a couple of unkind digs at Malin. Also, the kids told Ike that Tulley and Malin had a run-in shortly before the break, and Tulley was still fuming when they heard Malin tell Bernice she was going up to the balcony. And Liz recalled hearing Tulley remind the other teachers that all the kids disliked Malin and one of the older ones could have committed the murder. *Was she hoping to divert suspicion away from herself and the heated argument she and Malin had, only a few minutes before the body fell from the balcony?*

Ike must have been doing some heavy thinking too. Neither of them spoke for awhile, until Ike broke the silence.

"Let's see if there's any news about the terrorists," he said, turning the radio on.

They caught the start of a bulletin. "The FBI has announced that Hava Shukri, the elderly housekeeper for the recently captured members of a Manhattan al Qaeda terrorist cell who kidnapped a Manhattan woman last week, has been returned to Canada," a female newscaster stated. "Shukri, a deaf mute, rejoined family members in Montreal this morning. A native of Iraq, Shukri had been living in Canada for several years as a legal alien, dependent on the relatives with whom she lived. According to family members she was offered the New York housekeeping job at an extremely high salary by an Islamic man she met at her neighborhood mosque."

"I can understand why she'd jump at the chance," Liz said. "What are the odds on an elderly deaf mute getting a high salary job? And she was made to order for the terrorists."

"Yeah, I'll bet they couldn't believe their luck—finding someone who couldn't possibly know what they were up to." Ike agreed.

The newscaster continued, saying that a search of another apartment where some of the terrorists lived had uncovered a cache of weapons.

"Have the addresses of the two apartments been mentioned on the news?" Liz asked. "I haven't seen or heard anything about that yet."

"That'll be mentioned any time now, but it won't come as a surprise," Ike replied. "The locations of the apartments have leaked out. Residents of the first building and neighboring buildings couldn't help but be aware of the NYPD raid, and the FBI activity later had to be obvious in both buildings. I'm sure by this time the places where the terrorists worked are buzzing. All the employers had to do was put two and two together."

Continuing coverage bore this out. The newscaster made another announcement, saying that spokespeople for several firms where some of the terrorists were employed, had made statements expressing shock, and horror.

The location of the facility where the terrorists were being held was not disclosed. Liz remembered Dan saying the CIA might now be involved and they might have been taken to one of the CIA's secret prisons. She also recalled hearing that one of the terrorists was cooperating with the FBI. A cooperative terrorist might not have been sent to the same facility as the others, she thought. She wondered if he could be Alvino.

Suddenly, the newscaster came out with another statement. "Stand by for late breaking news about Chadwick

Academy's janitor, Dudley Baca, reported missing after last week's brutal murder of one of the school's teachers."

This made it sound as if Duddy had disappeared immediately after the murder.

"If I didn't know Duddy was in the clear, I'd think he was the killer," she said.

"Anything to get listeners' attention and keep them tuned through the commercials," Ike replied. "The only news they have about Duddy is he turned up in Bellevue and maybe something about his condition and when he's going to be released."

Sure enough, when the so-called late-breaking news came on, it was almost exactly as Ike had predicted. It closed with, "Baca is expected to return to his job at Chadwick Academy on Monday."

The mention of Monday reminded Liz that it was on Monday of last week that Malin was murdered. "It's been less than a week and you're ready to make an arrest," she said. "Nice going, Detective."

He flashed her a smile. "Nice going for you, too, Redlocks—you and your woman's angle."

She smiled in return. He never failed to acknowledge whatever help she gave him. This was one of the many reasons she'd fallen in love with him.

A few minutes later, he braked the car in front of the Moscarettis' building. She reached into the back seat for her overnight bag.

"I'll carry your bag in," he said.

"Thanks, but it's very light. Besides, the sooner you get to the lab, the sooner you'll be back here with the fingerprinting results."

"Okay." He gave her a quick kiss. "I'll see you in a couple of hours."

Rosa was waiting in the entrance hall when Liz let herself

into the building. "Hello, Dearie," she said. "We didn't have a chance to talk before you left Friday morning. Joe told me about the excitement Thursday night. I was sound asleep, and missed it."

"Excitement on Thursday night?" If Joe had told Rosa about the second terrorist attempt to kidnap her, Rosa seemed very unconcerned about it, Liz thought.

"I guess you were asleep too," Rosa said. "There was a fight on the street. Two men like they were out to kill each other, Joe said. He called the cops."

This explained, to neighbors and passersby, the presence of a squad car and police van outside the building on Thursday night, Liz decided. With the many serious crimes committed daily in Manhattan, reporters who'd looked into this hadn't considered it newsworthy.

Now she understood why there'd been no publicity. She recalled the FBI agents conferring with the other men at the scene. They were all in on the subterfuge, she decided—the agents, Musab, the other cops, even Joe.

Evidently Rosa considered the street fight too trivial for further discussion. "So how was the wedding?" she asked.

"Beautiful." She hoped Rosa wouldn't press for details. She wanted to pick up her mail, go to her apartment, and check her phone messages.

"You can tell me about it later," Rosa replied. "You got a stack of mail over yesterday and today and I know you want to see what came."

She handed Liz a packet of envelopes secured with a rubberband. "You got your phone and electric bills, but from what I could see, it looks like the rest is personal," she said.

Liz took the packet and started up the stairs, saying, "Thanks, Rosa."

When she stepped into her apartment she noticed the message light flashing on her telephone. She set her purse and overnight bag and her mail on the sofa and went to check on who'd called her while she was on Staten Island. Listening to the first message, she thought someone was playing a practical joke.

Oprah Winfrey wanted her as a guest on her show. Would Ms. Rooney kindly call the following phone number at her earliest convenience? *Yeah, right!*

She went to the next message. Larry King would like to interview her on *Larry King Live.* Would she please contact him as soon as possible at . . . She barely heard the number. *What was going on?*

By the time she got to the third and last message she wasn't surprised to hear that she was wanted for an appearance on *The O'Reilly Factor. All this might be for real!*

She quelled her excitement and told herself she'd better talk this over with Ike and see what he thought.

Turning her attention to the mail, she set aside the bills and began to read the letters. They were notes from friends and acquaintances who'd heard about her kidnapping and had written to say they were thankful she was okay. Their kindness warmed her heart.

With only one envelope still unopened, she picked it up and glanced at the return name and address. Her heart, already moved by the kind and thoughtful messages, began to stir with excitement. *The letter was from Ike's parents!*

Opening the envelope, she warned herself not to expect anything more than a polite note saying they would not be attending their son's wedding. But at least she'd tried.

Ike's mother had written the letter. She started by saying she and Ike's father had planned to answer her letter by thanking her for writing but saying their estrangement from their son was too great for them to consider attending the wedding. But before she composed the letter, news of the terrorist kidnapping broke.

"At first we weren't sure if you were the same Elizabeth Rooney our son was going to marry," the letter continued, "but your description on TV matched the description he gave us when he wrote to tell us about your forthcoming wedding. When it was mentioned on TV that the kidnapped girl worked for the medical examiner, we knew it was you. George had also told us that in his letter.

With rising hope, Liz read on. "We prayed for you, and after you were rescued by the New York police, including our son, we began to question the stand we'd taken against George so many years ago. Our bitterness began to fade away. We felt as proud of him being in law enforcement as we would have been had he chosen the profession of law itself, as we wanted him to do. We admitted we'd been stubborn fools and we'd wasted too many years.

"We saw you on TV, Elizabeth, and you impressed us as a beautiful, courageous young woman, and we're delighted you are going to be our daughter-in-law. We have written to George too, asking his forgiveness and telling him we wouldn't miss your wedding for anything in the world."

Liz felt her eyes misting. Part of loving Ike with all her heart and knowing they'd soon be married was the feeling of being wrapped in something soft and warming. His estrangement from his parents had had been like a harsh, chilling wind, threatening to penetrate the warmth. Now the threat was over.

She thought of phoning Ike. Although he rarely mentioned the rift, she sensed his deep-down regret and his heartfelt wish for a reconciliation. She didn't make the call. She wanted to see his face when she showed him the letter.

Chapter Twenty-five

Ike arrived later than expected. He came in the door apologizing, when he stopped short, glancing in the direction of the kitchenette. "What's that good smell? Have you been cooking?"

"I knew you wouldn't be back till dinnertime, so I threw something together," she said. She didn't tell him she'd gone out and bought the ingredients for beef stew—Gram's wonderful recipe. She'd made it for him once before, and he loved it. She was a fair cook when she had the time and put her mind to it.

Now he noticed the wine bottle and goblets on the table. "Champagne!" he exclaimed. "That's one of the bottles Big Tiny gave you."

"Chilled and ready for you to pop the cork," she replied.

"Are we still celebrating Sophie and Ralph's marriage?"

"No. Something else."

"Let me guess." He opened the bottle and poured the champagne. "How about Mr. Klein's apartment? That's cause for celebration."

"Guess again."

"Oh, I get it, he said, handing her a goblet. "You want us to drink to the solution of the Malin murder. I wondered why you didn't come at me with questions the minute I got here. You've decided who he killer is."

Before she could let him know the Malin murder had been temporarily relegated to the back of her mind, and why, he gave a teasing smile. "There's been a new development that wraps up the case, but I'm not telling you what it is till *you* tell *me* what makes you so sure you already know who the killer is."

A new development? He couldn't be talking about the fingerprints, she thought. But her excitement about his mother's letter took priority. "I don't know which one's the killer, and there's something you need to know before we discuss the murder," she said.

He looked at her in puzzlement. "What's going on?"

She handed him his mother's letter and raised her goblet. "Here's to our wedding and to your mother and father."

He scanned the letter in seconds. His smile told her everything he felt in his heart. "I'll drink to that!" he exclaimed, first touching his glass to hers, then following up with a kiss.

They sat down on the sofa. He held her close. For a few minutes all except this new happiness was forgotten.

"There's an old superstition that things happen in threes," she said. "We've overcome two problems in the last couple of days—first getting Mr. Klein's apartment, and now this. I wonder what the third one will be."

"I can't believe you forgot about the Malin murder, even for a few minutes," he replied. "That's number three." He gave her one of his teasing smiles. "We've got our killer."

Instantly, art teacher Gibbs, gym teacher Tulley and the tote bag again took over her mind. "Stop teasing me. Whose prints are we talking about—Gibbs' or Tulley's?"

"Neither. I never made it to the lab. We'll get the prints tomorrow, but they'll just be the icing on the cake."

He was still teasing her. "Will you please stop talking in riddles and tell me what this new development is?"

He flashed a grin. "Okay—on my way to the lab I got a call from FBI headquarters. The terrorist who owns the Mercedes and the apartment where you were held has been co-operating with the Bureau concerning al Qaeda activities. Now he's decided to cooperate with the NYPD. He told FBI interrogators he had information about the Malin murder."

"Alvino!" Liz exclaimed. "I thought all along he might not be as radical as the others."

Ike took a notebook out of his pocket and consulted it. "Yeah, Alvino Mancini, aka Hassam al Heriz. He gave us a written statement telling everything he knows.

Her hunch had been right. Alvino knew more than he was letting on.

"Did he say who killed her?" she asked.

"Yes—it was Gibbs," Ike replied.

Though she was halfway prepared for this, Liz felt a pang of sadness. Malin's taunts had driven the shy art teacher to the breaking point. And LoPresti knew—but how? And he told Alvino—but why?

She looked at him in puzzlement.

"I'll fill you in," he said. "Here's what Alvino said in his statement. A few days after school opened in September, LoPresti told him he'd gotten acquainted with the young woman dramatics teacher, and he'd suggested going somewhere for coffee after school. She made some lame excuse and declined, but that didn't bother him, he said. He wasn't strongly attracted to her. He just thought since they'd both be working on the school play, they could be friends."

Liz nodded. "That ties right in with what Alvino told *me*."

"Then, when the play rehearsals started, he found out

how verbally abusive the dramatics teacher was," Ike continued. "He told Alvino everyone connected with the play de-
tested her, and it made him angry that he'd been turned
down by such a disagreeable, undesirable woman. Then
when the principal's assistant told him the dramatics
teacher's real name was Malinbaum, and she'd shortened it,
he realized she was Jewish. He was enraged that an undesirable *Jewish* woman had spurned a Muslim man. According
to Alvino, he talked about it constantly, becoming increas-
ingly infuriated."

Liz recalled that the name change angle had crossed her
mind as a possible motive for hot-headed LoPresti to kill the
Jewish woman who'd brushed him off. But LoPresti hadn't
killed her—Gibbs had, and LoPresti knew it. *Where was
Alvino's statement leading?*

"Alvino said LoPresti told him that Malin was especially
mean and contemptuous toward the male art teacher," Ike
continued. "She started out ridiculing his work on the stage
sets. When she heard he lived with his mother and two
aunts—had been living with them most of his life—she began calling him a mama's boy and a wimp. She never let up."

"Gibbs, still living with his mother and aunts at his age,"
Liz said. "Sounds like he's dominated by women."

"Right," Ike replied. "And between the henpecking at
home and Malin's jibes at work, his life couldn't have been
any picnic."

"Gibbs is such a mild-mannered man," Liz said. "Malin
must have delivered an especially scurrilous taunt that day,
and he just snapped."

"Evidently, that's what happened."

"But how did LoPresti know about it?"

"Because he deliberately goaded Gibbs into it."

She stared at him in disbelief.

"It's true," Ike said. "He told Alvino he started talking to
the art teacher, telling him he shouldn't have to put up with

this constant abuse, and he should do something about it. He said at first he was just curious to see if the art teacher had the guts to stand up to her, but before long he told Alvino he beefed up his talks with Gibbs, hoping to stir him into doing something physical. He started pressuring him."

Liz thought back to the scene of her abduction, when Alvino had seemed reluctant, but LoPresti talked him into it. "I know what LoPresti is capable of," she said, "but it's hard to believe he could pressure Gibbs into killing Malin."

"It wouldn't be difficult for someone like LoPresti to influence someone like Gibbs," Ike replied. "He told Alvino he didn't suggest murder. He just kept at him, saying nobody should have to endure such insults, and the world would be a better place without people like her."

Liz pondered this. Tied to a trio of apron strings as he was, the closest to friendships Gibbs might have come were the two other teachers and the principal's assistant at Chadwick Academy. They'd formed a bond of mutual hatred for Marva Malin. LoPresti, especially, treated him with respect and spent time talking to him.

"Sounds like LoPresti wanted Malin dead, and he hoped he could get Gibbs to commit the murder for him," she said.

Ike cast her an approving smile. "That's it, exactly."

Liz pictured Gibbs caught in a crossfire of constant henpecking at home and nonstop ridicule from Malin at work. She recalled LoPresti's friendly manner toward Gibbs, backstage, and the comradely slap on the back.

"I understand how it could have happened," she said. "It was a Monday. Gibbs came to work after two days of domination by his mother and aunts. When Malin started in on him with the most demeaning jabs she'd ever delivered, it was the straw that broke the camel's back."

"And after the deed was done, LoPresti was so pleased with his strategy, he couldn't resist telling Alvino," Ike said.

As Liz pictured Gibbs encountering Malin in the balcony,

an idea struck her. "With Malin's tote bag the murder weapon, Gibbs couldn't have intended to kill her when he followed her up to the balcony. That means he won't be charged with premeditated murder, doesn't it?"

"You're right on track, Redlocks. But we figure he didn't follow her at all. He was already there when she came up. It makes sense that he would have wanted to see how his scenery looked from up there."

"Oh, I'll bet that's what happened. And when she realized he was there, she probably started jeering at him, telling him his backdrop looked terrible, and then went into her taunting. Only this time Gibbs thought of what LoPresti had been drilling into his head, and . . ."

"And when his suppressed anger exploded, he grabbed the bag, crushed the wooden part against her throat, and dumped her over the railing. Most likely his attorney will claim temporary insanity as a defense."

Liz's feeling of sympathy for the harassed art teacher soon gave way to a sense of closure. She now knew that Lo-Presti had goaded Gibbs into a murder he could not risk committing himself. She also knew the better nature she'd sensed in Alvino really existed. Perhaps, because of his co-operation with the FBI and NYPD, he'd be dealt with more lightly. Meanwhile, she'd hang onto a faint hope that he'd abandon his radical ideology and change his views of the country he believed to be a land of imperialistic infidels.

Picking up their empty wine glasses, she rose from he sofa and headed for the kitchenette, saying, "Believe it or not, I've had enough murder talk for a while. Let's eat."

"Suits me. I'm hungry," he said, following her.

He watched her ladle the beef stew into shallow bowls. "I hope that's the same great stew you made once before. Your grandmother's recipe, you said."

"It is," she replied, carrying the bowls to the table. "Let's have a little more champagne while we eat," she said. "I just thought of something else or us to celebrate."

"What—that you're getting to be a damn good cook?" he asked, refilling their glasses.

"No, but thanks anyway." She told him about the messages from Oprah, Larry King, and O'Reilly.

"Great," he said, raising his glass. "I'll drink to that."

"Then you think I should take them up on it?"

He quaffed some champagne. "Sure, why not?"

"Okay, I will." She took a sip from her glass and smiled at him across the table. "Imagine me on those big TV programs. I'll feel like a star."

She hoped it wasn't the champagne talking when he smiled back at her, saying, "You are and always will be *my* shining star, Liz Rooney."